M000316532

VITA AETERNA

JAY ALLAN STOREY

Non Sequitur Publishing
Vancouver, BC

Copyright © 2018 by Jay Allan Storey.

January 5, 2018

All rights reserved. No part of this publication may be reproduced, distributed or transmitted in any form or by any means, including photocopying, recording, or other electronic or mechanical methods, without the prior written permission of the publisher, except in the case of brief quotations embodied in critical reviews and certain other noncommercial uses permitted by copyright law. For permission requests, write to the publisher, addressed "Attention: Permissions Coordinator," at the address below.

Jay Allan Storey/Non Sequitur Publishing
190 – 1027 Davie Street
Vancouver, BC V6E 4L2
www.jayallanstorey.com

Publisher's Note: This is a work of fiction. Names, characters, places, and incidents are a product of the author's imagination. Locales and public names are sometimes used for atmospheric purposes. Any resemblance to actual people, living or dead, or to businesses, companies, events, institutions, or locales is completely coincidental.

Book Layout ©2013 BookDesignTemplates.com

Ordering Information:
Quantity sales. Special discounts are available on quantity purchases by corporations, associations, and others. For details, contact the "Special Sales Department" at the address above.

Vita Aeterna/ Jay Allan Storey. -- 1st ed.
ISBN 978-0-9917912-4-8

To my Mother and Father, for all their help and
support throughout my life.

ONE

....

CAM-SURFING

"Ten seconds, Alex," Richie's voice nearly blew out my eardrum. I put a foot out to stop my board, and turned down the volume on the earpiece.

"Do you have to yell?" I whispered into the mic of the controller on my wrist.

"Fifteen," he said, ignoring me, though his voice sounded a bit more normal this time. He always put on this stupid, serious tone like he was counting down a space launch or something.

I scanned the walls and rooftops with one eye, and watched the blinking light in my HUD, the 'Heads Up Display' implanted in my head, with the other. The tiny glow that showed I was in the clear was still green. So far, so good.

The cameras are usually easy to spot. SecureCorp want them visible so everybody will know there's eyes watching them. But sometimes they get sneaky and toss in a hidden one. It can be anything: a part of a light fixture, a fake electrical insulator, even just a tiny hole in the wall. But the cameras have a footprint, like the circle from a spotlight. There's a hack that shows the camera footprints like a bunch of intersecting ovals.

Whatever's on the display of your HUD sort of floats half-transparent in the space in front of you. The trick is translating what you see to the 3D space you're in. The footprints cover a lot, but not everything. With practice, you can visualize where they are, and avoid them. There's usually big enough gaps between them to squeeze through.

"One minute," Richie said. "You're doin' great. Keep it up."

That's how the game was played. 'Cam-surfing', we called it - seeing how far you could go without being tracked by one of SecureCorps's monitoring cameras. A lot of the kids played it. It really pissed SecureCorp off, which I guess was kind of the point. The hack we used also showed when a camera detected your presence. An indicator in the upper right of the display changed from green to red. It wasn't easy; the cameras are everywhere. You can't walk a block without being in range of at least one.

Cam-surfing was lots of fun, and I was really good at it.

We called ourselves the 'Lost Souls'. The name didn't mean anything, we just thought it sounded cool. We weren't really a gang, not like the *Killer Dragons*, or *Death's Heads*. We didn't commit crimes for money like they did, and we weren't into violence like they were. We just liked to take chances, and have fun (which are more or less the same thing).

Usually it was Richie, Jake, Spiro, and me.

Most of the time we just played against the clock, seeing how long we could go without being spotted. That's what I was doing now.

"Two minutes," Richie said in my ear.

I coasted on my board through the narrow gap between two camera footprints, standing up straight and pulling in my ass to clear them. Anything moving in the center of an alley or an intersection is toast - the cameras will pick it up right away. The most effective way to stay 'invisible' is to stick close to the walls. But you still have to look out for the wild card cameras. They point in weird-ass, random directions, and unless you spot them they'll screw you every time.

Just to make things more interesting, sometimes we'd find a way to bypass security for a building or an office, sneak in, and steal something. It was never much: a badge, a coaster, or a pen with the company crest - anything that would make a good trophy, that would prove you got inside wherever you were going.

The trophies were usually pretty much worthless, but the status for getting them was huge, and the penalties for getting caught were pretty steep. A friend of ours, Robbie, disappeared during a break-in about a year ago. The official line was that he was sent up to Juvenile Detention, but I don't know if I believe that - we never heard from him again.

So why did we do it? The excitement, the danger, the prestige, status, whatever. I guess it was kind of pointless, but hey, when you're sixteen years old in Tintown, the place where I live, and you've got nothing better to do...

Later tonight I was going to do something no kid had ever done before: I was going to break into a SecureCorp building. Since policing and security are SecureCorp's business, getting past their defenses was the ultimate challenge - and the ultimate risk.

3

"Four minutes," Richie said.

I jumped off my board and tried to look casual as a vehicle, a rare sight for Tintown, crawled up the street and passed me. It wasn't a RoboTaxi - it had a driver. There were no Corp markings, but who else would be driving something like that? Even most Corp don't pay much attention to what we do, but there was no point taking any chances.

My Cam-surfing record, and as far as I know the all-time record, is ten kilometers, more than a hundred blocks, in thirty minutes - half an hour. There's another hack that confuses the HUD's GPS locator, so for half an hour, SecureCorp didn't have a clue where I was. Half an hour being anonymous, invisible. That was probably longer than anybody in the city, even a Corp exec, ever had out of range of some kind of monitoring system.

The SecureCorp ads on HoloTV are always telling us that being monitored shouldn't matter if we we're not doing anything wrong. But it *does* matter. It was an incredible rush to know that for some period of time nobody, not SecureCorp, not my dad - not even Richie - could say for sure where Alex Barret was. For some short stretch of time I had something rare and priceless: privacy.

I'd gone around seventy blocks in just over twenty minutes when it happened. It almost always went that way - a hidden camera that I didn't spot until it was too late. A light on my HUD started flashing red.

"Shit!" I said.

"Busted!" Richie laughed into my earpiece.

I boarded back to the 'Center', the place we usually hooked up, in an abandoned warehouse on the outermost edge of Tintown. Richie and Jake were already there. I pushed aside the loose plank that blocks our secret entrance and squeezed through. As always, the place smelled like mold and rotting cardboard.

"Not bad," Richie said, standing near a beaten up old couch in one corner and tapping the HUD controller on his wrist. He was a foot taller than me, and built like a wrestler. You'd never guess that he knows more about hacking the system than almost any other kid in the city. "Not your best," he said, "but still better than anybody else I know."

A cloud of dust poofed up from the couch as I flopped down beside him.

"Practice makes perfect," I said.

Jake lounged nearby, in an armchair with all the stuffing coming out. "It helps that you can squeeze through every rat-hole in Tintown," he laughed, with another dig about what a runt I was.

"Screw you," I said.

"You still feel up to going for the big one?" Richie asked.

I shrugged. "You only live once, right?"

"You are one crazy dude," Jake said, shaking his head as he pushed himself to his feet and grabbed the board leaning against the chair arm. He stepped toward the exit opening. "Back here at nine?"

For something as dangerous as what I was planning, we had to wait. City security slackened off after nine PM.

Richie and I both nodded.

Jake smiled at me. "It's nuts, but hey, if you get away with it, you'll be a legend."

TWO

....

AT HOME

I boarded home to our apartment, on the fifth floor of one of the thousands of dumpy, disintegrating high-rises that were standard issue for
Tintown. The building loomed over my head as I climbed the outside
steps. Twisted, dripping pipes dangled at intervals from walls stained
with alternating splotches of bleached white and mildew black, like
some giant had been wiping his feet on them for a few thousand years.

You could tell which places were occupied. The mostly broken windows were blocked off with makeshift security bars made from chunks
of scrap metal, or had drying laundry flapping from them, and spider-
webs of wires spun out, gathering into bundles at the nearest standing
power pole.

When I walked into the living room Dad was leaning forward in his
chair watching HoloTV, like always - another stupid Safety Show. At
least the electricity, off when I left in the morning, had come back on.
Somebody must have climbed up again and re-jigged the rats-nest of
cables that siphoned off power from the electrical grid in the Corp

Ring. There were brown-outs five or six times a day in Tintown, and complete black-outs at least once a day.

Dad's chair was only a meter away from the HoloTV pedestal. He didn't see so good, and he couldn't afford glasses. He didn't look up. On the pedestal display, some loser dressed in a clown suit bent down, grabbed a big heavy box with both hands, tried to stand up with it, and clutched his back in pain. A serious-sounding narrator warned: 'Remember - always lift with your legs'.

The TV was blaring, as usual. Dad also needed a hearing enhancer for his HUD, but we couldn't afford that either.

"Dad," I yelled out to him.

He heard me, but didn't turn around. I went to the kitchen, grabbed a couple of food packets from the cupboard, and tossed them in the microwave. The packets were produced by FoodCorp, who just called them 'food' - we figured that was because it was never clear what the ingredients were.

Each packet was a thin plastic tray with an opaque film on top. You didn't know what you were getting until you heated one up and opened it. It didn't matter anyway. They almost always looked exactly the same - a dark brown mash. Nobody in Tintown could afford a pet, but my girlfriend Cindy's rich, and she's got a cat. She showed me once what she fed it, and it looked exactly like what we eat most of the time.

Once they were heated, I carried both packets to the living room, set one beside my dad, sat down on the couch, and opened my own. Yep, no surprises there. I attacked it anyway. Cam-surfing always made me hungry.

"Your dinner's there," I said to him.

He nodded and continued staring at the TV. That was his response to everything.

I guess I couldn't blame him. He'd gotten a raw deal on his Appraisal. His body was shriveled and bent, his skin mottled and wrinkled, and his wispy white hair almost gone from his head. He looked ancient, but in fact he was only forty-five years old. He'd 'negged out'. That is, the result of his Appraisal had been negative, less than one.

The way it was told to me at the co-op school, every species on earth's got an expiration date, like the food packet on my lap. Their metabolisms all run at different speeds, which means that some have a long lifespan, some not. The lifespan of a typical human is around eighty years. The lifespan of a dog is less than fifteen. I hear the lifespan of some trees can be more than one thousand.

About sixty years ago, long before I was born, scientists came up with this process, Appraisal, that 'resets' the metabolism of the person it's applied to. Appraisal can slow the aging process, so the affected person will live up to X number of years for every year of an 'average' human.

In Appraisal jargon, X is called the Life Extension Factor, or LEF. The LEF is a fraction, usually between one and two, based on an average age of 80. If you've got a LEF of 1.1, your life expectancy is 80 X 1.1 = 88 years. A LEF of 1.5 (I wish) would give you a life expectancy of 80 X 1.5 = 120.

But this is the bizarre part: people don't just live longer, their entire metabolism is affected. So, just like a fifteen-year-old human is way younger in real terms than a fifteen-year-old dog, a seventy-year-old with a high LEF is like a thirty-year-old with a low one. That's why on HoloTV you see seventy-year-olds playing squash, competing in Iron-man races (and winning), and all kinds of other stuff that used to only be done by the young.

But, like most of the scientists' brilliant discoveries, Appraisal comes with some serious hitches. The effect is different for everyone it's applied to. Person A could have their lifespan doubled while Person B had almost no change. Even worse, in rare cases, like my dad, one in one hundred thousand they say, the LEF is less than one. Not only did Appraisal not lengthen his life, it actually shortened it. My dad's LEF was 0.6, which means his life expectancy is 80 X 0.6 = 48. We call this 'negging out'.

Over the years I've heard of a few people with LEFs over two. They say that only happens for about one in a hundred thousand, like negging out. The highest I've ever heard of is two point five, but that might be bullshit.

And the killer is, Appraisal can only be done once. Doing it a second, third, or whatever time has no effect. The result is irreversible, and there's no way to predict what it will be. They say it's not dependent on genetics or any other known biological factor. No matter who you are or how much money you have, once it's done, Appraisal can't be undone; you've just got to live with the result. Even so, almost nobody ever refuses it.

Seems like the Barret family is cursed. My mother's Appraisal was negative too, though just barely. It didn't matter anyway, because she died of cancer eight years ago. You could have a LEF of three and still die early, from disease or an accident. I guess it's always been tragic

9

when somebody dies before their time, but I think it's worse now, 'cause in most cases your 'time' can be so much longer.

Dad's depression about his Appraisal, and then my mom's death, turned him into some kind of zombie. I don't think he'd even bother feeding himself if I wasn't around. What makes it so sad is that if he'd just chosen not to have the Appraisal in the first place, which he could have done, he probably would have lived to be something like eighty. But, like I said, there was no way to know ahead of time.

Travis, my teacher at the co-op school, says Appraisal has had a major impact on society. Knowing they're going to live longer, people are a lot more in tune with taking care of themselves. Nobody wants to get some chronic injury they're going to have to live with for the next hundred and twenty years.

I guess that's why the Safety Shows are so popular. People can't seem to get enough of hearing how to properly lift heavy objects, climb stairs, step off curbs, etc. Sound boring? You bet it is, but they're the most watched shows on HoloTV.

Even Dad watches them, which is a joke; there's no point unless you're going to live to a hundred or something. What does he care if he throws out his shoulder lifting a box the wrong way. He'll be dead in a couple of years. It's just something to do, I guess. He's got nothing else.

THREE

....

TINTOWN

Like I said, the place I live is called Tintown (don't ask me why - nobody seems to know). Tintown is a 'Quarter' - an area of about five hundred square blocks. It's one of thousands of tiny self-governing knots of people that make up The Quarters - part of a huge urban center. They say it used to be a great city, but now most of it's falling apart, and a lot of it's abandoned. A long time ago they moved everything that counts somewhere else - to the southwest. I wouldn't know about any of that - it all happened before I was born.

The ones who've made it big in the world, the ones we call the Elite, live in a gated community to the south called the First Circle. I've been to the edge of it a couple of times with Cindy. There's actually this massive wall around it to keep the riff-raff (like me) out.

Living in a sort of giant ring around the First Circle are the workers and managers of the Corps, the corporations that produce all the goods and services the world needs. Most of the factories and offices are there too. There's no wall around the Corp Ring, and nothing to stop us going there, but if we hang around too long they find a way to get rid of us.

According to Travis (though I'm never sure whether he's joking, psycho, or serious sometimes), there used to be thousands of businesses, pumping out a huge variety of stuff, and almost everybody could afford at least some of it.

Now, there's only six, so besides SecureCorp there's five others.

FoodCorp, as I mentioned, produces the food packets we eat. **BuildCorp** designs and builds all large building projects. **InfoCorp** is responsible for all the stuff broadcast over our HUDs and on HoloTvs, and for training and education. **TechCorp** designs, builds, and maintains all the high technology stuff.

And last, but definitely not least, **MediCorp** is responsible for everything to do with medicine and health. Cindy says they're really good. Here in the Quarters our medical plan is we hope we don't get sick.

Together with TechCorp, MediCorp are responsible for installing the HUDs. Everybody in the city, and the world, for all I know, has one. They' attached to your optic nerve and powered by your body heat. The HUD allows you to access the network from anywhere, automatically. My HUD is as much a part of me as my ears and eyes.

Scattered around the Corp Ring like flies on a dead dog, there's the rest of us. We live where we can. Here in the Quarters, there's no services to look after us (who would pay for them?), so if we don't do something ourselves, it doesn't get done. A few lucky people have landed jobs in the Corp Ring, doing stuff the Corp workers don't want to do, and that can't be done by robots - things like sweeping floors, cleaning toilets, and working in the sewers. If it wasn't for the money those guys bring in, we'd probably all starve to death.

We can handle the crime, power outages, and garbage. What everybody lives in fear of is getting sick. If you get sick in the Quarters, you better hope your immune system will save you, 'cause nobody else will. And when you die, your body might lie around in the gutter for weeks until somebody gets tired of looking at it and dumps it somewhere.

Travis says there's a cure for what my mom had, if we'd had the money. It's horrible to think that she didn't have to die, but I guess, like they're always saying on the newscasts, that's the way it should be - survival of the fittest. It was our fault. Me and my dad. We should've made more money. We should've done whatever was necessary. If we had, she'd still be alive.

A lot of the old city's empty. That's why we managed to snag our own little apartment. It's tiny, and it's kind of a dump, but it's got electricity (when it's working) and running water.

In the Lost Souls, we pretty much stick to The Quarters in general, and Tintown in particular. The other Quarters don't like strangers hanging around (neither do we). Once in a while we venture into the Corp Ring, but that's always dangerous. If SecureCorp grab you, you never know what they'll do.

But there's an even larger ring outside all the others. Everybody calls it 'The Dregs'. It's almost completely abandoned; the only people that hang out there are the homeless and criminal gangs. It's a dangerous place. When we were kids our parents used to tell us scary stories about it to keep us out. The stories worked, and still do. In all our dodgy adventures, we've never dared to go there.

☼

I always found it depressing at home, so I usually got whatever I needed and got out of there as fast as possible. Tonight, I had an hour or so to kill so I hung around in my room. I tried to relax, preparing for the run later, even though there really wasn't any way to prepare. You just did it and hoped you didn't get caught.

Always in the back of my mind was my own Appraisal, which was coming up fast. After what happened to both my parents it was tempting to refuse it, but I knew that wouldn't happen. I shoved all thoughts of it out of my mind, and finally fell asleep.

When I woke up it was almost time to leave. I got my stuff together and headed out. My dad was still sitting watching HoloTV. This time it was a newsreel. Hap Happerston, the announcer that usually handles 'feel-good' stories, was gushing about some guy from the Quarters, Burt Harper, who'd made it big.

"Burt's Appraisal was nothing special," Hap beamed. "It was what he did with his life that counted."

Hap went on to explain how Burt, once an enforcer with the Death's Heads gang, had graduated to the bottom ranks at BuildCorp, risen quickly by systematically eliminating his rivals, and was now living the good life. A 3D image of a huge yacht appeared on the pedestal, with this bozo standing on the deck, smiling ear-to-ear, a bikini-clad babe under each arm.

Burt's rivals had never been heard from again. "We have no idea what happened to the poor guys," Hap said, laughing. "But wherever they are, nobody can pin it on Burt." Hap winked at the camera. "Hey, it's just business - nothing personal."

"I'm going out," I said to my dad.

He didn't acknowledge me, just stared at the TV. I headed off on my board to the Center to meet Richie and the others. On the way, I got a call on my HUD. It was Cindy.

See you later tonight? she texted.

You sure you want to come? I answered her. *It'll be boring for you.*

I didn't really want her there. I knew she'd be pissed at what I was going to do.

Don't you want me around? she texted back. I smiled, imagining a cute pout sweeping across her face.

Sure I do, I answered, resigned. *I'll see you there. Ten o'clock.*

By that time, it would all be over.

FOUR

....

BREAKING IN

The others, Richie, Spiro, and Jake, were already at the Center by the time I got there.

"I was starting to think you were gonna jam out," Richie laughed as I squeezed through the opening.

I just sneered at him.

"You guys ready?" I said.

I scanned through the hacks listed in my HUD, double-checking that they were all there and ready to go.

Richie double-checked his own list. Finally, he smiled. "Okay - beat it."

I headed back out. "Good luck," he called after me.

Not wanting to take any chances, I boarded to within about ten blocks of the target, then strapped the board to my back and Cam-surfed on foot. On the way I passed one of the thousands of Se-cureCorp posters that dotted Tintown. Superimposed on a backdrop of the city, the face of Charles Wickham, the CEO of SecureCorp and one of the most powerful men in the world, stared down at me, pointing his finger, as if to warn me off what I was about to do.

Twenty minutes later the target came into sight. I felt good. The intel from the web was that it was one of SecureCorp's less important locations. Looking at it seemed to confirm that. It was a crumbling brick building at the outer edge of the Corp Ring. Walking by, you'd never guess what it was. We figured that, seeing as it wasn't an ultra-modern monolith like most Corp buildings, security wouldn't be as tight. At least that was the theory.

A crypted message had come in a few days ago about a flaw in the SecureCorp monitoring system. Richie and Spiro had rigged up a hack to utilize it. I volunteered to test it out. You never knew for sure whether these messages were some loser pretending they were clever, or maybe even deliberately trying to mess with the Cam-surfers. Some of the kids even claimed that SecureCorp themselves put some of the hacks out to catch us.

But this one came from a trusted source (if there was such a thing). Anyway, you only live once, right?

"I'm going for it," I whispered into my controller.

All I heard at the other end was an intake of breath. I flipped off the messaging functions in my HUD. There couldn't be any more communication until I said so. We all knew that if I got nailed I'd be on my own. I wouldn't expect, or even want, the others to help me.

The target door was in sight. It was some kind of delivery entrance, but it still had cameras focused on it, and a surveillance drone passed by every fifteen minutes. The hack the guys had come up with was awesome. Richie had set up my HUD's ID cast so it would simultaneously freeze the outside camera images for ten minutes - any longer and the video motion monitors would register a warning - and crack the electronic lock on the door. They claimed that all this would be undetectable by SecureCorp. Well, we'd see.

We'd cased the place enough times to work out the schedule of the drones. all I had to do was wait until one had just passed, to give me enough time to get inside, grab whatever I could, and get out again before it returned. Piece of cake - in theory.

My HUD said nine-thirteen PM. The next drone run should be at nine-fifteen exactly. I positioned myself at a corner, in a camera gap with a view of the door, and waited. The drones could detect the bat of an eyelash for a radius of ten meters, so I had to stay perfectly still. Part of my head was exposed as I peeked around the corner, but the drones weren't as good at detecting and identifying shapes at a distance if they weren't moving.

Exactly two minutes later I heard the faint hum of the drone. My spine stiffened as it shot around the corner of the SecureCorp building. Its non-reflective black exoskeleton was almost invisible at night, but we had another hack that edge-detected the outlines and enhanced the image. It was still just a blur, but it was a blur you could follow, a bright mesh of stitching against the night, outlining its insect-like frame.

It stopped for a few seconds, scanning. I was sure I hadn't moved. I fought against my fear and willed my body to stop shaking. The drone headed toward the door. If it saw me, there'd be nothing to indicate it. I'd find out when the SecureCorp goons surrounded me with their guns drawn. All I could do was stand still and pray I was in the clear.

The drone hovered for a while, then took off. I waited for one minute after its last echoes had faded away. Then I exhaled, stepped out from around the corner, and took one last look. It was gone.

I studied the door. Assuming the hack worked, I could get inside without getting caught. Problem was, nobody knew what was on the other side. This was a SecureCorp building - anybody who'd seen the inside was either part of that organization or wasn't coming out again. That's why all I was planning to do was sneak in a little way, see if there was something I could grab, and run for my life. If I made it in and back out again I'd be a legend. If not, I'd be toast.

I scanned the connecting alleys in every direction, the blood thumping in my ears. There was nobody around. I held up the controller on my right wrist and made one last scan of the door, with detection on. The glow of a spotlight circled it like a halo. The cameras were there - two of them. I wouldn't know whether the hack worked until I was almost in front of them.

I lifted the bandanna tied around my neck to cover the bottom part of my face. If a camera caught me I'd be harder to identify. I swallowed hard and snuck toward the door. My HUD showed the proximity. With one more step I'd be in range. I was at the point of no return. I either had to activate the hack and pray that it worked, or walk away.

I pressed the button on my controller to turn on the hack. There was nothing, no alarm, no indication that anything had changed. After a couple of seconds, my HUD said the cameras were frozen. I was breathing hard as I rushed up to the door and tried the handle. Open!

I had to hurry. The hack would expire in less than ten minutes. I pulled the door open. I was facing a long, dimly-lit hallway. High on the right-hand wall about halfway down was another camera, but I was sure I could squeeze past it. I slid inside and closed the door behind me, my heart hammering against my ribcage.

The door thunking shut jolted me back to reality. *What the hell was I doing?* But I was in. I edged along the closest wall, out of range of the camera. The motion detectors that dotted the hallway appeared on the HUD as yellow dots. The hack was supposed to disable them as well. There were no boots pounding toward me and no screaming sirens, so it must have worked.

There was a door a few meters along the wall I had my back against. Light streamed out through a small window at head height. I made for it, holding my breath. When I got there, I put my ear against it. Silence. My body shook as I stood on tip-toes and peeked through the window. I was staring down another hallway, about twenty meters long, with another door halfway along it, on the right. That door was open, and light spilled out from it to the hallway floor. Beyond it, the hallway continued for a few meters then took a right. My HUD didn't show any alarm on the door in front of me, and it was out of range of the nearest camera.

I hesitated for a few seconds, then took a deep breath, turned the handle, and opened it. Nothing. I breathed out as I stepped inside, gently eased it shut and rushed down the hall.

I was so stressed out that at first I didn't notice the humming sound in the outer hallway. When it finally registered, it was unmistakable - a drone, headed in my direction. It was almost at the door I'd just come through. I raced to the door ahead of me, and ducked inside just as I heard the first door click open.

20

I moved away from the opening, pressed my back against the inner wall, and held my breath. I glanced around. The room was large, and brightly lit. There was a single examination table in the center. I looked closer and froze. There was a guy strapped to it. He looked impossibly ancient: thin white hair, pale, mottled skin hanging from him like cords. At first I thought he was dead. Then he lifted his head. My heart just about stopped.

The drone hummed along the hallway outside. It paused at the open door beside me and hovered for a few seconds, while I stood just out of sight, shaking. Finally, it continued down the hall without coming inside. The old man was staring at me. In a few seconds, the drone hummed by going the other way. I heard the outer door open and close again, and the hum faded into the distance.

I was about to take off, then I remembered why I was here. With one eye on the old guy, I checked the bench beside the closest wall. Nothing. Finally, I noticed a card storage case in one corner. It had a keypad on top - protected by an electronic combination. I grabbed the top and pulled on it - it was locked. There's no way I was going to carry the whole thing around when I left, and anyway it was anchored somehow to the bench.

I glanced back. The old man's lips started moving.

"Help me," he whispered, in a voice like dried leaves.

I couldn't just leave him. I approached the examination table. There was a strap across his chest, and another one across his ankles. Both straps were buckled down at the bottom of the table where the guy couldn't reach. I checked my watch - less than seven minutes. In a panic, I undid the straps.

"Can you walk?" I asked him.

He tried to slide his feet off the table, but they barely moved. He closed his eyes and his fists clenched.

"They drugged me," he said. "It's no use."

I felt like a jerk, but there was nothing I could do for him. I'd be lucky if I got out of here myself.

He lifted a shaking right arm and pointed. I followed his hand. He was pointing at a poster taped to the wall beside the card case. It showed a golden sun rising over a range of mountains. Below it was a caption: Celebrate Our World - 11-10-64.

"That's what you want," he said.

I glanced back at him. He was still pointing. Suddenly it hit me. I rushed to the card box and entered the numbers from the poster on the keypad of the storage case. A tiny light on the top turned green. I checked on the old man. He'd dropped his arm. I grabbed the lid of the unit and it opened.

Inside were a set of cards. Most of them didn't look that interesting. I didn't have much time. I grabbed one at the back that had the SecureCorp gold-shield logo in one corner. In the other corner was a line drawing of a butterfly. I scanned it with the HUD controller. No locator, or at least the locator wasn't enabled, so it would be safe to take it.

I stuffed the card in my pocket, and turned back to face the old man.

"It's alright," he said, with the saddest of smiles. "Save yourself. Get out while you can. They'll be back in a few minutes."

I took off. When I got to the hallway door I peeked through the little window. The main corridor was empty - there was no sign of the drone.

I checked the time and drew in a breath. I'd been inside for eight minutes. The hack was about to expire. If I didn't make it through the exit and out of camera range in two minutes I was dead.

I slunk along the hallway as fast as I could. I reached the door, and opened it a crack. A SecureCorp cycle was crawling by. The rider didn't look my way - just routine. I closed the door and waited. I checked the time - twenty seconds.

They ticked by: fifteen, ten. I opened the door again. The cycle was just disappearing around a corner. Seven seconds. I opened the door and slipped outside.

Three seconds. I took off like a bullet.

FIVE

....

THE PRIZE

Back at the Center, my hands were still shaking as I pulled the 'trophy' card out of my pocket and stared at it. Richie leaned over my shoulder to see. It was kind of disappointing. Plain white on one side, with the SecureCorp logo and the butterfly drawing. The other side had two columns of numbers in the center. It wasn't that impressive. It didn't even really prove I'd been in the building.

"What do think the numbers are?" Richie asked, obviously not that impressed either.

I shrugged, and shoved the card back in my pocket. "I'm not going back to find out, I can tell you that much."

While I'd been on my way back, Spiro and Jake had made a run to steal some beer. They picked up my girlfriend Cindy on the way. It was too dangerous for her to go anywhere near our side of town by herself.

I told them not to tell her what I was doing, so I was pissed when they showed up and she knew all about it.

24

"She asked why you weren't there to pick her up," Jake whispered to me. "I had to say something."

I explained to her what I'd done. It sounded stupid even as I said it. I showed her the card.

"So that's what you risked your life for?" she asked, nodding at the card. "Collecting souvenirs is one thing, but breaking into SecureCorp? Are you crazy?"

"Hey, I made it out," I answered, puffing out my chest. "Nobody's ever gotten inside a—"

"You're going to get yourself killed," she snapped, shaking her head. "For a stupid card. And it doesn't even do anything."

"It might," I said defensively.

"Nothing that would do *you* any good."

I stepped forward to hug her. She pushed me away. "If you're going to keep doing stuff like that, I don't want to see you anymore."

She moved away to a corner with her back to us.

I went over and put my arm around her shoulder. This time she didn't resist. "Hey, we're just fooling around," I said. "I promise I won't go near SecureCorp anymore. That scared the shit out of me anyway."

"I don't want to lose you," she turned and whispered into my ear.

"You won't," I whispered back. "Forgive me?"

Finally she smiled, and kissed me.

I took her hand and we joined the others. We proceeded to get hammered to celebrate my run. I showed Jake and Spiro my trophy. They said it was great, though I got the feeling they were underwhelmed. I didn't tell any of them about the old guy. It was so creepy, and I was still trying to figure out what was going on. I felt guilty about leaving him there, but what else could I do?

Anyway, I'd done something no other kid had ever dared to do - broken into a SecureCorp building. It was a great feeling, but something else overshadowed all our laughter and back-slapping. It was like we all wanted to say something, but we were all afraid. We'd talked about it so many times before, but back then it had been something in the distant future, something we could kick down the road and worry about later.

Now it *was* later. We were all about the same age, so we'd all be having our Appraisals sometime this year.

Richie brought it up first. It pissed me off. I didn't really want to talk about it.

"I'm not worried," he said. "Everybody in my family's done okay. I'll be in the high teens."

"It's got nothing to do with heredity," Spiro said. "They proved that a long time ago."

Richie sneered at him. "They're full of it. I'll do okay."

"I'll outlive all of you losers," Jake laughed, a bit nervously I thought. "You wait - I'll be a two."

"Good luck," Richie said shoving Jake's shoulder. "You'll be one of those white-haired forty-year-old guys sleeping in their chairs with the HoloTV on and..."

He blushed and glanced over at me. Nobody else spoke. "S...Sorry Alex," he finally said.

I just shrugged and looked at the ground.

"What about Spaz, here," Jake said. He nodded his head toward Spiro. "Bet he negs out big time."

Spiro's face turned red and he clenched his fists.

"You shut the fuck up!" he yelled at Jake. He stood up, ready for a fight.

"Settle down," Jake said. "I'm just joking."

Spiro stood shaking for a few seconds. "And don't call me Spaz," he mumbled as he finally sat back down.

"What about you, Cindy?" Richie said. "Your daddy's rich. He should be able to buy you a good one."

"I don't want to talk about it," she said. She looked scared. I took her hand.

"Screw you, Richie," I said. "Leave her alone. Anyway, you know it doesn't work like that."

"That's what they say," Jake said, "but who really knows."

"Shit, you guys are touchy," Richie said.

He looked at me. "Anyway, what about you?"

I was annoyed with the direction the conversation was going. "How the hell do I know?" I said. "Whatever happens, happens. Let's just shut up about it."

I'd just turned sixteen. I was the oldest, so I'd be going first.

My Appraisal was just one week away.

SIX

....

THE QUARTERS

Tintown is managed by sort of an ad-hoc council. If you're lucky, they'll pick you to do odd jobs around the Quarter, sometimes for money, but usually for barter, like food, or medicine.

A few years ago, my dad got hired to help pick up the garbage that the rats and stray dogs didn't get to. He makes enough to keep us going, but he's constantly got to fight to keep his job. Like I said before, it's survival of the fittest - the way they're always telling us - the way it should be. But Dad's not as healthy as he used to be. He's slowing down.

The luckiest guys are the ones who work security. They take care of anybody that gets out of line, and defend our Quarter against attacks from outside. The job's dangerous, but you get lots of barter, and lots of respect. If I was bigger, that's what I'd do when I'm old enough. But jobs like that are hard to come by. They probably wouldn't want a runt like me, and even if I snagged one I'd have to fight like hell to keep it.

Since the Corps are all private and for profit, none of them lift a finger without getting paid, and the amount they do is directly proportional to how much they get. For instance, BuildCorp is responsible for collecting garbage. How much they collect, and how often, depends on how much they get paid. If they're not paid anything, they don't do anything. If the garbage piles up and rats and disease are everywhere, too bad.

Like all good private enterprises, the Corps would all like to swallow each other. Travis, my teacher at the co-op school, says they've reached a standoff - they jockey for position and dominance, but mostly they put up with the status quo.

Here in the Quarters there's a few small backroom setups: corner stores, repair shops. But if they grow to any size the Corps either absorb them or drive them out of business. Then there's the black market, which the Corps are constantly trying to shut down. With all the stuff on HoloTV about free enterprise and competition, you'd think the Corps would approve. I guess when it doesn't bring in money for them, suddenly it's evil. But for us, buying from the Corps is just too expensive. For us, the underground market is all there is.

Life in the Quarters can be tough, but they say it used to be a lot worse. The newscasts talk about how in the past, every time you made a dollar you had to pay part of it to the government. They called it 'taxes'. Nowadays we're free from all that. Whatever we make, we keep - period.

Travis says that's a joke - that if what you make is pretty much zero, which it is for us, not having to pay any of it back isn't a big advantage. According to him, a lot of the stuff the Corps do now used to be done

29

by the government and paid for by taxes, and since everybody paid a share, and they didn't have to make a profit, it ended up costing less.

Sounds like a stupid idea. Why pay for stuff that you might not even want or need? Anyway, now we're free - free to follow our dreams. We don't have to depend on anybody else's help. Anybody - even people like us from the Quarters, can make it big and join one of the Corps - even the Elite.

Back when Mom was alive, Dad used to say I could make something of myself, even though we're poor. If I got a good Appraisal, I'd have time to get really good at something and one the Corps would have to hire me. I notice he doesn't say that anymore.

Mind you, Dad doesn't say much of anything anymore.

☼

It's weird. For almost everything I do, Dad doesn't seem to give a shit. He never asks me where I'm going, who my friends are, even whether I'm happy. Mind you, it's not just me - as far as I can tell my dad doesn't give a shit about anything or anybody.

That's why it's so weird - about school. I have to go. He's fanatical about it. He can't actually force me - he can barely walk. But he makes my life miserable if I don't go, hounding me and getting on my back. Since he cut down on his work schedule, that's pretty much the only reason he ever takes time off from watching HoloTV. I keep offering to take over the garbage work for him, but he gets mad and tells me to concentrate on finishing school. In the end, it's easier to go than listen to him. Anyway, as pathetic as my dad is, I still feel like I owe him something.

Of course, like everything, regular school costs. There's only one proper one in the Quarters, but even when Dad was working full time it would have been too expensive. Now that he's old and sick, there's no way. Our only choice is the co-op school. It's not really even a school - just a couple of people from the neighbourhood who volunteer to teach the local kids.

I don't really mind going. I actually might have liked what they call higher education (that is, anything above about grade eight), if there was such a thing in the Quarters, and if I didn't have to spend most of my time fighting to stay alive.

Travis, the teacher that shows up most of the time, is what you'd call eccentric, but he's basically a great guy. He seems to take a special interest in me. He says I'm one of the few of his students that's got an 'inquisitive mind'. When you're teaching people as ignorant as we are, you could say pretty much anything and they wouldn't know any better, but he's confirmed enough stuff that I actually know about for me to give him the benefit of the doubt.

After all the time we've spent together, I still don't even know his last name, or what he does when he's not teaching us. He just shows up at the allotted time, like the rest of us (when I say 'the rest', I mean the three or four that can be bothered). I asked him once where he got all his education, but he wouldn't tell me. I found out from one of the other kids that he had a daughter about my age, though I've never met her. Apparently, she went to the regular school - who knows how he could afford that.

Travis taught me to read and write, and some math and science. He tries to teach me what he calls history, too, but it sounds like bullshit to me. Anyway, what's the point of hearing about stuff that happened before you were even born? You hardly ever hear anything about it on the HUD or on HoloTV. If it was important you'd think they'd talk about it. Nobody cares about it - nobody except Travis, that is.

And he likes to talk about philosophy and politics. More lame subjects. He goes on about democracy and freedom of choice and all that, which I don't get. How could you be any more free than we are right now?

Anyway, like I do every Monday and Wednesday, I boarded down to an abandoned office building a few blocks from us, where they'd set up the co-op school. More history. More philosophy. More politics. Boring.

At a break between classes I cornered Travis in the courtyard outside. Most of the time he managed to make classes pretty interesting, but today was a snoozefest.

"Maybe you find it boring," he said, "but it's stuff you need to know."

I laughed. "I need to know about politics?"

He gave me that look he had.

"What's the difference between the Freedom Party and the Enterprise Party?" he said.

"How do I know?" I said. "Anyway, who cares?"

"Well, they're the only two parties you can vote for. If they stand for the same thing, why vote?"

"You have to vote. It's the law."

He held out both his hands with the palms facing up, like he was balancing something in them. "Look, if I force you to choose between a red ball and another identical red ball, do you actually have a choice?"

"I don't want a red ball," I laughed.

He droned on and on. I got tired of listening to it.

"Shit, man," I said. "All you do is complain. What more could we want? We got free speech, we got the vote - we *have* to vote. Anybody who works hard can get rich—"

It was his turn to laugh. "What good is free speech when there's nobody to hear you?"

"I can talk to you," I said, "and Richie, and my dad—"

"But you can never reach a large crowd. You could never broadcast on the net to people's HUDs. You could never talk on HoloTV. You could never change anything."

"Sure I could. I'd just have to make enough money."

"And how would you do that?"

I looked at my feet. I had to admit it was a pretty stupid idea.

"You'd have to be in one of the Corps," he answered for me. "Even then it would be tough. And in the incredibly unlikely event that you managed to claw your way up the ranks to a position of power, your agenda would be the same as all the guys in the Corps now."

I was getting annoyed. "If things needed changing," I said, "I'd change them."

He stared at me, like he was studying me.

"You know," he said, "maybe you would."

He glanced over at the other kids kicking a ball around the court-yard, then turned back.

"Let me ask you this," he said. "Have the government and the Corps ever given you anything for free?"

I laughed again. "Why would they do that? If you want stuff you have to pay. Everybody knows that."

"But in fact, there's two exceptions to that rule," he said, smiling.

"Oh yeah?"

He nodded at the HUD controller on my wrist. "There's the HUD. Don't you think it's strange that everybody gets one?"

I shrugged. He was always coming up with stuff like this. I can just barely remember when I got my HUD. I think I was about seven or eight years old. Travis says they're a pretty recent thing, developed within the past fifty years. So I guess there was a time when nobody had them. I can't imagine what it would be like without one.

"Everybody - even bums living on the street - get the HUD," Travis said. "Why do you think that is?"

I shrugged again.

"The same reason they sell the HoloTVs for almost nothing," he said. "Control." He pointed at his own head. "The HUD feeds you in-formation, but it's *their* information - the information *they* want you to know. If you can access something on the HUD, it's because they want you to have it. If they choose not to show it to you, it might as well not exist."

For once I thought of a comeback. "What about the hacks?"

I figured I had him on that one. Hacks like the one that confuses the HUD's GPS locator, and the ones we use Cam-surfing, are pretty

34

common. They've never done any real damage, which I guess is why the crackdown hasn't been harder.

At first Travis' eyes opened wider, like I'd reminded him of something. The look disappeared, and his brows came together. I smiled. I'd stumped him.

"That I can't answer for sure," he finally said, "but I don't think the kids are coming up with this stuff on their own."

"What do you mean?"

"I mean they're getting help. Maybe there's people in the Corps... Then again, if you can hack into the system, it's probably because the Elite want you to."

"Why would they want that?"

He looked me in the eye. "There's no way for us to know exactly why they're doing something, but if you know how their minds work, you can guess."

I looked down and shook my head. "And you know how their minds work?"

He stared out at some distant point beyond the courtyard. "I know enough," he said.

I was starting to tune out, like I usually did when he got on one of his rants.

"You know there was a riot last night?" he said.

I looked up. "What?"

"A riot. People in the streets, throwing rocks and bottles. In ShakeTown, the next Quarter over. They're desperate. No jobs, no money, no future - the Elite have walked a fine line, leaving just enough to keep the public quiet. But they're getting greedy, putting themselves in danger."

"You're so full of it," I laughed. "I would have seen it on my HUD."

"You think so? Like I said, if they don't choose to tell you about it, it's like it never happened."

"Well, if it's so secret, how do *you* know about it?"

He leaned in toward me and whispered. "I was there. The SecureCorp thugs opened fire. A bunch of people died."

I stared at him. "I don't believe you."

He shrugged. The riot thing was new, but I was getting a little bored with the conversation. I thought about changing the subject, but I couldn't think of anything. Then I remembered.

"So, what's the second thing?" I asked.

"Second thing?"

"You said there were two things they gave us for free — what's the second one?"

He smiled. "Appraisal - they pay for everybody to have it, even you. Why do you think that is?"

I stood there like a moron. I've got to admit the thought never occurred to me before.

"You're so smart," I said. "You tell me."

"Because they're looking for people," he said.

"People?"

"People who respond to Appraisal - in a certain way."

"What do they care?"

His expression turned dark. "For all they go on about freedom and democracy, it's the farthest thing from what they want."

"So, what *do* they want?"

"Everything," he said. "They want everything. And they've almost got it. The only stumbling block is Appraisal. They can't control it. They have to put up with the results the same as everybody else. They can't stand that.

"They've poured trillions into research trying to find a way to change the outcome, but nothing's worked. That's why they give the Appraisal to everybody. They know that statistically a certain number will be worth studying."

"You can't know all this," I said.

"You're right," he said. "I don't know. I'm just guessing. But it's the only explanation."

"Who's this 'they' you keep going on about? The government? Everybody knows what bozos *they* are."

He smiled at me. "I don't think you're quite ready to hear about that yet."

SEVEN

....

APPRAISAL

The week before my Appraisal appointment crawled by. I didn't feel like talking to anybody, not even Cindy. Then something happened that seemed like some kind of bad omen. One day I showed up at the co-op school and Travis wasn't there. I asked around. Nobody seemed to know what happened to him. There's a couple of other teachers, but they're not much more educated than I am, and I've never connected with them like I did with Travis. As the days crept by he still hadn't shown up. I was already feeling bummed out about the Appraisal. This just made it worse.

When the day finally arrived, I got up and got dressed, just like always, though I knew it would be like no other in my life.

"I'm going," I called to my dad from the front door. He just sat staring at the HoloTV.

At the Appraisal clinic, I avoided eye contact with everybody in the waiting room. I knew they'd all be freaked out. Hey, I was freaked out myself - who wouldn't be? It didn't help that both my mother and father had gotten negative Appraisals. Everybody swears heredity's got nothing to do with it, but it's hard not to worry about it.

The clinic closest to us was in an older concrete building just inside the Corp Ring. In the waiting room, a bunch of kids, most about my age, sat fidgeting on the plastic chairs spaced along the walls. Some had their parents with them. Most, like me, were alone. I confirmed my appointment at the front desk, then found an empty chair in a far corner.

There was nothing left to do but wait. I stretched out my legs, laid back my head, and closed my eyes. I tried to focus on something pleasant.

I thought about how Cindy and I first met. It was about a year ago, when me and Richie were Cam-surfing. Usually we only did it at night, but we were bored and needed some excitement. We staked out the Museum of Democracy, deep in the Corp Ring. As usual, we got there by latching onto the backs of empty RoboTaxis and letting them tow us on our boards. Government buildings were always more of a challenge to get into, and we'd just gotten ahold of a hack that was supposed to unlock some of the museum doors.

The hack worked; we made it inside through a delivery entrance. The place was actually open, so technically we could have just walked in as visitors, but it cost and we had no money to pay, even if we wanted to, which we didn't. Anyway, they would have taken one look at us and told us to get lost. The hack was also supposed to give us access to some of the inner offices - much better for trophies.

Vita Aeterna

That was when I saw her. She'd snuck away from the group on one of her school outings. Later she told me she'd lied to them and said she had to use the bathroom, but then she took off to explore.

She came around a corner and caught us just as we were breaking in. She was wearing a school uniform: plaid skirt, a blinding white blouse with a school tie. Her blond hair curled around the shoulders of her uniform jacket. Her reckless blue eyes bored into me. I thought she was the most beautiful girl I'd ever seen.

She took one look and knew what was going on. I figured for sure she'd scream or rat us out or something, but she didn't do anything.

"Looking for souvenirs?" she whispered.

At first we were both too shocked to say anything. Finally, I just nodded my head.

"I know where you can get some good ones," she said.

Richie and I looked at each other. It could be some kind of trick. She tilted her head to the right, and started walking. I turned and followed her.

"Are you crazy, man?" Richie whispered, trailing after me. "She's gonna turn us in to security."

"I don't think so," I whispered back.

"My names's Cindy," she said when I caught up with her. I was in love.

She seemed to know where she was going. Once or twice we saw uniformed people, but we managed to hide before they spotted us. We eventually reached a door that said 'Storage #2'.

"Here," she said, nodding at it.

I tried the hack. We heard a click. Richie and I looked at each other. I shrugged and turned the handle. It opened. I half expected a squad of SecureCorp soldiers to jump out from behind it. The room was empty of people, but we stood for a few seconds with our mouths hanging open. It was the storage room for the entire souvenir shop. There were shelves and shelves of stuff - a trophy-hunter's paradise. Richie and I grabbed a couple of the best ones we could find.

"We better get out of here," Richie whispered.

"Thanks," I said to Cindy as we backed out the door. She smiled. It seemed ridiculous to even suggest it, but hey, you only live once. I said: "I want to see you again."

She didn't say anything. She punched something on her controller and her HUD address came up on my display. I gave her one last smile. I felt ten feet tall as we took off with our trophies.

After that me and Cindy were together all the time. Sometimes I felt like a loser with her; she had all this money and opportunity and this incredible education, while I had nothing, and could barely read and write. All I had was what I learned from the volunteer guys like Travis in the Quarters.

There were holes in my education you could drive a truck through, but she never laughed at me or said anything about it. Sometimes she'd correct me about something, but she always did it with love. Cindy...

Something bumped against my feet and I woke from my daydream. Some old lady was trying to get by. She gave me a nasty look. What was she doing here anyway? She must have been Appraised back in the Stone Age. I pulled in my legs and sat up straighter, but laid back and closed my eyes again after she passed.

My mind spun ahead double-time. I thought about the milestones in people's lives: birth, marriage, children, and of course, finally - death. All of them had been around in some form for as long as people existed. And none of them had changed all that much since then - except the last one. The newest milestone, Appraisal, had been around for less than a hundred years, but it was a doozy.

I heard muffled voices behind the door in front of me. I lifted up my head and opened my eyes. The door opened. A girl, about my age, stumbled out, crying into a handkerchief. A nurse in a white uniform had an arm around her shoulders, comforting her. The girl removed the handkerchief and blew her nose. For a second, she looked up and her eyes met mine. I cringed. This was exactly what I'd been trying to avoid.

I couldn't help studying her face. It did look a little wrinkled - nah, that had to be my imagination. There's no way you'd see anything this early. The girl staggered past and out the door. I laid back again. Thinking about it was a drag. I tried to blank out my mind and I must have fallen asleep.

I woke with a hand on my shoulder. I jumped and drew back. The same nurse, the one that was comforting the girl, was standing beside me.

"Mr. Barret?" she said. Her eyes were sad.

I nodded. *How can somebody handle a job like that?* I thought.

I followed her through the door the crying girl had come out of and down a hallway. By this time I was totally wired. She pointed to a small room on the right and I went in. She shut the door and I waited.

For my whole life I'd been able to put the whole issue of Appraisal out of my mind. Now the moment that every kid my age looked forward to with a mixture of anticipation and dread, was finally here. I thought about trying to go back to sleep, but now I was too strung out.

I figured I was probably screwed. Talk about bad genes. My mother, my dad. There was something screwy about my uncle's Appraisal too - my dad's brother. I'd never met my uncle Zack. I always assumed he was dead. Dad would never talk about him, or what happened to him, but it must have been something bad. Another negative Appraisal, I figured. Seemed like everybody else in my family had gotten screwed. Hey, why not me too?

I thought about how I'd react to the result. If it was bad, I'd accept it and be a man. There was no way I was going to end up like the girl I saw in the waiting room. Or like my dad...

If it was good, I'd be - what was the word - humble. I wouldn't flaunt it and look down on the unlucky bastards with low multiples like some of the older kids I'd seen. If it was mediocre, well - that's what most people's was anyway. Nothing wrong with that.

A different nurse knocked softly, opened the door, and led me to another room, with a raised bed and benches full of tools and instruments.

This is it, I thought.

In a few minutes a man in a lab coat came in, carrying an electronic notebook.

"Mr. Barret," he said, smiling. He reached out his free hand and shook mine. "I'm Doctor Ryman. I'm going to do your Appraisal today."

I swallowed hard, as the reality hit me.

"Just relax," he said. "It won't hurt a bit."

He swept a hand toward the bed, and I climbed up on it. The nurse held out a tray with an electronic hypo. It looked a lot smaller than I was expecting. Such a small gizmo producing such huge consequences. Dr. Ryman picked it up, checked the dosage reading, and pressed it against my upper arm. I felt a slight pinch, like Cindy did when she was teasing me. Dr. Ryman put the syringe back on the tray and the nurse carried it away.

They both took off for about ten minutes, left me lying on the bed, shaking. When they got back, Dr. Ryman took a blood sample. That was a more involved procedure than the actual Appraisal. I watched my red blood filling the test-tube. It looked normal enough.

What an idiot, I thought. *How would you expect it to look?*

Dr. Ryman stepped back and took off his gloves.

I was lying there like a dummy waiting for something else to happen, but the nurse just motioned for me to get down from the bed. She led me back to the room I'd been in before.

'Anticlimactic' - yeah, I thought. *That was the word.*

Funny, I didn't feel any different, even though I knew the injection could transform my life. Twenty minutes later Dr. Ryman walked in. He sat there for a few seconds, staring at me like I was some kind of freak.

What's the deal? I thought. *Is he trying to psych me out or something? Is this part of it?*

"Mr. Barret?" he said.

Is that all anybody says around here?

I nodded.

His face twisted into this weird expression. "I'm afraid there's been a bit of a glitch."

"What?" I said, like a moron. "They gotta do it again?"

He just sat there staring at me. I tried to figure out exactly what his expression was, and I felt a lump in my throat when it finally occurred to me - it was fear.

"Would you follow me, please?" he said.

We left the room and headed down the hall. At the very end was another room with a narrow, padded bench on one side and a chair against the far wall. It looked a lot like the one I'd just been in, but something was different.

"Please wait here," he said. He shut the door and I jumped when I heard the thunk of the latch outside. I tried the handle. I was right - it was locked.

"Hey," I pounded on the door. "What's going on? What the hell are you trying to pull!"

That was when I figured out the difference between this room and the one I was in before. My shouts faded into the walls and disappeared instantly. It was a hardened, sound-proof cell. I was a prisoner.

I pounded on the door for another twenty minutes before I finally gave up. I sat down and tried to figure out what was going on. I'd been preparing for all kinds of different scenarios my whole life: high, low, even negging out. This wasn't like any of them. I'd talked to older kids

45

about how their Appraisals had gone, and none of them had mentioned anything like this.

My hands were shaking. Strung out and exhausted, I lay down on the bench. Maybe it was stress or something. Maybe it was the injection. Whatever it was, in a few minutes I fell asleep.

When I woke up there were voices in the room. Two white-coated men were standing just inside the open door. I jumped up and rushed at them. I was hoping I could push them out of the way and get out of this place. They each grabbed one of my arms. Before I could even yell anything one of them pressed an injector against my shoulder, and everything went black.

EIGHT

....

A PRISONER

When I woke up I had no idea how much time had passed. My head was pounding like bombs were exploding inside my skull. I tried to sit up, but the pain almost made me pass out. I closed my eyes again, lay back down, and waited for the pounding to subside.

A few minutes later I tried again and finally made it. The room was about twice the size of the one at the clinic. It looked like a hotel room. It had a proper bed, which is what I was sitting on, and a night table with a lamp. There was a couch in the farthest corner, and a coffee table and a single chair. There was a bathroom off to the right.

What it didn't have was a HoloTV, a phone, or any other way to receive or send information.

And there was something even more freaky, something I hadn't experienced in living memory. My HUD wasn't working. I frantically pushed buttons on the controller, but nothing happened. It was sickening - like part of me was missing - like there was a gaping hole in my reality.

Now I really did feel sick.

I swung my legs over the side of the bed. The throbbing in my skull intensified, and I tasted bile in the back of my throat. I stumbled for the bathroom, collapsing to my knees, my head over the toilet, just in time to puke my guts out. Thank God there was a bottle of painkillers on the sink. I staggered to my feet, gulped down three, and headed back out to check the door of my room.

Surprise, surprise - it was locked.

What the hell's going on? I thought. *What did I do?*

I lay down and slept for another twenty minutes. When I woke up I felt something like normal again. I'd just gotten back out of bed when the handle of the door turned. I moved to a corner next to it, positioning myself so I could make a run at the opening.

I crouched down, ready to spring through the gap. As soon as the door opened, I flew towards it. Unfortunately, the space was occupied by two burly guards: one in some kind of uniform, the other in a white tee-shirt. Both of them were a foot taller than me. I threw myself against them anyway. They grabbed my arms and forced me back into the room.

A third man walked through the now open door. He was smaller and more intelligent-looking, with slicked-back hair and black-framed glasses. Like Dr. Ryman, he wore a white smock and carried an electronic notepad. Unlike Ryman's, his smock had a small symbol, like a stylized butterfly, on the lapel. It looked familiar, but I couldn't figure out where I'd seen it before.

"What the fuck am I doing here!" I yelled at them.

"Settle down, Alex," the man in the smock said, smiling. "Nobody's going to hurt you. Have a seat."

He closed the door and motioned to the chair next to the coffee table.

I struggled against the guards, but finally relaxed. There was nothing else I could do. I sat down in the chair. The guards moved away but stood by the door. The white-smocked man took a seat on the couch.

"First, let me introduce myself," he said. "My name is Doctor Charles Knowles. You can call me Chuck."

"Well screw you, Chuck," I said. "What are you trying to pull?"

Chuck's smarmy grin gave me the creeps. Somewhere behind it was the same expression I'd seen on Dr. Ryman's face.

"Settle down," Chuck said. "We just need to do a few more tests - to make certain there are no side-effects."

"You drug me and kidnap me and lock me in this room, just so I can have some tests?" I said. "And what's with the goons?" I nodded at the two men by the door. The uniformed guy, a gorilla with a square, over-sized jaw, sneered at me.

"I apologize for that," Chuck said. "There was a bit of a mix-up. It's important that we do these tests. We didn't want you running off before we got the chance."

"Some mix-up," I said. My head was still throbbing. "So do the fucking tests and let me out of here. And what the hell is my Appraisal? That other doctor never even told me. Why doesn't my HUD work in here? And where am I anyway?"

"All in good time, Alex," Chuck said, putting a hand on my shoulder. He nodded to the guy in the tee shirt, who opened the door and took off. "Don't worry," Chuck said to me. "Everything's fine. We'll do our little tests and get you out of here as quickly as possible."

I relaxed a little, but the whole thing still felt like bullshit. The door opened and the guard that had left reappeared with a bundle of clothes in his hand.

"Put this on please, Alex," Chuck said.

I stood up. My head exploded with pain. The throb that had been fading away rushed back like a tidal wave. I swayed sideways. Chuck reached up and held my arm to steady me. After a few seconds the pain finally subsided. I got undressed and put on their stupid hospital gown, one of the ones where your bare ass is sticking out the back.

Each of the guards took one of my arms. They opened the door and led me down a hallway. It opened into large, empty room with several examination tables, mobile instrument carts, and giant over-head lights. I tried to pull away and the guards tightened their grips.

"Don't be so jumpy," Chuck smiled. "You'll be out of here in no time."

I was still groggy and confused, but one thing was becoming crystal clear: I needed to get out of this place - right now. I relaxed like I wasn't going to fight them anymore, waiting for a break.

Even if I got away from them - where would I go? I didn't even know where I was. I didn't care. I had to try. We reached one of the examination tables and Chuck swept his hand towards it. The guards let go of my arms so I could climb up. I put my hands on the table. There was still a guard on either side of me. I swung my legs up onto the table like I was going to lie down, but then I didn't stop, I just pushed myself off the other side. That put the table between me and the others.

I took off and started running. I could only see one exit. I had to run in a wide circle to stay out of the reach of the guards, and by the time I got to the door they'd caught up with me. One of them took a flying leap and tackled my legs. I fell forward. My head bounced off the floor and I was gone.

☼

Days, then weeks, went by. Three times a day some orderly-type, always accompanied by at least one burly guard, would bring me a meal - the only bright spot about being here - it was actually real food rather than FoodCorp packets. Other than the guys who worked there, I never saw another soul.

The part about letting me go was bullshit, but the part about testing was true, at least so far. They still hadn't said anything about what they were actually after. They hadn't done anything bad to me (though I had a sickening feeling they were going to). They'd taken blood samples, urine samples, hair samples, and done body scans. Everything they did was slow and deliberate, like they were worried about making a mistake.

The rest of the time I was trapped in my room. One night I had a dream - about my dad. It was just after my mother died. I was about eight years old. Already most of his hair was gone, and what was left was completely gray. He was apologizing.

"I was selfish," he said, his face already lined with defeat. "I knew I wouldn't be around to look after you, but we wanted a child. I always thought your mother would be there after..."

I woke up, the dream still fresh in my mind. I thought about my mother. The fact is, I don't remember much about her. Once in a while I'll have a flashback. It's never an actual image - I don't even remember what she looked like. When I try to visualize her, it always comes out like one of those interviews on HoloTV where they blur somebody's face to hide their identity.

I never remember her face, just the little details you'd think weren't that important: the warmth of her body as she tucked me into bed, the rhythm of her voice as she read me to sleep, even the smell of her hair as she bent down to kiss me good night. At least I tell myself I remember - it was a long time ago.

Living without her's not terrible. It's just - emptiness - like nothing's there. And I don't miss her. You don't miss what you never had, or at least don't remember having, I guess.

I wondered what my dad was doing right now. Would he be able to take care of himself if I wasn't there?

In all this time they still hadn't told me what my Appraisal was. At this point I wouldn't have believed anything they said anyway.

Every day the goon in the uniform, who I'd nicknamed 'Brickhead' because of his square, angular skull, would show up at my room. We'd march along a series of antiseptic white corridors and through a series of doors. Sometimes Chuck would be with him. Most of the time we'd be alone. Some of the doors were secured with biometric panels.

Either Chuck or Brickhead would unlock them by pressing an index finger on the sensor.

There's dozens of labs in this place, but we almost always ended up at the same one. Twenty minutes later Chuck would show up. They'd force me down on the exam table, and the sessions would begin. By the third week I figured they must have done every test, probe, and scan it was possible to do.

They were preparing for something, and it was pretty clear I wasn't going to like whatever that thing was.

NINE

....

WALTER

I hadn't been able to use the HUD since I got here. The building must be shielded somehow, and the staff either had theirs turned off or were using some frequency I couldn't read. It was horrible, like having one of my legs cut off or something, or like being deaf or blind. The world didn't seem normal anymore. It was like somebody had erased part of it.

That's why I nearly shit myself when Brickhead was taking me on my usual jaunt down the hallway toward the lab, and an image suddenly floated in front of me. It was a hologram, a standard projection like anybody would have in their living room, but produced by my HUD. Even more shocking was what I was looking at. It was the old guy I'd seen when I was Cam-surfing and broke in looking for a trophy.

It's hard to describe what he looked like. The closest I can come is that he looked dead. He wasn't dead, but he looked dead. Like the life had been sucked out of him. He looked like a corpse that was somehow reanimated and still walking around. I jumped when I saw him. I checked to make sure Brickhead hadn't noticed. When I glanced over, the goon gave me his usual sneer, like he'd like nothing better than to beat the living crap out of me. I had enough sense not to let him know what I was seeing.

"I mean you no harm," the image spoke in my earpiece. His voice was tired and weak, like every breath was an effort. "I'm your friend."

Maybe he was some kind of plant - put there to make me think there was somebody I could trust, though you'd think they'd use a guy who didn't look like he was about to drop dead to do it. Anyway, why should they care whether I trusted them or not? I hadn't figured that out yet.

"I can see and hear you," the image said.

I gave him the finger.

"Yes, I saw that," he said.

"Just testing," I said.

"What?" Brickhead turned and glared at me. Luckily, he hadn't seen my finger gesture.

"Nothin'," I answered. Brickhead gave me a shove just for good measure, and we continued.

"Sorry for contacting you now," the image said. "I only had a small window of opportunity when the monitors were down. My name is Walter. *They* can't know about this." He inclined his head toward the guard. "I'll contact you again."

My mind was racing as Chuck performed yet another barrage of tests. Who was this Walter guy? Was he for real, or were Chuck and the gang trying to mess with my head? And what was wrong with him?

If he was as out of it as he seemed, how did he manage to contact me without them knowing?

Again, nothing much happened. More blood samples, urine samples, hair samples, body scans. When it was over they took me back. I was confused. I hadn't seen any more of Walter (or seen anything at all on the HUD). I started to think it was some kind of dream. When Brickhead shoved me back in my cell I was so stressed out I just collapsed on the bed.

I closed my eyes, hoping to get some sleep, but images kept swirling through my head: my dad, Richie, the Lost Souls, Cindy…

I thought back to a couple of months ago, when Cindy had snuck me into a HoloSurround chamber in the Corp Ring. She'd picked out the 'Rustic Farm' track, kind of a hokey, girl track, but I didn't mind. It was the first, and probably the last, time I'd ever experienced something like that. It was like a dream, but I remember every detail.

We entered the chamber, and the lights went down. When they came up again, it was mid-afternoon on a blazing summer day in the country. A breeze was shaking the branches of the trees surrounding the gigantic field where we stood. Little parasol-shaped dandelion seed pods wafted through the air, dragonflies buzzed overhead, crickets hummed in the tall grass. It was like the first summer of the world, like it must have been for Adam and Eve on their first day in paradise.

Cindy took off, and I chased after her. I flew across the field, and nearly lost my balance in the chase. Ahead, Cindy giggled and raced toward the old barn on the north side. She turned back and glanced at me, her face glowing with an inner light. For a fraction of a second, time stopped, like God had taken a snapshot and captured this one instant of joy and happiness - Cindy's backward glance frozen in place, her smile like the rays of the sun overhead. It was like I paused in mid-air, feet off the ground, lips parted, the laughter caught forever on my face.

I remember studying the frozen scene like I was some kind of ethereal being, floating above it all.

I still can't believe it, I thought. *I can't believe that she's in love with me.*

The moment passed and time started up again. My feet touched the ground and I caught up with Cindy near the barn. She giggled as I wrapped my arms around her and gently guided her down into the long grass.

She ran her fingers through my hair and gazed into my eyes, inviting me in. Without thinking, I leaned down and kissed her. It was like nothing I'd ever experienced before, like she was all that existed, like the world began and ended with her.

We lay for a long time without speaking.

Finally I said, "Let's make a pact."

"What?" she laughed.

I hesitated, petrified that she'd say no, or even laugh at me. "That we'll always be together."

"Really?" she answered.

"Do you love me?" I said, dreading the response.

"More than anything," she gazed into my eyes and smiled.

"And I love you," I said. "So it's settled. We'll be together forever, no matter what."

57

She sat up and looked at me. "But what about my dad?"

An image rushed into my head of her father's bloated, red face glaring down at me in contempt.

"He'll come around," I said, trying to sound more confident than I felt.

"And Appraisal," she said. "What if we're not compatible?"

"You sound like you're trying to get out of it."

"No way," she said. She twirled a lock of her blond hair around one finger. "If we really love each other it doesn't matter. I don't care - do you?"

I felt better. "No, I don't care," I said.

She lay back down and put her head on my shoulder. "Let's be in love and stay together forever, no matter what."

I wanted this moment to be frozen in time, like Cindy's backward glance.

A knocking sound snapped me out of my day-dream. At first I thought it was at the door, but then I realized it was in my head. I sat up on the bed and rubbed my eyes. My HUD fired up again and there he was.

He told me he was a prisoner, just like me.

"How can you see and hear me?" I whispered. I still didn't really believe anything he was saying, but it's not like I had anything better to do.

"The building is wired with microphones and cameras," he said. "They want to monitor what you're doing. I've devised a hack that diverts their feed for a short period."

"You're the guy I saw before," I said. "So, we're in the building I broke into?"

He nodded.

"Sorry I didn't help you before," I said, looking at the floor.

He shrugged. "There was nothing you could have done..."

"How long have you been here?"

"More than twenty years," he answered. "When I arrived, I was the same age as you."

I cringed. "What! What multiple are you anyway - point five or something?"

"I don't know," he said. He looked down and shook his head sadly. "No one's ever told me. But I don't think my apparent age has anything to do with my Appraisal. They did experiments..." He swept his hands along either side of his body.

"*They* did that?" I swallowed hard. I still didn't really believe him. "So, what am I doing here?"

"I don't know," he said. "They've never told me anything. Every day they take me to a room, perform their tests, and bring me back."

I shuddered, imagining the past three weeks stretching out for twenty years.

"They'll do anything to get whatever it is they want," Walter said, yanking me back to the present. "Kill, maim, cripple for life. Nowadays they only do the preliminary tests here. Soon they'll move you somewhere else - somewhere with much heavier security. You must escape."

"You're telling me," I said. "But I've been studying this place for weeks. There's no way out."

"There's one way," he said. "And I know what it is."

"If you know a way out, why haven't you escaped a yourself?"

"It takes two," he said.

"So nobody else has been here in twenty years?"

"There have been many."

"What happened to them?"

He smiled sadly. "This facility is being phased out, and some were transferred to the new one, as you will be. I'm so broken that it's probably not worth moving me. The experiments take a great toll. Some didn't survive. For some reason they have been more careful with me."

"They've hardly done anything to me so far…"

"Then you must be very special indeed."

T E N

....

E S C A P E

Walter and I talked for a week or so, mostly at night, after all the poking and prodding was over. So far, my luck had held out. They still hadn't done more than a few minor tests. We never talked for very long. Walter figured we had about ten minutes at a time before Chuck and the rest figured out that something was going on.

"For twenty years I've studied them," Walter said one night. "It took years to modify my HUD controller and produce the first hack - that gave me access to their system.

"Luckily, I had lots of time," he gave another one of his sad smiles. "Sometimes their experiments made me sick. After one I almost died. Most times I felt well enough to work. I never gave up on the idea of getting out of here." His right hand clenched into a fist. "I have vowed that, one way or another, I will escape this place."

We went over his plan in detail. I still wasn't sure I trusted him, but I had nobody else, and no other prospects.

He lifted a shaking hand to scratch his cheek. "Are you sure you're in shape to get away?" I asked him.

His mouth formed a hard line. "Don't worry - I have enough strength to do what's necessary."

"They're going to shit themselves when they find us gone," I said, smiling.

He nodded and gave me a strange look. There were still some details he hadn't explained, but he told me I'd understand when it all went down - that I should just play along.

Finally the day came for the escape. Brickhead was herding me down the hallway, as usual. Walter said that the routine was that Brickhead would lead me to one examination room, and just after that, Chuck would lead Walter to another (they didn't need Brickhead or any other goon for Walter; he was too old and decrepit to put up much of a fight). That way, Walter and I would never actually see each other.

This time, as Walter had instructed, I dragged my feet and stalled. Brickhead was getting pissed off, but I ignored him. It was a fine line, slowing as much as possible, but not so much that he'd figure out that something was up. He pointed to a closer hallway on the right instead of the regular one further away on the left.

"We got something special planned for you today," he smiled.

I'd be around the corner and out of sight in a few seconds if I didn't do something. I started acting like I was out of it. I staggered and veered over so that I bumped right into Brickhead.

"What's your problem?" he snarled, shoving me away.

I pretended to get mad. I stopped and turned to face him.

"You looking for a beating?" he said. He put a hand on the club on his belt.

I stared at him for a few seconds, stalling, waiting as long as I dared. Then I started walking again, as slowly as I could get away with. Out of the corner of my eye I finally saw Chuck leading Walter into an examination room we'd passed already. I didn't dare look or I'd tip off Brickhead, but when he was turned the other way, I stole a glance. Since that time I first broke in, I'd never actually seen Walter in person. His expression was a weird mixture of fear, anger, and determination. The corner of his mouth curled up in a loopy smile. He gave me a barely perceptible nod.

A few seconds later there was a loud shout and both Brickhead and I turned back to see what was happening. Walter was wrestling with Chuck. I saw a flash of light reflecting off a metal blade. Brickhead started running toward them. I ran after him. I got closer and saw a scalpel in Walter's hand. Chuck was trying to disarm him.

Walter broke away from his grip and slashed the side of Chuck's neck. Chuck screamed as blood spurted out. He forgot about Walter and tried to stop the flow. His hands were covered with blood. Brickhead was almost there. I was right behind him. I stuck out my foot and he went down hard. I jumped forward and landed on his hips, and something cracked. He screamed, flailing around like a dying fish.

I looked up and saw Walter grab a pair of cutters from the cart beside the examination table. Chuck was lying on the floor, blood still spraying from his neck. He was barely moving. Walter lifted Chuck's right hand, stuck Chuck's index finger in the jaws of the cutters, and snapped them shut. Chuck screamed again, for the last time.

Walter stood for a second holding the severed finger.

"Come on!" I yelled, gesturing at him.

He just shook his head and gave me another one of his sad smiles. He held up the finger and pointed at me.

"No!" I screamed.

Brickhead staggered to his feet and there was something in his hand - a gun. He pointed it at Walter. Walter tossed the finger at me just as Brickhead fired. A patch of red bloomed on Walter's chest and he went down. I caught the finger and started running.

The finger was covered with blood. I wiped it off on my gown. Tears streamed down my cheeks as I ran. I could hear Brickhead's limping footsteps pounding after me. I heard a gunshot, and a hole was blasted in the wall above my head. I got to a corner and flew around it, finally out of his sight. I reached the inner doors and fumbled to press the finger against the scanner. The access light went green and the latch clicked. I flung the door open and tore down the hallway. A siren started blaring.

Two more doors. I wasn't sure if they'd be disabled with the alarm. The first one opened. I got to the second. I pressed the finger against the scanner but nothing happened.

I willed myself to stop shaking, wiped it again on my gown, and tried again. It worked. The doors were still operational, but wouldn't be for long. I flew down the final hallway to another door. Suddenly my HUD was working. I must have passed through whatever was screening it. Another alarm kicked in.

I tried the finger on the final door. It didn't work. I tried three times. The place was in lock down. I was screwed.

I fought to stay calm. My restored HUD reminded me of the night I'd broken in to steal the trophy. I'd used the hack to fool the system into opening the door. My hand was shaking as I punched the controller buttons to set up the hack again. I prayed to God they hadn't changed anything.

Brickhead limped around the corner. He started firing as soon as he saw me. I screwed up one of the codes and had to enter it again. The bastard was only a hundred meters away. His shots were getting closer. Finally the HUD light went green. I held my controller wrist up to the panel. The lock clicked open.

I smashed through the door into darkness. It slammed shut behind me. As my eyes adjusted I could see I was in a short hallway with a single door at the end. I pounded down it and glanced back just as three bullet holes punched through the door behind me. Pencil-thin beams of light from outside played on the floor. One last panel at the hallway door. Green! I pushed it open.

I was outside.

ELEVEN

....

ON THE RUN

I flew around the nearest corner and down two or three alleys, hoping to lose Brickhead. It must have worked. I heard his lopsided footsteps thumping in the distance, but I never saw him again. I'm sure at least a few of the cameras recorded me running away, but once I calmed down, my Cam-surfing experience paid off like I never would have thought. It was night. I checked my HUD. Thank God it was working again. It was eight-thirty PM.

I was still in the Corp Ring. There were cameras everywhere. I had to slink around walls and down alleys trying to stay out of their view. I was still wearing the hospital gown with my bare ass hanging out. I'd be screwed if anybody saw me. Luckily, there was hardly anybody on the street. I crossed back into Tintown and made for home. I couldn't think of any place else to go. I wondered if Dad would even still be alive, without me there to help him.

When I finally got to the apartment, Dad was watching the HoloTV, like always. He didn't look up when I walked in.

"Dad," I called out to him.

"Where've you been?" he said, without turning around.

"I gotta talk to you," I said louder, to drown out the audio.

He finally turned and scowled at me. "I just want to see this."

"It's important," I shouted. I walked over and turned the TV off. He was pissed, but he didn't get up.

"I was watching that," was all he said.

"It's about my Appraisal," I said.

He waved me off again and stared at the empty pedestal, like there was still a show on. I crouched down in front of him so he had to look at me. I hadn't been that close to him face to face for a long time. His hands were wrinkled like old parchment and speckled with age-spots, his face was lined and mottled, snow-white wisps of hair ringed the blotchy pink dome of his head.

He looked like he was about to nod off. I put my hands on his shoulders and shook him. His eyes opened. I looked into them and shuddered. There was a sadness I'd never noticed before, like staring down into a grave. For the first time in all the years we'd been together I felt like I understood what he'd been through.

He finally noticed my gown. "Why are you dressed like that?"

"Somebody's after me," I said. "They wouldn't tell me my Appraisal. They took me to some special hospital but I ran away."

His eyes opened wider and he stared at me.

He put a hand on each arm of his chair and pushed himself up to a standing position. I'd never seen him react so strongly. It was like he'd been asleep and had just woken up. I stood up, facing him. He staggered sideways and backed away from me.

"What?" I said.

"You," he whispered. "It can't be."

He was shaking, still backing away.

"What the hell's going on!" I yelled.

"Vita Aeterna," he whispered, his voice trembling with fear. "It's impossible."

It occurred to me that the look he was giving me was the same one I saw on the doctor's face after my Appraisal.

"Run," my dad finally said. He jerked his head toward the door, his eyes wide with terror. "Run and hide."

Sirens blared in the distance, getting closer.

"Run!" he shouted at me.

I jumped up and headed for the door.

"Find your uncle Zack - Hurry!" he yelled.

I backtracked to my room, grabbed my pack, and threw in some clothes - and everything I could find that seemed important.

"Forget that!" my dad screamed. "Get out now!"

I'd boarded to my Appraisal, so my regular board was gone, but I had an older, even more beaten up one in my room. It would have to do. I grabbed it, rushed to the front door, flung it open and flew out into the hallway.

"Don't come back," my dad called after me.

I ran outside and tore down the street in a panic. The sirens were right around the corner. It was too late to get away. I flattened myself against the wall inside an alcove. A SecureCorp van flew by me, siren wailing.

I took a chance and peeked around the wall. The van stopped at my building. Soldiers pounded out of it, up the stairs, and through the entrance. I waited a few minutes. I had to know what they were going to do. It was a hot night and our window was open. Shadows flicked across the wall in the living room.

I heard them screaming at my dad, heard his voice mumbling back. A few minutes later the shadows converged at the living room window. There was a gunshot and a loud crash. I watched in horror as a body was jammed through the makeshift metal security bars and tossed five floors to the street below.

It was my dad.

✧

Richie's apartment building looked at lot like mine, but the dark hid a lot of the dinginess and decay. I'd Cam-surfed there, after cowering in the shadows as the soldiers rushed out of our building and took off in the van, then changing into the clothes I'd brought. I had nowhere else to go.

I made my way to an abandoned parkade nearby that the Lost Souls had used a few times before, one that we could access out of sight of any cameras. Using our code name for the place, 'Dungeon', in case SecureCorp were listening, I texted Richie to meet me.

At first he didn't believe it was me. He finally agreed to come, and showed up at the meeting place. Half the parking stalls were occupied by rusting skeletons of cars, most stripped down to almost nothing by years of scavenging.

"You're s…supposed to be dead…" Richie stopped short when he saw me. His face was pale, like he'd seen a ghost. We hid behind the hulking frame of what was once a delivery van. "They told us at co-op school," he said. "They had an announcement about it. Some kind of scooter accident. We even had like - a special ceremony, you know?"

"I'm not dead," I said. The twinge that had been running up and down my spine for a while now tightened like an iron clamp.

"I can see that," Richie said. "What the hell's goin' on?"

"That's what I'm trying to figure out. How'd Cindy take it?"

"She hasn't been around either - for a while we thought maybe you two had run off or something. Then we heard…"

"What? About me being dead?"

"No, that was later. It was Cindy. We heard she negged out big time."

I stepped forward and grabbed him by the front of his shirt. "Fuck you."

"I'm telling you, she negged out," Richie said.

It was hard to breathe. It was like somebody had nailed me with a baseball bat. For a few seconds I couldn't talk.

"What was her score?" I finally said. My brain was paralyzed.

"Bad. I think something like point five."

My gut twisted in knots. It wasn't possible.

"You better not be messin' with me," I said.

"Talk to her," he said. "Don't just take my word for it."

"Have *you* talked to her?"

"Nobody has. Like I said - nobody's seen her for weeks."

"Then how do you know?"

70

"It's in the grapevine, you know - everybody's talking about it."

"You're so full of it. There's no way she's got an Appraisal that low. That would give her a life expectancy of less than forty."

"Hey, don't take it out on me," Richie said. "I'm just telling you what's going around. It's not my fault."

"Well you shouldn't be repeating crap like that about Cindy," I said, letting go of his collar. "She's supposed to be your friend too."

"All I know is what I heard."

I told him about the kidnapping and escape.

"Wow, that's messed up," he said. I'm not sure he really believed me.

"Have you ever heard of anything like that happening?" I said.

He shook his head. "Beats me. Maybe you're super-negative or something."

"What?"

"You know, like point two or something."

"If I was point two I'd already be dead of old age."

"Oh, yeah - well you know what I mean. After all, your mum and dad..." he looked at the floor.

"By the way," he said, looking up again. "I got a one point five. Not bad, eh?"

"That's great," I said.

He just stood there, like he was waiting for something. I think he was pissed because I wasn't cheering about his news, but I had more important things to think about.

"I need a place to hide," I broke the silence.

"What?"

"I told you - they're after me. After I escaped I went home. My dad told me to run away and find my Uncle Zack. They came to our apartment." I found myself choking back tears. "They killed him."

Richie stood with his mouth open. "K...Killed him?" he finally said.

"I need a place," I said. "Just for a few days - till I figure out what's going on."

"What are you talking about?"

Richie stepped back, his eyes bugging out of his head. I realized that in the space of one day I'd witnessed three people killed - one of them my own father. What *was* going on?

"I wouldn't ask," I said, "but I've got no place else to go."

Richie stared at his feet. "Look, man, if it was a regular thing..."

"Forget it," I said. "I'll find something."

I started to walk away.

"Hey, what if they came after me or something?" Richie yelled after me.

I waved him off without turning around.

TWELVE

....

CINDY

I headed for another hideout we'd come across cam-surfing, a tiny room in the basement of a building not far from the Dungeon. Its only window was broken, but it had bars so you couldn't get through. There was a long section that was out of sight from the street. You could jam something against the inside of the latch-less door to keep people out. Nobody ever came around anyway.

I sat on the floor and sifted through the trending news on my HUD. There was nothing about me (big surprise), and nothing about Chuck, or anything else that had happened, just the usual chatter about our freedom and everybody's potential for success.

I had to think. 'Find your Uncle Zack', my dad had said, which didn't make any sense. Uncle Zack was supposed to be dead. I'd only heard about him a couple of times growing up. I always figured he was like some black sheep of the family that nobody wanted to talk about. From the little I heard there was some problem with his Appraisal. Us Barrets and the Appraisal - I swear we're cursed. I never really paid much attention, but now that I thought about it things got kind of quiet whenever his name was mentioned.

I fished through my pack. I'd tried to grab everything that was important, but I'd only had a few seconds. I exhaled as my fingers touched the pouch where I kept my personal stuff. I couldn't remember whether I'd grabbed it or not. It took a few minutes to find what I was looking for. Our family info card was an old, cheap one, and didn't have any broadcast ability. I was grateful for that. I scanned it with my controller and the results materialized in my HUD.

There was hardly anything about Uncle Zack on the card - his birth record, a couple of old pictures of him, my dad, and my grandparents, some notes from the coop school. But at one point all mention of him stopped, like he'd disappeared. I worked out how old he would have been at that point - sixteen - the same age I was supposed to have 'died'.

There was no mention of this Vita Aeterna, whatever that was. I was dying to look it up, but whoever I was up against must have boatloads of money. You can bet they'd be on the lookout for anybody using that search term. I didn't even dare look up anything about my uncle, for the same reason. I rifled through the other stuff in the pouch. The card I'd stolen from SecureCorp was there. A lot of good that was going to do me. I almost tossed it, but then changed my mind.

I had no idea what was happening to me, and where I'd end up tomorrow, but there was one place I had to go, no matter how much of a risk I'd be taking.

✧

Cindy's house was deep inside the Corp Ring, which was far more dangerous for me than Tintown, where nobody really gave a shit what you were doing. Maybe I was just paranoid, but it seemed like there were a lot more SecureCorp guys than usual everywhere I went. There were more cameras in the Corp Ring, and a lot fewer places to hide. Normally I would have been gawking at the gleaming sky-scrapers and mansions I was passing as I Cam-surfed through the streets, but now I had more important things to worry about.

I was careful, and made it to Cindy's without being seen. I'd been there a few times before, but I still pulled in a breath at the sight of it. It was like a palace, three stories high with vaulting roofs like a mountain range.

I hid between a couple of bushes and cased the place. There were a few lights on in the lower level, but I couldn't see anybody inside. The light in Cindy's room upstairs was off.

I clenched my fists thinking about what Richie had said. I still didn't believe it. I had to see her and hear it from her in person. Her dad hated me, so I knew he wouldn't lift a finger, but I hoped maybe Cindy might find a way to help me.

I checked the grounds, and up and down the street. There was no sign of any SecureCorp, or anybody else for that matter. After about twenty minutes I worked up the guts to go and knock. Normally I would have thrown a pebble at her window or something, but I couldn't afford to stand out in the open for too long. Anyway, from what I'd heard she might not even be there.

Cindy's dad opened the door. His overflowing bulk filled the whole frame. When he saw who it was, for a second the contempt on his bloated face was the same as always. Then his jowls smoothed out as his lips tightened into a smile so broad it looked like it was hurting him.

"I want to talk to Cindy," I said. I tensed and stepped back, expecting him to grab me and rat me out to the authorities.

"Why don't you come in," he said instead, still smiling.

I was so stunned I just stood there like a moron. He'd never invited me into his house before. Usually if he even caught me on the grounds he'd threaten to call SecureCorp.

He stood aside and held the door open. I walked through it; I had to talk to Cindy. I craned my neck and scanned around the massive foyer, bigger than our whole apartment. Ahead of me, a curving marble staircase swept up to the next floor. A thousand points of light wheeled across the tiles beneath our feet. I tilted back my head and saw a gigantic crystal chandelier hanging ten meters above me. For a few seconds, I almost forgot where I was and who was standing in front of me.

I finally shut my gaping mouth and came back to reality.

"Mr. Edwards," I said.

"Call me Tom," he said.

Somehow his being nice to me creeped me out even more than when he hated my guts. I leaned my board against the wall. He sneered at it for a second, like it was going to contaminate the place, then, like he'd remembered something, smiled again.

I followed him to another huge room off the foyer. The curved platform of a three-meter-wide HoloTV pedestal stood against one wall.

An oriental carpet the size of a city block covered the floor. Expensive looking antiques balanced on ornate wooden tables, and potted plants taller than me stood beside the wine-coloured plush leather furniture.

"Have a seat," he said, sweeping his arm toward one of the couches. "I'll get you a drink of water."

"I'm not thirsty," I said.

"Don't be silly," he said. "I insist."

He waddled off through a door to the kitchen. I sat down on the couch. I heard him turn on the tap and the water seemed to run for ages. I was about to get up and check on what he was doing in there when he stuck his fat face around the door frame.

"Be right with you," he smiled.

Something was wrong.

I heard a faint beep from his HUD controller. That's when I knew.

I got up and started for the door.

He was coming out of the kitchen. To my surprise he was actually carrying a glass of water. He dropped it when he saw me trying to run. I couldn't believe a guy with that much bulk could move so fast.

I got to the door first, but realized he'd locked it when I first came in. I started to twist the deadbolt knob. His massive ham-like fist reached out, grabbed my wrist and tore my hand away.

His face turned an even brighter shade of red, and the veins stood out on his neck as he stood there, still gripping my wrist like a vise. Beads of sweat stood out on his forehead. His mouth twisted with my wrist as he sneered at me.

"I've got you now, boy" he said, his hand trembling. "SecureCorp will be here any minute."

"I didn't do anything," I said.

"You little prick," he said. He twisted harder, driving me down to my knees. "All the decent, hard-working, successful people in the world that are condemned to early deaths, and you…"

He shook like he was going to explode.

"What *about* me?" I yelled up at him.

"It's impossible." He said - to himself. It was like he was in some kind of trance.

"What?" I said. I thought maybe he was losing it.

He wasn't even looking at me anymore. He was staring at the floor, or really his belly because I don't think he could see the floor.

"While my sweet little girl…" He hauled back on my wrist until I thought it would break.

"Where's Cindy!" I screamed, cringing with pain.

He snapped out of it. "Don't you defile her memory by saying her name," he said through half-clenched teeth. His words sprayed at me, like he was foaming at the mouth.

"What do you mean, *her memory*?" I said. "What happened to her!"

For a second it looked like he was going to faint. He relaxed his grip on my wrist. It was enough. I twisted it out of his hand, jumped back, and started running. He lumbered after me, cornering me in the living room. I grabbed a lamp on an end table. He smiled and pulled a gun out of his pocket.

I threw the lamp at his head. The gun went off, but missed. I jumped behind the couch I'd been sitting on. Two or three more shots went off and holes exploded through the leather back beside me. I crawled to the far end, followed by more exploding holes. There was a big glass sculpture on another end table, hidden behind the base of a potted plant. I reached up and grabbed it. I heard him stomping across the room, heading around the couch to get at me.

I was only going to get one chance. He couldn't see me right away because of the plant. I got up on my haunches and tensed, ready to jump. As soon as he appeared I sprang past him carrying my glass weapon. He fired, but he wasn't fast enough. I landed, found my balance, and kicked at his gun hand. He screamed and the gun dropped to the floor. I lifted up the sculpture and brought it down on his head as hard as I could. He crumpled like a dynamited building and lay still. Blood gushed from his scalp, soaking into the plush weave of the carpet.

Sirens blared in the distance. I looked for the gun and realized he was lying on top of it. I couldn't move his huge bulk. I managed to jam my arm under his folds of fat, and groped for the gun, but couldn't find it. He was lying face down. I stared down at the bulge in his back pocket. I remembered I had no wallet - they still had it at the hospital. I worked the wallet out and opened it. Only a couple of dollars.

I checked through his cards. I was in a panic but I needed his fingers to deactivate the security on them. I found a MoneyAll card and pressed his thumb and forefinger against it, and it fired up, showing two thousand dollars in 'Unsecured Cash'. The blare of the sirens was getting closer.

The thought surfaced: *'It's impossible'* - *what was he talking about? And how did he know?*

I shuffled through the other cards and found one that was totally black. I pressed his thumb and finger on it and it. An image swirled into life - a logo - a butterfly, like the one on Chuck's smock, with the letters 'VA'. I stared at it, trying to figure out what it was. The letters were familiar. I'd seen them before. Suddenly a lens appeared in the right-hand corner and a tiny picture of my face appeared under it.

Shit, I thought. *A camera.*

I let go of his fingers, but the card stayed on, with my picture locked on it. I couldn't leave it here. I shoved it and the MoneyAll card in my bag, stuffed the wallet back in his pocket, and took off. By this time the sirens were right outside the house.

I ran to the front door and grabbed my board. Just as I got there a car screeched into the driveway. I ran for the back. I'd been to the place before so I knew there was a back door, but I'd never been inside. It took a few precious seconds navigating through all the rooms for me to find it.

My hands shook as I fiddled with the lock. It finally clicked open. I flung the door open, flew down the back pathway and into the night.

THIRTEEN

....

GETTING MONEY

My first priority was to get out of the Corp Ring. Back in the Quarters there was a lot less SecureCorp presence. I'd be dead if I stayed here. It was like some death-race version of Cam-surfing. Even just playing I'd managed to avoid the cameras for a half-hour at a time, and that was when my life wasn't on the line. I had a lot more incentive now.

Just as I crossed over into the Quarters, Richie's avatar came up on my HUD. I was confused. I figured SecureCorp could fake stuff like that.

Then some text came up. *The Stump Factory - 20 minutes.*

Since he mentioned the Stump Factory, I knew it had to be Richie. That was the Lost Souls' code for one of our meeting places, an old abandoned prosthetic warehouse not far from our apartment. I thought about my dad... No - put it out of your mind. Only a handful of my friends knew about the place. Unless one of them had ratted on me...

I had to take a chance.

81

"Don't let them see you," I texted back.

☼

"Tintown's crawling with SecureCorp," Richie said, when he showed up at our meeting place near the warehouse. "I'm not sure whether they're looking for you or they're here for some other reason."

"Sure you weren't followed?" I said.

"You know me better than that," he smiled. "I felt bad about not helping you before," he said, looking at his feet.

I told him what happened with Cindy's dad. I didn't mention that I might have killed the guy.

"What about Cindy?" he asked.

"I don't know," I lied.

We snuck past a couple of cameras and through a gap we'd set up ages ago. We headed for a space inside where the crew used to meet.

"A friend of my mother's negged out real bad," Richie said as we moved. "I think she was like a point six or something. Both her parents were one-point-fours. She ended up dying of old age before either of them did."

"I wish they'd never invented that shit," I said. "It's against God's laws or something."

"I'll put you up," Richie offered when we finally got there. "I'll hide you somewhere—"

"No," I said. "You were right the first time. Two people already died trying to help me. I don't want another one on my conscience."

"Then what—"

"I need a place to lay low for a while, someplace way off the grid."
Richie looked at the ground, thinking.

"We found a—"

"It can't be a place any of you guys know about," I interrupted him.
"They might try to get to me through you. There's nothing you can do
- don't worry - I'll find something. I gotta figure out what's going on. I
need a crypted phone. You said you knew a guy—"

"I know a guy," Richie answered, "but he's an asshole."

I shrugged at him. "Not like I've got a choice. Problem is, I've got
no money."

"I can help you with that," Richie said. "I haven't got much, but you
can take it - I'll go get it."

"Too dangerous. They'll know we hang out. If they're not watching
you already they will be soon. Anyway, I got a way to get money. Then
I'll work something out with your guy."

"Don't call him my guy. He's no buddy of mine. You sure you want
to deal with him?"

I nodded. He contacted the guy and arranged a meeting place.

"Thanks," I said. "I owe you."

"Keep me in the loop - somehow," he said.

✿

It was rare to find a working streetlight in Tintown, but I guess the
MoneyAll machines rated special treatment. The glow shone down
like a halo on the machine I'd picked out for my attempt at getting
some cash. Just finding one was hard enough. Nobody used cash

anymore; just the act of trying to get some would probably raise a red flag somewhere. Hardly anybody in the Quarters even had a bank account. I hid in the recess between two buildings, checking it out.

The machine had two features that might allow me to use it without getting caught. First, it was in a location I knew really well - one I'd Cam-surfed lots of times and could escape from at top speed. Second, it was within running distance of a hiding place. One not so close that SecureCorp could set up a dragnet around it, but close enough that I could get there (or at least get out of sight) before they got to the machine.

The little square in front of me was deserted. There were cameras, but no more than usual. Of course, there'd be a camera on the machine itself, so they'd know it was me when I actually used it. There was no way I could avoid giving myself away. My only hope was that I could get the hell out of there before they could catch up.

Of course, the card would have a PIN number. Cindy had stolen it once or twice, without her dad knowing. I knew what the PIN was. All I could do was pray that her father hadn't changed it.

I didn't doubt that they could even stop the machine from giving me money - it all depended on how fast they figured out it was me at the machine, and that I had Cindy's dad's MoneyAll card. I'd been smart enough to put his wallet back, so it might take them a while to work it out. Anyway, the longer I waited the more likely it was that they'd block access.

I took a deep breath and took one last sweep around. Nothing. I snuck as close as I could, and tried to see where the camera (or cameras?) would be. I couldn't tell, but you could bet they'll make it next to impossible to use the machine without them seeing you.

I considered pulling the bandanna I had around my neck up around my face, but decided against it. As soon as they saw somebody trying to hide their appearance they'd have a swarm of drones dive-bombing me. At least without it the facial recognition software would take a few seconds, especially if I could angle my face to make it harder to recognize. I approached from the side, and mentally rehearsed what I was going to do when I got there. My plan was to jump in front of the machine, stick in the card, enter the PIN, extract the cash, and take off.

My heart was hammering in my chest as I leapt out with the card in my hand. I shoved it in the slot. I could imagine all the monitors in some SecureCorp bunker lighting up with my picture. My hands shook as I entered the PIN in a panic. Success! I went for the full amount: two thousand dollars cash. Lights started flashing around the top of the machine.

The display said: 'Four Hundred Dollar Limit'.

"Shit!" I said under my breath.

I confirmed the four hundred. I'd already been here too long. I stared at the slot waiting for the money. There was a whirring sound and a stack of twenty twenty-dollar bills seemed to take forever popping into the tray one by one. I waited for the card. Nothing. My hands were shaking. It was taking too long. They were screwing with me.

It finally popped out. I grabbed it and turned to run. I glanced back just as a picture came up on the screen. A guy in a SecureCorp uniform.

"Remain where you are," the guy in the picture said. "You cannot escape. A car will arrive shortly."

Yeah, right, I thought, as I made a bee-line for the nearest shadows. *I'll just wait here like a moron.*

"Remain where you are," the voice echoed off the walls of the alley, "you cannot escape."

I was so scared, at first I didn't even pay attention to the cameras. Then I calmed myself down and went into Cam-surfing mode.

☼

I'd only gone a few blocks when a faint hum approached from the south. I checked the warning light in my HUD. It was still green - I hadn't triggered any cameras. Seconds later a swarm of drones screamed around the corner and started circling my head.

I batted at them and got a couple, but there must have been a hundred. I'd never seen that many in one place before. Sirens started blaring in the distance, getting closer. All the drones had cameras and GPS; I had to lose them or I was screwed.

I took off, with the swarm tearing after me. I didn't have time to get to the hiding place I'd planned on. As I ran, I scanned around for a building with an open door. I finally spotted what looked like an old factory, now all boarded up. I headed for one of the doorways that had a couple of the boards torn off. As I reached it, a feathered dart embedded itself in a board beside me - a tranquilizer - some of these things were armed.

One board blocked me getting through. I yanked on it, the drones dive-bombing me and the sirens getting louder. The board finally came free. I used it to bash at some of the closest drones. I got five or ten, but there was still lots left.

I squeezed through the hole. A bunch of drones flew in after me before I could jam the board back in place. Some of the original boards were still lying around; I used them to plug every hole I could find. As I worked I could hear the swarm hammering against the outside walls like some kind of freaky hailstorm.

The ones inside were hovering around me. I found another loose board and smashed at them until they were all dead. Suddenly I thought about the MoneyAll card. I fished it out of my pack. A tiny red light blinked in one corner. A locator - no wonder they found me. It must have been triggered when I accessed the bank machine. I didn't want to destroy the card, I might still need it. And I couldn't disable the locator without the old man's finger.

From the gears, lengths of tubing, and chunks of metal strewn around the floor, the place must be an old appliance factory. I used our standard trick for disabling cards with locators. I found a scrap of thin metal sheeting, managed to break a piece off, and folded it around the card. It would be a pain to carry, but the metal would shield the signal until I could come up with something better.

I remembered the other card, the black one with the camera. It had turned black again, and I couldn't see any sign of a locator. I stuffed it, along with the one I stole from SecureCorp before, inside my makeshift shield just in case. I'm not sure why I was keeping them. I guess I didn't want to toss anything I might be able to use later. I tied my bandanna around the shield so the cards wouldn't fall out.

Vita Aeterna

Then I ran. Outside, in the distance, sirens rounded the building and gathered at the point where I'd escaped the drones. I headed for the corner farthest away and hunted for a way out. I heard the drones had some kind of smell sense like a dog, too, but so far no more seemed to have made it inside. I found a broken window, climbed out, and took off.

FOURTEEN

....

THE CRYPTED PHONE

"No money, no gizmo," Richie's contact, a guy named 'Fatso', said.

He'd been showing me a crypted phone in an alcove in the darkest corner of another underground parkade on the outermost edge of the Quarters. The yellow light from the display on his comm-glasses danced over his forehead as he leaned against the rusted-out hulk of a vehicle. I didn't want to mention the four hundred dollars until I knew what to expect from him.

Fatso's appearance was totally at odds with his name. Skinny and emaciated, his withered, spider-like limbs were so thin that he wore a mechanical exoskeleton to hold himself up. It was a flashy one too, a carbon-filament job that must have cost a fortune. I'd seen his condition before. It was yet another of the wonderful side-effects of the Appraisal that happened one in every couple of million cases. Because of his condition his HUD didn't work properly - hence the comm-glasses. There was only one way somebody like him could get enough money to get their hands on gear like that - by screwing over people like me.

It occurred to me that I was going to be spending a lot of time with guys like Fatso, now that I was a fugitive. In the Lost Souls we knew a few tricks; these guys knew a lot more: how to get around without being seen, ways of encrypting and scrambling net accesses so that the broadcast's location couldn't be determined. They also knew a lot about helping themselves to stuff that belonged to other people.

But I needed the phone. To find out what was going on, I had to hook up to the deep net, and there was no legal way to do that without the connection being monitored and, eventually, my ID and location given away. But like everybody, Fatso was only interested in money.

"I've got a MoneyAll card," I said.

"Is it yours?"

I looked at the ground.

"If it's hot, it's worse than nothin'."

He stuffed the phone in the pocket of his coat and turned to leave.

"Wait," I finally said. "I've got cash."

He turned back. "How much?"

"Four hundred."

He stared at me, probably trying to decide whether he could jump me and take it. It looked like he decided against that.

Instead he just said: "Not enough."

"How much more do I need?"

"Four hundred might do for a down-payment," he laughed, as he turned away again.

"It's an emergency," I said to his back.

"Not for me," he said over his shoulder as he strolled toward the exit, the joints of his exoskeleton clicking faintly as he moved.

"Look, I'll sign an IOU or something," I called after him. "I gotta figure out what's going on. They're saying I'm dead."

Fatso stopped in mid-step. He turned back to face me.

"You're dead?" he said.

I nodded.

I took a step toward him. "I know we're not friends or nothin', but it took a lot for me to escape. Two people died trying to help me. I don't—"

"Hold it," Fatso said.

He reached up and pressed a button on his comm-glasses. His eyelids fluttered like he was having some kind of fit while he accessed the net.

"Wow, you *are* dead," he said.

"I told you..."

The eerie light from his glasses scuttled across his eyelids like a crawling caterpillar. A thin smile formed on his lips.

"What are you doing?" I said.

"Nothin'."

"You called somebody."

"Bullshit."

I turned to run. He tried to block me, skipping into my path like a spider and extending his arms like metal pincers. I jumped aside and managed to skirt around him. The tricked-out performance of his exoskeleton gave him a huge speed advantage. There was no way I could hope to outrun him. Again, sirens wailed in the distance. He easily caught up with me.

I noticed that he was careful to never turn his back to me, and when I took a good look at his suit I figured out why. A thin bundle of wires, almost hidden but accessible if you approached from the right angle, ran from his hips up to a single filament running up his back. As he reached to grab me I jumped sideways, dove to the ground between his legs, and reached up under him.

He twisted around so fast I couldn't believe it, but not before I'd curled my right index finger around the exposed section of his wiring harness. I screamed, as searing pain shot through my finger, but something gave, and his legs started twitching grotesquely beneath him. He staggered in place, legs spasming, unable to move. I took off as fast as I could down the alley.

"Get back here," he screamed. "They're gonna get you anyway. Might as well let me make a buck off it."

I stopped. The sirens were getting closer. There wasn't much time. I needed the phone. I rushed back toward him.

"That's more like it," he laughed.

He lifted his pincer-like arms to grab me. I jumped out of the way. His legs were still convulsing and he couldn't keep up. I reached down into his coat pocket. He saw what I was doing.

"Get out of there!" he screamed.

I grabbed the phone and held on. He wrapped a vibrating arm around my head. Even with the damage he was incredibly strong. I stomped as hard as I could on his sandaled foot.

He screamed and let go. "You broke my foot you little shit!"

The sirens were around the next corner. I reached down with my free hand, grabbed his left ankle, and pulled as hard as I could. The foot lifted, and Fatso started to sway. I jumped out of the way as he crashed to the ground. I took off. He lay there, thrashing like he was having a seizure.

"Get back here!" he screamed. "Help me! I'm gonna get you, you bastard!"

I flew out of the parkade. A SecureCorp squad car passed me but I was hidden in the shadows.

☼

In our old Cam-surfing game, nobody was actually looking for us. Cameras randomly picked up stuff all the time, but the crime detection algorithms weren't that accurate, and rumour is that normally, not many of the camera feeds had anybody actually watching them.

Now, my gut told me there'd be an army of eyes scouring every camera. I couldn't afford to be seen. It was slow navigating through the camera footprints, but I've done it enough times. I felt safe on that score. When we played the game, there was always some kind of time element involved. Now I could take as much time as I wanted, so in theory I should be able to Cam-surf indefinitely. I traveled for about half an hour, to the deepest reaches of the Quarters, desperate for a place to hide.

I was exhausted, about to give up and just collapse in a corner somewhere, when I spotted an abandoned car factory. I prowled around for about ten minutes before I found a loose panel I could use to get in. It was still night; this deep in the Quarters there were no streetlights - even outside you could barely see where you were going.

Inside, it was black as a cave, but after a few minutes my eyes adjusted well enough that I could navigate. I had to pick my way over the piles of debris on the floor, terrified of making any noise. I reached what looked like the factory floor. The skeletal remnants of the construction robots cut into the darkness. I couldn't be sure there was nobody there. The only sounds were the scurrying of rats up and down the hallways.

I could make out a room off to the east side, and I headed for it. It looked like it had once been some kind of office. There was an overturned desk, half-demolished. Somebody had already scavenged it for sellable metal.

A couple of chairs lay in one corner. I grabbed a plastic one that would be less likely to be infested, stood it up, sat on it, and pulled out the phone.

The crypted phones foiled the SecureCorp location software by randomly switching between cell towers all over the city. They never stayed with any one station for more than a few micro-seconds, so there was no way for the software to triangulate a position. They also encrypted all messages so they couldn't be read from outside.

What they couldn't do was hide what information you were trying to access. Since any information SecureCorp was worried about was flagged and would send an alarm somewhere when anybody tried to access it, I still had to be careful about where I surfed. Right now, I figured that trying to do a search on Vita Aeterna would be a real bad idea. It was probably a search term that almost nobody but me would use. I had a feeling I wouldn't come up with anything anyway.

In fact, I wondered what I *could* access without triggering some kind of response. In the end, I decided I had no choice but to trust that the phone was secure. Like I expected, there was nothing on Vita Aeterna. I checked on my Uncle Zack. Officially, he died in an accident with a RoboTaxi. I'd been right before. He was sixteen, the same age I was supposed to have 'died'. I did a search for Dr. Charles Knowles. I got a slew of results. I sifted through some of them. Chuck was a mid-level drone at the Appraisal section of MediCorp.

I opened my eyes wide when I read one line in Chuck's list of roles: *Special Liaison to the CCE*.

The CCE, the Council of Chief Executives, is made up of the CEOs from all six Corps. They're kind of folk heroes for most of us. Everything we hear on the HUD or on HoloTV points to government waste as the root of all the misery and poverty we deal with every day. The CCE are constantly recommending ways to reduce red-tape and eliminate regulations, based on their massive experience efficiently running the Corps, but the government never seems to listen.

Charles Wickham, the CEO of SecureCorp and one of the most famous people in the world, is also the head of the CCE. If the CCE are folk heroes, then Wickham is their Robin Hood. He's the public face of the organization, and his picture is everywhere.

An election is coming up in a few months. The public can't wait. The polls say the Freedom Party is more hated than any in living memory. All kinds of negative stuff has been coming out about them for the past year or so: party officials caught redirecting government money to themselves, accepting bribes, eliminating opposition. As always, it's not the stealing and dishonesty that's the problem - after all, if you can make money doing something, there's no rules - by definition. What infuriates people was that the Freedom Party were stupid enough to get caught.

Anyway, we're itching to vote so we can throw out President Foster and the Freedom Party and give the Enterprise Party a chance to clean things up. The Enterprisers also hint that they'll give more power to the CCE, something everybody wants, but that never seems to happen.

Let's face it - the CCE are the only ones you can believe, since they're not actually part of the government. Charles Wickham has proved time and time again how government waste, inefficiency, and red tape are strangling the economy and keeping the common people in poverty. The CCE have worked their asses off trying to do something about it, but the government blocks them at every turn.

The new Enterprise Party leader, Dan Holloway, sounds like a good guy. He swears he'll clean up the 'rot' created by the Freedom Party, and cut through the masses of red tape like the CCE are always recommending. He's even hinted that he'll consult with Charles Wickham about how to run things, but we've heard all that before.

There's a movement to try to ditch the government altogether and let the CCE run everything, with Wickham as leader, but whenever anybody mentions the idea, the CCE themselves shoot it down. They say it's important to preserve democracy and let whatever government we've elected rule. I've always respected that about them.

It's every parent's impossible dream for their child that he or she would grow up to be a member of the CCE. I've never heard of anybody in my neighbourhood getting up that high, but they say it could happen.

Everybody's hoping that Holloway and the Enterprise Party will finally give the CCE more control, and we'll have the prosperity the CCE always say is just around the corner.

It was insulting that an asshole like Chuck would have any connection with the CCE. I searched for a picture of Chuck and found one. There he was - same smarmy, arrogant sneer on his face. I thought about Walter and wanted to reach in and wrap my fingers around Chuck's neck. He'd gotten his, anyway.

I poured through the web chatter for any news of Cindy. It was sketchy, but from what I could find, she'd OD'd on some kind of street pain-killer, during the time I'd been held prisoner at the clinic. They tried to say it was an accident, but I knew her better than that. I hadn't been there to help her or comfort her. She'd died alone, not knowing where I was, or what happened to me.

On top of all this I was still trying to deal with my Appraisal. All this had gone down right after I'd gotten it. It had to have something to do with that. But what did Dad mean? What did *he* know about it? The image of his body smashing through the window and onto the pavement resurfaced, and suddenly I was crying. It was like the tears just flowed out of me spontaneously.

Dad and I had never been close. In fact, I always thought he hated me, or at best didn't give a shit. Now he'd given his life for me - the second of two people to do that in the past few days. It was all too much.

I hung my head and cried until there were no more tears left. I didn't even care if anyone was around to hear. I cried for my dad, cried for Cindy, cried for Walter, cried for all the people who'd been screwed by the Appraisal. I cried and cried, then collapsed from exhaustion on the filthy concrete floor.

FIFTEEN

....

INTO THE UNKNOWN

When I opened my eyes the next morning it took me a while to remember where I was. I turned my head and scanned around me. I was still lying on the floor of the office where I'd passed out. For a few seconds I dared to imagine it was all a bad dream. Then reality came rushing back.

I sat up and rubbed my back and my eyes, and tried to piece together all that had happened. My dad had been so panicked about Vita Aeterna. I guessed that it was some kind of organization. I figured the first thing I had to do was find out for sure. But even before that, I needed food, and water, and I needed a safer place to hide.

I got ready to move. It was a pain carrying around the folded chunk of metal that shielded the cards. I decided to look for something better. Even in daylight the inside of this place was gloomy, but I could see well enough to have a look around. I'd been lucky so far; I hadn't seen another soul. Still I tried to step lightly through the dust and debris in the hallways.

Vita Aeterna

In the southeast corner, I found a room that looked like some kind of electrical repair shop. Workbenches lined three of the walls, and smashed circuit-boards and pieces of broken equipment were lying around. I sifted through some of the junk and hit pay dirt - a conductive bag used for holding static sensitive parts. I'd seen them before in the computer shops in the Corp Ring.

It was just a little larger than the cards and flexible, like an ordinary plastic bag. I checked the bag for holes, brushed the dust off a nearby stool, sat down at one of the benches, and opened my metal shield just enough to get the bag in. There was no sign of a light on the MoneyAll card, so it wasn't getting to the outside.

I slid the bag over all three cards and folded the top over. Then I pulled the metal shield away, ready to put it back if the MoneyAll lit up. Nothing happened. I smiled. For the first time since my escape, something had gone right.

Holding up the transparent bag, I examined the black card I'd taken from Cindy's dad, and my heart just about stopped. It had turned a deep blue, almost ultra-violet. I didn't have the owner's finger to open it up, so I had no way of figuring out what it was. Part of me wished I'd pulled a 'Walter' and taken the finger with me, but I don't think I had the stomach for that - not yet, anyway.

Worse still, the ultra-violet card now seemed to be stuck to the SecureCorp card I stole Cam-surfing, which now had a line of moving light flashing up and down one side.

Shit! They were talking to each other. I had no idea what they were saying, but there was no way it was good. I kept the bag sealed, but worked the two cards around and gripped them, trying to pry them apart. No way - they'd somehow melded together. Travis talked about this 'nanotechnology' that made stuff like this possible, but I'd never seen it.

The joined cards were a bit thicker than a normal card, and I could still see a thin seam between them, but they were now a single unit. I guessed that by the time they finished whatever they were doing, the end result would look like a regular card. But - a card that did what?

I was about to toss them in a dumpster some place and get as far away as possible, but when I pressed on the black/ultraviolet one the same butterfly logo I'd seen at Cindy's place swirled into view, with the same two letters - VA. I remembered where I'd seen the butterfly before - on the SecureCorp card, and Chuck's smock... Then I realized why the letters were familiar - VA - Vita Aeterna. I was pretty sure they couldn't communicate outside the bag, so I decided to keep them.

I found an elastic band and wrapped it around the bag, to make sure it couldn't fall open accidentally. Now I could tuck the cards, inside their protective bag, into my pack. I doubted if I could ever use the MoneyAll card again, but kept it, just in case. As if to remind me of the situation, I heard another siren in the distance, heading my way. It wasn't safe for me in the Quarters.

I found regular plastic bag, stuffed the four hundred into it, then stuck it in my shoe. I switched off all the messaging functions of my HUD. From now on, the only way I'd communicate was with the crypted phone. I confirmed that the phone was still in my pack and headed out, boarding and Cam-surfing northeast.

Vita Aeterna

There was only one place I might have a chance of escaping my pursuers. When I hit the farthest edge of Tintown, for the first time in my life, I kept going.

SIXTEEN

....

BENNY

There's no distinct boundary between the Quarters and the Dregs. The garbage just gets deeper, the streets are more broken down, and the atmosphere is more desperate. My plan was to venture a little way in - far enough to be out of sight of SecureCorp, but close enough to dash back to the Quarters if things got too rough.

From what I've heard, the Dregs is basically empty, so there's fewer cameras, and a hardly any SecureCorp patrols. It's probably as dangerous as everybody says, but it's also the place I'm least likely to get caught.

I pushed on, still heading northeast. The buildings I passed were crumbling: shards of glass lining the window openings like broken teeth, walls black with mildew, moss, and even plants sprouting from every available crack. Most were ancient skyscrapers, so many that the streets were in shadow, even though it was still morning.

My HUD picked up the occasional camera, but they were so far apart that Cam-surfing was a breeze. Good thing, because I couldn't

103

use my board. My footsteps crunched on a fist-thick layer of dust, garbage, chunks of cement, and broken glass.

I had no idea where I was going, or what I was looking for. Right now, I just wanted a hiding place - somewhere I could take a breath and think about what to do. I headed down one of the main streets, sticking to the shadows.

I'd walked for about twenty minutes when I saw an orange glow spilling from around the next corner. I snuck along the wall toward it. When I got closer I could hear voices - at least two - both male. I crept up to the corner of the wall, leaned out, and poked my head around.

Two guys in rags were sitting around a fire they'd built on the sidewalk next to a skyscraper. A couple of broken wooden chairs - their fuel - lay on the ground beside them. They were both holding sticks over the fire with some kind of meat skewered on them. The savoury smell wafting over reminded me how hungry I was. I thought about how I could get some. Maybe if I just introduced myself...

I jumped when a third guy appeared around the corner behind them. I jerked back, and a chunk of the brick I was gripping broke off and thudded to the ground. One of the seated men lifted his head, saw me, and pointed. As he turned, his stick moved closer to the flames, and I lost interest in sharing - what was skewered on it was a rat. The two seated guys jumped up and dropped their sticks, and all three ran toward me.

I took off. They followed for a while, but soon they were staggering, not running. After a few minutes they gave up and I was alone. I decided I had to get to someplace inside. I kept going, on edge, ready to run and hide at the first sight of danger. I was surprised to see an entire family – mother, father, kids, scurry into a doorway and slam the door as I rounded one corner. I saw kids and old people alone. Once or twice they saw me, but we both kept our distance.

I walked for an hour or so, until there were no more people around. I spotted a dilapidated building that looked like a good prospect for a hideout. Like all the others I'd come across here, it was worse than any in the Quarters - filthy and surrounded by piles of debris. I found an entrance that had once been boarded-up, but the boards had been torn away and lay in a pile just inside. The open door made the place easy to get into, but raised the question - who removed the boards in the first place?

I took a chance and stepped inside. The interior was dark, but there was enough light to make out where I was going. A hallway with doors off either side ran ahead of me for about fifty meters. I was about to start down it when a voice behind me said:

"Hey, where do you think you're going?"

I froze, and turned to locate the source. Half in the shadows of a graffiti-plastered pillar on my left stood a guy in his early twenties (I think - let's face it, it's hard to know). He towered over me - at least six feet tall. He had a few days' stubble on his face, and he looked like he hadn't washed in at least that long. His brown hair stuck out wildly from his head. There was an ugly scar ten centimeters long beside his right temple, and his right eye seemed to wander.

He was wearing what I guess was once a business suit, like what the big-wigs in the Corps like to wear, but it was torn, tattered and filthy. The top buttons of his shirt were gone; he'd fastened the collar together with a safety pin. What was left of a necktie was wrapped around the collar. It looked like he'd tried to tie it properly, like the big-wigs, but he must not have known how, 'cause it was tied with a regular square knot. The tie was all torn and filthy too, and the bottom part was missing, like it had been ripped off by a wild animal.

He was trying to act tough, but when I looked closer I could see he was shaking.

"Can't you read?" he said. He nodded at a torn piece of cardboard tacked to the wall where I'd come in. "Rent - $2.00" was scrawled on it in a shaky hand.

"Rent?" I said. His eyes were wild and distant. He didn't look dangerous, but I was ready to run.

He gestured around at the junk, dust, broken furniture, and collapsing walls. "To use the offices."

I started to laugh, but stifled it when I looked at his face. He was dead serious. Instead I said, "So - what - you own this place?"

He straightened up and puffed out his chest. "I own all these places - the whole block. I'm a entrepreneur."

"Well, I haven't got two dollars," I said. I wasn't going to tell him about the money in my shoe.

He scowled and took a step toward me. "Then you're in big trouble."

"Look," I said, stepping away, "I didn't know this was your place. Maybe I should just take off."

I started to turn back toward the door. He moved closer. I spun around and put up my fists in case he came at me. He jumped back, startled.

"I don't want any trouble," I said. I put a hand on the door jamb and lifted one of my feet to step out.

"Wait," he called. I stopped and turned back.

His expression softened. "I'm havin' a special right now - first week for free."

He stepped away and gestured for me to come in. I was pretty desperate. I was hungry and exhausted, and I needed a place to hide. I introduced myself.

"I'm Benny," he said, shaking my hand.

Benny led me to his 'office', a filthy, debris-strewn room with the remains of a desk in one corner. What must once have been a computer sat on the desk, surrounded by rotting stacks of used paper. Several other pieces of junked equipment were scattered around. I couldn't make out what any of them were.

"This is my command center," Benny said. "This is where it all happens."

"What all happens?"

He shot me a look of annoyance. "My corporate empire," he gestured around him.

A government poster tacked to the back wall was all but blotted out with graffiti written with a black marker. The words 'Fuck You' were scrawled over a photo of the president, and comments like 'bastards' and 'go to Hell' surrounded it.

Benny noticed me looking at it. "You're not with them, are you?" He staggered back in fear and disgust.

I laughed. "Do I look like I'm with the government?"

He relaxed a little. He leaned forward and whispered. "They've got spies everywhere."

On another wall was a picture of Charles Wickham. The head of the CCE stood confidently in front of some fancy building, with his arms folded across his chest, the light from above reflecting from his silver buzz-cut, a confident sneer on his craggy face. That poster was untouched by graffiti and, unlike most of the room, looked like it was cleaned regularly. Benny was obviously a lot more positive about him.

"Someday, we're gonna kick some government ass," he said, nodding at the CCE poster as if Wickham and him were buds. "Someday soon."

The walls of the room were plastered with pages ripped out of magazines. I glanced at a few - all were either anti-government or pro-CCE.

For the first time I noticed that there was no HUD controller on his wrist. I studied the scar on his head and froze. The silver HUD access connector on his right temple was missing. He was the first person over five years old I'd ever seen that didn't have a HUD.

"What happened?" I asked, pointing at his scar.

"Those government bastards tried to brainwash me with their evil bullshit," he rubbed the scar like he was remembering something painful.

"But it's hooked into your optic nerve," I said. "How'd you get it out?"

"It's like a poisonous plant," his hand shook as he rubbed the scar again and screwed up his eyes. "You just dig in and pull it out by the roots."

I cringed. "That must have hurt."

"Made me blind in one eye," he said, "but it was worth it." His voice dropped to a whisper. "What do think I'm doin' here, anyway?"

I shrugged.

"I'm underground, stupid," he sneered. "I'm gathering intelligence. I'm like a... 'field operative'."

In one corner was a huge stack of old food packets. He noticed me eyeing them and handed one to me.

"I'll put this on your tab," he said.

I checked the expiry date. It had expired a month ago. The packets were vacuum-sealed, and technically didn't have to be refrigerated, but that was getting pretty old. Anyway, it's not like I had much choice. I ripped it open and scooped out the brown mash with my fingers. I might not starve now, but I might die of food poisoning. He threw in some stale crackers, which tasted like cardboard. We left the office and he showed me the remains of an old kitchen where there was a supply of water.

"I'm glad I ran into you," I said, feeling better, but wondering what would happen when the rotten food hit my system.

Benny was out there. It was a long-shot, but I figured I might as well see what he knew. "I'm looking for information on some people. An org—"

"Don't say any more," he whispered, putting a hand on my shoulder. "They might by listening."

"So, you know who I'm talking about?" I asked.

He narrowed his eyes and nodded. He drew me closer.

"What do you want to know about them?"

109

"Who they are," I said. "What they're after."

He laughed and shook his head. "What they're after - yeah - what they're after. That's a good one."

He turned and stared at the wall for a long time and didn't say a word.

Finally, he turned back and put his lips next to my ear.

"You're CCE, aren't you," he said. "This is a test - I know. You want to see how much I found out."

I played along. "I can't fool you. So how much *did* you find out?"

"I can do better than tell you about them," he whispered. "I can take you."

What the hell? I thought. *I'm not sure I want to go anywhere with this guy. Maybe I better give up and get out of here before he loses it completely.*

Too late. He grabbed my arm and started dragging me out of the room.

"Hey, forget about it," I said, trying to pull free. He seemed to have flipped into some kind of hypnotic state. "Hey, asshole!" I yelled. "Let me go! I changed my mind. I don't give a shit who they are."

He wasn't listening. He dragged me across the entire building and through a hole blasted in the wall at the opposite end. We headed down a filthy alley. He wasn't even trying to avoid the cameras. I looked around and realized that this deep in the Dregs there were almost none anyway, and the few I saw looked broken. I checked my HUD and it wasn't registering anything.

"There's no cameras?" I said.

He finally spoke. "Smashed 'em all. Nobody came back to fix 'em. Nobody ever comes around here."

I finally gave up and went along. We traveled a few blocks, then entered another abandoned building. We climbed a half-demolished set of stairs for three floors, headed down a hall littered with garbage, and turned right into what had once been an office. A gigantic hole had been smashed out of the inside wall. The center of the building was open, and you could look through the hole right down to the bottom floor. There had once been an atrium with a garden. Most of the plants had died. Some of the hardier vines had spread around to cover the walls.

Benny sat down near the hole and closed his eyes.

"What now?" I asked.

"We wait," he answered.

I thought about trying to get out of there. The guy was obviously unstable, but so far he'd been harmless. There was a chance that he might actually know something, or at least might lead me to somebody that did.

He sat there like some kind of Buddha statue. He wasn't going to say anything else. I figured I might as well wait. I thought of filling the time checking the crypted phone, but wasn't sure what he'd do if he knew I had it. I cleared some of the debris from a section of the floor, laid my pack down for a pillow, stretched out, and went to sleep.

I woke up. Somebody had a hand over my mouth and was shaking me. I opened my eyes and looked up. It was Benny. He put a finger to his lips. I nodded and he removed his hand. I sat up and rubbed my eyes. There were voices in the space down below. Benny leaned in close to my ear.

"They're here," he whispered. He pointed down toward the voices.

I moved closer to the hole in the wall to look down.

"Careful," he whispered. "Don't let them see you."

I leaned out just enough to see a small group in the atrium area, sitting in a circle, talking. It was pretty dark, and they were about fifty meters away, but I could see them well enough to tell they were homeless and dressed in rags, like Benny. I didn't know much about Vita Aeterna, but I figured it was pretty unlikely these guys were them.

Unlike Benny, they all had HUD controllers on their wrists. They were passing a bottle around, talking and laughing.

"This is them?" I whispered to Benny. "They look like a bunch of drunks on a bender."

Benny scowled at me, annoyed. "That's their cover. Don't you know anything?"

"So what are they doing here?"

"Lookin' for me," Benny sat up straight and smiled. "But they'll never find me."

I heard a noise toward the door behind us. A voice said, "I thought we told you not to come back here."

We turned to look. A guy was standing in the doorway with a gun in his hand. He was young, tall and thin, with a scruffy dark beard.

"It's my building," Benny said. "I can…"

"Cut the bullshit," the guy said. "We don't want to hear about it." He nodded at me. "Who's your little friend?"

I got to my feet. "I can speak for myself." I probably should have been more careful. He had the gun, but his attitude pissed me off.

He raised the gun and pointed it at me. "Well I can blow your head off if I feel like it, and nobody - including this bozo -" he nodded at Benny, "will give a shit." He cocked the firing mechanism. "Now, what are you doing here?"

I stepped back. "Name's Alex," I said, losing the attitude. "I've been living on the street." There was no way I was gonna tell him the truth.

"For how long?"

I winged it. "A few months."

He scanned me up and down. I realized that my clothes, which weren't anything special, weren't rags either.

"How come we've never seen you before?" he said.

"What?" I said. "I gotta come and announce myself to you guys whenever I'm around?"

He stepped forward and pressed his gun barrel against my forehead. "This is our turf, and yeah, you *better* come and ask permission to be in it." He sneered. "If you were living on the street you'd know that." He waved the gun toward the door. "Let's go."

"No!" Benny yelled.

"I wasn't inviting you," the guy sneered at him. "You can get lost."

"If I come down, he comes with me," I said.

"You're not in a position to bargain," the guy with the gun said. "Anyway, you should pick a better class to be loyal to."

SEVENTEEN

....

THE GANG

We left Benny and navigated down the garbage-littered stairs to the bottom. The group didn't look any better close up. There were four guys, including my captor, who introduced himself as 'Tory', and three women. I guess it was party time. They were passing a bottle of something around, laughing and shouting. They were all dressed in rags, and they all had this gaunt look like the life had been sucked out of them.

They took my pack and the board strapped to my back. Tory held a gun on me while one of the others frisked me. The guy was so pissed he didn't notice the cards, which I'd moved to an inner pocket of my pants, and didn't find the money in my shoe. One of them pulled the crypted phone out of my pack and held it up, smiling. I moved to grab it, but Tory cocked the gun and pressed it against my head. I stepped back.

"Take care of it," Tory said to the guy.

I watched as he stumbled off, hoping to see where he put it, but he went around a corner and I lost sight of him. Tory shoved me forward and told me to sit down with the others. After the big deal he'd made about taking me down there, nobody really seemed to care whether I was there or not, but they still wouldn't let me leave.

At first they didn't want to share their booze (which was okay with me), but as they got more hammered, they changed their minds. I wanted to keep my head straight and maybe make a run for it once the rest of them passed out or something, but they got suspicious when I kept turning down drinks, so I gave up and joined them.

I told them about my Cam-surfing, and there was talk of me joining - like that was some kind of honour. Anyway, they said the head-man, Cash - the guy who'd end up making that decision, was off negotiating with the leader of another group.

I asked Tory about their gang.

"We help each other stay alive," he explained as they passed the bottle around. "We sneak into the Quarters, even the Corp Ring sometimes, and steal enough to survive, like the thousands of others out here. We stay together for protection. If SecureCorp catches any of us we're dead."

"Thousands?" I said. "Bullshit - the Dregs are practically empty."

Tory laughed. "Empty? Who've you been listening to?" he nodded at the HUD controller on my wrist. "That?"

The others joined in laughing. I felt my face turning red. "Well, how else are you supposed to know what's going on?"

They all laughed again.

I explained how Benny and I had met. I didn't mention anything about looking for Vita Aeterna or Uncle Zack, or what happened to me. They seemed to buy that I was just a regular street kid.

"Where'd you get the money for a crypted phone?" Tory sneered.

I looked at the floor. "I didn't. I stole it."

I looked up. They were all staring at me.

My eyes locked with Tory's for a few seconds. Finally he shrugged. "Anyway, who gives a shit. Cash'll find out what's up with you when he gets back. Have another drink."

☼

About an hour later the leader, Cash, finally showed up. He looked pretty much like the rest, in his twenties (I guess), ragged and un-washed, but with a little more intelligent glint in his eye. As soon as the others saw him they quieted down. The bottle was almost empty anyway, but they shoved it under a jacket - like he wouldn't notice.

Cash took Tory, who I guess was sort of his right-hand man, aside and talked to him away from the others. Tory pointed at me a couple of times. Cash looked over at me and smiled. It gave me the creeps.

Finally, Cash and Tory both came over. I stood to face them.

Cash stuck his face in mine. "Who the fuck are you?"

I felt my body shaking but I didn't move. "What's it to you? I was just minding my own business. It was you guys—"

"You're in our territory - your business is our business," he said. He shoved me back on my heels. "Tory says you're supposed to have been livin' on the street for a few months."

116

"Yeah," I said. "So?"

He sneered. "You haven't been out here for more than a few days." He stared at my clothes. "What the hell are you up to?" He smiled again. "You told Tory your name was Alex."

I cringed. *Why the hell did I tell them my real name?* I thought. *He's heard about me.*

Cash nodded at Tory, who left and returned with a couple of the other guys that were sitting around.

"I gotta take off for a while," Cash said. "I got some people to talk to - figure out what to do with you."

The others rushed forward and grabbed me. I tried to break free but they had me pinned.

Cash turned and walked away. They dragged me to a small room nearby, threw me inside, and locked the door. I pounded on it for a while and screamed, but they all ignored me. I could see a shadow moving occasionally through the crack under the door - they'd left a guard outside.

I sat down on the bare concrete floor with my head in my hands. After all that had happened - and Walter and my father giving their lives for me to get free...

I scanned around the room, hunting for a way out. There was nothing. Even if I could break through the wall somehow the guard would hear and I'd be put somewhere else. The room was around the corner from where the main group were sitting, but I could still hear the noise from the drinking party getting louder. They must have gotten another bottle from someplace.

Vita Aeterna

☼

Twenty minutes later the party was in full swing - lots of shouting and laughing. I'd given up on escape for now. I slid down against the back wall, hoping to get some sleep, but images kept swirling through my head: my dad, Walter, Richie, the Lost Souls, Cindy…

I clamped my eyes shut and tried to drive the reality out of my mind. Cindy - I guess I always knew our relationship was doomed, even if all this hadn't happened, but I thought at least she would be out there somewhere - a little patch of beauty and love in a world that didn't have much of either. That alone would have made my life a little easier to take. But now…

I looked up when the guard outside the door made a funny noise. It was like he was about to yell but got cut short. There was a series of thumps on the other side of the door. The guard grunted and there was a snapping sound.

A few seconds later there was the tinkling of a set keys, the door opened, and a figure filled the entire doorway.

It was Benny.

"We gotta get out of here," he said.

"You got that right," I agreed, smiling. "I've never been so happy to see somebody."

Benny stepped aside and I saw the crumpled body of the guard lying motionless on the floor beside the door, his neck broken.

Mental note, I thought. *Benny isn't so harmless after all.*

We snuck toward a door at the far corner of the atrium, away from the sound of the partiers.

We were almost there when a guy rounded the corner, unzipping his fly. He looked up and spotted us. Benny moved to run after him.

I grabbed his arm. "You'll never catch him in time - we better move."

The guy started yelling and we started running. I glanced back over my shoulder. Tory appeared, running after us with the gun in his hand. He raised it and fired. He was too far away to hit anything.

Benny and I tore through the doorway. He didn't even slow down as we switched direction into a corridor full of debris. I guess he knew this place inside-out. There was still yelling behind us, but it was farther away. After a half-dozen twists and turns we made it to a hallway that looked like it led outside. The yelling was moving away, like our pursuers had taken a wrong turn.

We reached a door, but it was boarded up from the other side. Benny stepped back and kicked at it, and couple of the boards broke, leaving an opening. We squeezed through and we were outside. We took off, trying to put as much distance as possible between us and the gang.

"Thanks a lot, man," I whispered when we finally stopped for a breather.

"You make sure you tell them about me," Benny said.

"What?"

He lowered his voice to a whisper. "The CCE - you'll tell them how I helped you."

I'd almost forgotten about that. "Yeah - yeah, sure I'll tell them. You did good."

I felt like a jerk playing him like that, but I wasn't sure what he'd do if I told him the truth. We walked for another twenty minutes. Finally he stopped and pulled a couple of stray pieces of junk away from the wall of an abandoned building. There was an opening behind them. He may be unhinged but he knows this place. We crawled in, then he pulled it all back in to cover the hole. We were in another hallway. We walked down it to another room full of debris, and sat down in a clear space on the floor.

"What did I tell you?" Benny said. "Those guys are a menace."

At first I wasn't clear what he meant. In all the confusion, I'd forgotten why we hooked up with them in the first place.

"Thanks for getting me away from them," I said, "but those aren't the guys I'm looking for."

Benny looked nervous. "So - who?"

I hesitated, wondering how he'd react.

"They're called 'Vita Aeterna'," I finally said. "Heard of them?"

His face was blank. He shook his head. He genuinely didn't seem to know anything about them. I pushed on.

"I'm also looking for my Uncle Zack," I said. "He disappeared a long time ago - before I was born."

He stared at me. "Disappeared?"

"I thought he was dead, but now I'm not so sure."

Benny's body stiffened. "Could be Dead Shift," he said. "What do you want with Dead Shift?"

"Dead Shift?" I said.

"I see them sometimes," he said. "They call them that because they're all supposed to be dead - whatever that means."

"Do you know where I can find them?"

He looked at the floor and wrung his hands together. "You don't want to find those guys."

I couldn't help thinking that somewhere buried within the tangled web of his mind he had the information I was looking for.

"Why not?" I asked.

He rubbed the scar on his right temple. "I don't want to talk about that." For a second I thought he was going to make a run for it. He was shaking. "Who are you, anyway?" he asked, rocking back and forth, suddenly suspicious.

"Relax," I said. "You can trust me. I'm just doing research."

He settled down a bit.

"You don't have to get involved," I said. "But do you know anybody that might know where I can find this Dead Shift?"

For a few seconds he was silent.

"You'd really be helping us out," I said, hinting that the CCE were behind it all.

He perked up at that, eager to help.

He leaned in close to me and whispered. "There's these guys called 'The Rebels'. They're trying to get rid of the government." He said the word 'government' like he was biting off something that tasted bad. "I tried to join them once…"

He looked down again at the floor. I figured it was best not to ask what happened.

"They might know," he continued. "I heard that sometimes they talk to the Dead Shift."

"Can you take me to meet with these Rebels?"

He started fidgeting again. He got up and paced back and forth in front of me.

"You don't have to come," I said. "Just tell me where I can find them."

He started whispering to himself, clenching and unclenching his fists: "No, I won't fail - I won't! I'll measure up!"

He turned to face me. "They move all over. There's a couple of places I've seen them before. I'll take you."

EIGHTEEN

....

THE REBELS

There was no further sign of the gang, so we rested for an hour or so, then headed out. Benny led me through yet another maze of alleys. It was daytime, but surrounded by masses of skyscrapers, we were always in the shadows. Every one of the places looked abandoned.

This was like another city I didn't even know existed. There was nothing here - no people, no vehicles, no cameras. Just crumbling ruins and piles of garbage. I thought we had it bad where I lived, but this was something else. I wondered at all the work that went into the buildings towering over us. Now they'd been left to rot. What happened?

Benny was shaking.

"Why don't you wait here," I said, trying to let him off the hook. "It's better if I go to meet them alone. Just give me the directions."

He ignored me and kept moving. A couple of hours later we reached a huge open square with an ancient-looking stone building in the center. I'd never seen anything like it. It had pointed spires that

123

swept up from the roof, and what was left of a big round window with shards of coloured glass in some kind of pattern. There was a big cross at the front - a church. It looked ridiculously out of place in the midst of all the giant skyscrapers. Benny stopped. He was petrified.

"Is this the place?" I asked him. "This is where you saw the Rebels?"

He nodded, staring at the building like it was going to fall on him.

"In there?" I asked, gesturing at the church.

He nodded again, faintly. I turned and headed for it.

I looked over my shoulder. Benny was still hanging back.

I stopped and called to him. "You coming?"

He finally stepped toward me. It was like he was dragging himself forward. I turned back and continued walking.

We reached the massive archway at the front. The wooden doors, which looked like they'd originally had some kind of picture carved into them, were in shreds. I walked inside. There were lots of holes in the walls, and even though there wasn't much light outside I could see well enough. I looked behind me. Benny was stuck at the front door, mumbling to himself - I guess trying to talk himself into coming in.

I turned back. I was standing in a gigantic open space. The floor was made of wooden boards. The ground underneath must have buckled, because the floor bulged up in the middle, like a huge pimple. A lot of it had been ripped up, probably for firewood. Here and there were scattered what was left of some benches. Ahead of me, at the far end of the building, was a maze of tubes of all different sizes, some round, some - the biggest ones - square.

I hiked over the bulge in the middle, avoiding the numerous holes in the floor, and reached the jumble of tubing. Stuffed into the center of the back wall, almost buried by the tubing and other junk, was what was left of a keyboard, like for a piano.

"A pipe organ," I whispered to myself. I'd heard of them, and seen pictures, but I'd never seen one for real.

I turned and looked back. Benny was standing on the highest point of the floor, like he was at the top of a hill. He was staring down at me. He took one step forward. I heard a board creak - but it didn't come from him - and it didn't come from me.

A voice came through my HUD, "Alex Barret, you need to come with us."

"Benny, you bastard!" I yelled up at him.

"What?" he said. He turned and looked back. "I didn't do anything, I swear," he yelled back.

A shot echoed through the building. Benny collapsed and slowly rolled down the incline of the floor in my direction. He came to a stop almost at my feet. A swarm of soldiers appeared on the floor/hill above us, their weapons drawn. From their ink-black business suits, like what the big-wigs wear only made out of bullet proof fabric, their black ties, and the blood-red stripe across each of their chests, it was clear who they were.

SecureCorp.

Benny started to push himself up.

"Stay down!" I whispered to him.

They rushed down the slope toward me. There was nothing I could do. When they reached me, one moved to either side and gripped each of my arms.

The leader, a weathered, skinny guy with a pock-marked face, stood in front of me, staring. Beside him stood Cash, the leader of the gang who'd held me prisoner. A thin smile curled up on his lip.

"Didn't I tell you, Weber?" Cash turned to the pock-marked guy. "Where else was he gonna go?"

"Help my friend," I said, nodding at Benny.

Cash sneered at me, then stepped over and kicked Benny in the head. Weber's expression didn't register anything. He and the others ignored Benny and led me out the way I'd come. I fought to get free but there were too many of them.

We marched out the front archway and into the relative light of the outdoors.

"I haven't done anything," I protested, struggling against the hands gripping me.

"Shut up," Weber said, without emotion.

The group turned and headed south, toward the Quarters, dragging me with them.

"Wait," Cash said, grabbing Weber's shoulder.

The leader turned his head and glared down at Cash's hand, like it had contaminated him. He held up his own hand and everybody stopped.

Cash saw the look and removed the offending hand. "I found him," Cash said, "like I promised. Now let's have my reward."

Cash held his hand out.

Weber turned to face him. He didn't say a word. In one fluid move-ment, he hauled a gun from the holster at his belt and shot Cash point-blank in the chest. Shock registered on the gangster's face as he stared down at the gushing wound. Then he toppled over and was still.

"Let's get out of this shit-hole," Weber said.

He holstered his gun, waved his hand again, and we continued marching, like nothing had happened, leaving Cash's lifeless corpse in the street.

We marched through the rubble and shadows. I hung my head and trudged along, devastated. After all I'd been through - it was all over. And Benny had probably died trying to help me - another life on my head.

About ten minutes later, we'd just entered the junction of a cross-alley when there was the pop of a gunshot and the front man in our group went down. The soldiers rushed for cover as more shots took out several others near the front.

Weber motioned to the two guys holding me, then ran off directing the others as a gun battle went on. My captors dragged me behind what was left of a dumpster. All around us the firefight raged, shouts, screams, running boots, gunfire.

After a few minutes I heard grunts on either side of me and my two guards collapsed to the ground, blood pooling beneath them. I scanned around in panic, expecting to be next. Nothing happened. I was about to take off when a new pair of arms grabbed me and started dragging me backwards.

I finally got a look at my new captors. They were rough, like the gang I'd met before, but their clothes were clean and they had determined looks on their faces.

"Stay quiet," one of them whispered. "We're on your side."

The gunfire echoed into the distance as they led me down another series of alleys. We finally stopped, and one of my new captors talked to somebody on his HUD. He nodded to his partner.

"Who are you guys?" I said.

"You'll find out soon enough," one of them said. "For now, keep it down. We're not out of danger yet."

I could still hear gunfire, but it was sporadic. Then it stopped altogether. After about twenty minutes we stopped in front of a side door for one of the abandoned skyscrapers. The guy in front pulled out a key, unlocked it, and we went through. Inside was a massive open space. Far in the distance were a few doors to what looked like offices.

The guy holding me nodded to his right. We twisted and turned down a bunch of hallways until we finally reached another large empty space. All the debris had been cleared out, and there were cots positioned against the walls.

In one corner were several desks and chairs. We sat down on a couple of the chairs and waited.

After a few minutes another group came into the room. I was shocked to see that two of them were holding up Benny, who was limping and looked pretty badly injured, but was alive. They led him to one of the cots and laid him down.

Before the guards could stop me, I rushed over. A woman was bending over him.

I grabbed her arm. "What are you doing!"

"I'm trying to save your friend's life," she answered over her shoulder.

They'd gone to the trouble of bringing him back here, so I assumed she was telling the truth. I stared down at Benny. He was unconscious. Blood from a wound in his side was soaking into the cot. The woman cut away Benny's shirt. The wound was nasty and still bleeding a lot.

"Is he going to live?" I asked.

"If I can stop the bleeding," the woman said. "You should leave me to it - there's nothing you can do. I'll come and let you know what happens."

"Don't worry," a familiar voice came from behind me. A hand was placed on my shoulder. "She'll take good care of your friend."

I jumped and turned. I couldn't believe what I was seeing.

NINETEEN

....

REUNION

Standing beside me, like some ghost out of the past, was my old school teacher, Travis. I stood there with my mouth open. He smiled, enjoying my confusion.

"Surprised?" he said.

"I figured you were dead or something," I said.

"Not yet," he laughed.

I was speechless, still trying to process what was happening.

"What are you–" I finally blurted out.

"Doing here?" he interrupted me.

He smiled. "Some of my views were filtering back to the Elite, and pissing them off. I was already affiliated with this group part-time. It would have been full-time as it was if it wasn't for Laura." I raised an eyebrow. "My daughter," he said, and I nodded. "The previous Rebel leader was killed during a raid." Travis closed his eyes for a second, remembering. "Meanwhile, I got wind that SecureCorp were planning to make me disappear. I beat them to it and went underground."

"You always were paranoid, man," I laughed. "Since when do they care what you say? It's a free country."

He gave me this annoying sort of patronizing look. I told him all that had happened. He shook his head slowly as I described my Appraisal and the aftermath.

"We heard about you," he said when I was finished. "We've been keeping an eye out. Lucky we found you before they got you out of the Dregs. I'll tell you one thing. They really want you bad."

"But why?" I said. "What did I do?"

He motioned with one hand, and led me to a room with a few boxes and a large table in the middle.

"Let me guess," I said as we walked through the door. "You guys are planning to overthrow the government or something."

It was his turn to smile. "Not quite."

He nodded toward a couple of the boxes. We went over and sat down on them. We were alone.

"What do they want with me?" I asked. I was so glad I'd run into him. Maybe finally someone could tell me what was going on.

"I'm not sure about that," he answered.

"What the hell's the deal with my Appraisal?" I said. "Nobody's even told me what it is." I looked into his eyes. "Do you know?"

Something changed in his expression. He shook his head. "All I know is that SecureCorp are desperate to get you back."

"There's something happening," I said. "Something weird. According to my friend Richie, I'm supposed to be dead."

A light seemed to go on behind Travis's eyes, then it disappeared.

"Does that mean something to you?" I said.

Vita Aeterna

He shook his head. It was so good to meet someone I knew, and share what was happening to me, I kept going.

"My dad talked about something called Vita Aeterna. I think it's some kind of organization."

Travis' eyebrows came together. "Don't know them. I can make some inquiries…"

I studied his face. This time he really didn't seem to know.

"My dad also told me I should find my Uncle Zack. I don't understand what he was talking about. Uncle Zack's supposed to be dead."

Again, a flash of something crossed Travis' face.

"Dead?" he asked. "How did he die?"

"He fell hitching on a RoboTaxi forty years ago," I answered.

"What's going on?" I asked.

He smiled and put a fatherly hand on my shoulder. "I don't know. But together we're going to find out."

The woman that had been taking care of Benny appeared at the door. She smiled over at me. "Your friend is going to be okay."

I relaxed a little - one less person dying on my account.

Travis gestured for her to join us. "This is Patricia Treadwell," he said. "She's our doctor-in-residence. She was a doctor to some of the Corp heads before she got fed up."

Treadwell offered her hand and I shook it.

She gestured with her head back to where she'd been treating Benny. "We've stitched him up - he's resting. I'd leave him for now - you should be able to talk to him later."

"G…Great, thanks," I said.

We got up and Travis took me in to meet the others.

"What do we want with him?" One of the men, a bearded, intense-looking guy named Rolf, complained after Travis had introduced me. "We're just drawing attention to ourselves for nothing. We don't know anything about him - he'll give us up."

I opened my mouth to say something, but Travis put a hand on my shoulder and shook his head.

"I know him," Travis said. "And I don't want anything bad to happen to him. Yes, it's a risk, but if SecureCorp are so hot to get him, keeping them from getting him is probably a good idea."

I tensed. Not all the Rebels were happy I was here.

☼

"I feel a lot better," Benny said a few hours later, as I knelt beside the cot he was lying on. "I'm just kinda tired."

"You're a tough guy." I smiled at him. "It takes more than a SecureCorp bullet to take you out."

"But why are SecureCorp after you?" he asked. "It's some kind of test, right?"

I hesitated. I wasn't sure how to answer him. "Yeah, something like that," I finally said.

"You'll tell them?" he said.

"What?"

He winced in pain as he leaned over and whispered. "You know, *them* - you'll tell them I took a bullet."

"Yeah." I patted his shoulder. "I'll tell them."

The run-in with Rolf had made me edgy. I leaned in and whispered. "What do you know about these guys? Can we trust them?"

"I don't know," he answered. "They hate the government, so they should be okay. But I heard them say something bad about…" He leaned closer and mouthed the words, 'Mister Wickham'.

"I know the leader, Travis," I said. "He's a good guy, but I didn't know about any of this…" I gestured around the room with my head. "Makes me wonder what else I don't know about. It's too bad. I had a crypted phone in my backpack that I could have used to do some research, but that asshole gang took it."

"I could…" Benny started to say. He put out his hands and tried to push himself up.

I stopped him. "You're not doing anything right now. Just get some rest."

Benny lay back down and closed his eyes. Dr. Treadwell was examining another patient in a far corner. She stood up and turned to leave. I caught up with her as she was going out the door. I asked her about Benny.

"He's lost a lot of blood," she said as we walked, "but the wound was pretty superficial. He should okay once his stitches heal."

I stared at her. "Did you really quit working for the Corps to be here?"

She smiled. "I'm not the only one. It happens more than you might think."

"What do you mean?"

She nodded toward the main work area. "You don't know about Travis?"

I shook my head.

"Travis was once a senior programmer at InfoCorp. He gave it all up, to join our cause."

"What!" I turned and stared where she'd been looking. "No way - nobody would do that."

Dr. Treadwell smiled. "You'd be surprised at what people will sacrifice for what they believe in."

She turned and walked away. My head was spinning. I thought about it - the things Travis knew about, the mystery of where he'd come from. It seemed impossible but...

I realized that I was pretty exhausted too. I found Travis again. I couldn't help looking at him differently after what Dr. Treadwell had said. He arranged for a cot for me not far from Benny. As soon as I lay down I passed out.

☼

I woke with a hand shaking me. "Alex," a voice said. "Alex, wake up." I sat bolt upright and stared around in confusion. Then I remembered where I was. Light was pouring through a nearby window - it was morning. I looked over. The voice belonged to Travis. His hand was on my shoulder.

"Your friend," he said, his expression grave. "He's disappeared."

TWENTY

....

REAPPEARANCE

It didn't seem possible that Benny could sneak away from this place. I didn't think he could even walk.

"Somehow he got past the guards," Travis said. "It would be impossible for anybody to break in unnoticed, but they're not watching as closely for people leaving. His wound was pretty severe. We all thought he was too injured to go anywhere. Obviously that's not true."

"Benny might be a bit slow," I said, "but I can't believe how well he knows these streets. If he's gone, we'll never find him."

"He's put all of our lives in danger," Travis said. "We're going to have to move. They're packing the stuff up as we speak."

"What?" I said. "Because of Benny? He'd never tell."

"We can't afford to take a chance."

"I'm sorry," I said, hanging my head.

"It was my decision to rescue him," Travis said. "It's me that's responsible. Anyway, moving's not that big a deal. We've done it so often we've got it down to a science."

Travis didn't seem like the same easy-going eccentric who'd taught me at the co-op school. Now he had an angry edge, something I'd never seen before. I had a fleeting thought that the Rebels might have gotten rid of Benny, then made up the story about him leaving. But then why save him in the first place? And why move if he wasn't a threat? I put the idea out of my head. Anyway, I had no way of finding him. If he'd wanted me to know where he was going he would have told me.

After a wash and a quick breakfast of some kind of mashed grain, I followed Travis over to a group that was packing up the sleeping area. They were folding up the cots, which were made from thick canvas strung across hinged tubular frames, and piling them on a wheeled cart.

"You can give them a hand," Travis said, gesturing at the group.

I nodded and joined them, collapsing the nearest cot and carrying it over. Nearby was a young girl, probably about my age. She had light brown skin and dark, curly hair tied back in a ponytail. Something about her was familiar. She looked up, caught me eyeing her and smiled. I felt my cheeks flush. I looked away and concentrated on cot folding.

Fifteen minutes later all the cots were ready. A couple of guys tied them down on the carts and wheeled them away. The guy in charge directed us to another room, to start packing up the cooking utensils. I tensed when the girl moved up to walk beside me.

"You're Alex, aren't you," she said.

I looked up, shocked. "Do I know you?"

She laughed and her face lit up. "Sort of. I came to a few of your classes at the co-op school."

I thought back. I couldn't remember. Finally it came to me - a skinny kid that showed up for class a couple of times. But she didn't look like this...

Suddenly I realized who she was. "You're Travis' daughter."

She nodded. "I'm Laura," she said, holding out her hand.

I shook it. Travis had never mentioned to anyone in class that she was his daughter, and I guess nobody asked. She'd only come a couple of times.

She had black eyes and a smile that overflowed with life. She was really cute, but I felt a stab of guilt even looking at another girl so soon after what happened to Cindy... Suddenly it all came rushing back and my throat tightened. I felt tears welling in my eyes. I looked away.

"Are you okay?" I heard Laura's voice, and snapped out of it.

"Yeah, I'm fine," I said, pulling myself together.

We headed for a door at the far end of the room.

"It must have been rough to go on the run like this," I said, fighting to take my mind off things.

She shrugged. "Yeah. I'm still sort of getting used to it. It's a hard life, but we've got no choice now."

I imagined what her life must have been like before, if what Dr. Treadwell had said was true. If she'd really gone from the luxury of the Corp Ring to living in squalor and on the run, she didn't show any bitterness about it.

We split up again as the guy in charge directed us to different tasks. I didn't see her again that day. I tried to focus on what was happening with Travis and the rest of the Rebels. I asked Travis about trying to find out if Uncle Zack was still alive.

"I'll get some of the tech-savvy guys to check into it," he said. "While we're waiting, maybe you can help us out. We can always use another man."

✧

The move went pretty smoothly. Like Travis said, they had the process down to a science. Our new digs were several hours away, in a monster building with a row of steps running up to a wide terrace, with big stone pillars at the entrance. I guess they'd scouted out lots of potential hideouts ahead of time and picked one far enough away from the one we'd been at. The building had running water, which was pretty awesome.

Even with all the Rebels' experience, it had taken half a day to pack, and another full day to complete the move. I felt like I was responsible for it and all the disruption it had caused. I had no control over Benny, but he'd been taken in along with me. Some of the Rebels were already down on me. This wouldn't help. I still felt guilty when I found myself keeping an eye out for Laura, but anyway I hadn't seen her since that first time.

A few days later we were settled in. I helped around the place, doing odd jobs. One day we were hauling some equipment up the front steps, which was pretty tiring work. During a break I stepped to one side to get my breath, and caught a movement out of the corner of my eye. I scanned around. At first there was nothing. Then I saw it again, beside a building to the north. I glanced over at the guards on either side of the steps. They hadn't seen anything. I kept an eye out, careful not to let the guards see me. I didn't want to alert them until I knew what was going on.

Finally I saw it. Benny. He peeked out from the corner and waved. He was in a position where only I could see him. I took a chance and looked in his direction, nodding to let him know he'd gotten my attention.

Tonight, he mouthed the words, pointing at the north side of our new hideout. I nodded again, though I wasn't sure how I was going to swing it.

I'd been assigned a cot in a large room with a bunch of other guys. It was nothing fancy, but it beat sleeping some alley waiting to get my head bashed in. But it made it hard to slip away. I wondered what Benny was up to. He was probably wise not to show his face back here after running off like that, but why did he leave in the first place? And now why was he back?

I decided there was no point in sneaking around. Late that night I just got up headed for the front door. A guard with a rifle was posted just outside of it.

I moved to push past him. He shoved his rifle out and blocked me.

"I'm going for a walk," I said.

"I can't allow that," the guard said.

I stepped back. "What do you mean? Am I a prisoner here or something?"

The guard hesitated. "It's a safety thing," he said. "It's dangerous out there."

I stared at him. I knew he was right. It was dangerous, but was that the only reason?

"I need to stretch my legs and get some fresh air," I said. "I won't go far."

He stood for a few seconds in the moonlight, studying me. "You can walk along the side of the building," he finally said, "but stay in sight."

I gave him one last look. At some point I was going to have to test whether I was free to leave, but not right now.

"Okay," I nodded, and started walking.

The guard moved out past the northeast corner so that he could watch me. I had nowhere to go anyway. I just headed down the wall, like he'd instructed. I wasn't sure how I was supposed to find Benny. I assumed he'd contact me somehow.

I walked right to the end, to the farthest corner, and turned to look back at the guard. He was still standing there, where I'd left him, nervously, with his rifle at the ready.

I stared into the blackness ahead of me, waiting. I respected Travis and the Rebels, but there was something else going on. I'd see some of them whispering to each other and stealing glances at me when they thought I wasn't looking. I kept bugging Travis about trying to find out more about Uncle Zack. He always claimed that they were working on it, but they didn't seem to be working very hard.

I glanced around, looking for Benny, trying not to be too obvious. There was the sound of a cough to my right. I froze. The space behind

141

the building was in shadow even in the daytime, and now it was late at night - all was blackness.

"Hi," a voice whispered. A large shape stepped into a nearby patch of moonlight, behind the building, out of view of the guard.

It was Benny.

"Where have you been?" I whispered back. I made sure my back was to the guard so he wouldn't see my lips moving.

"Around," he said.

"Keep it down," I whispered. "They're watching me."

He reached into his inner jacket pocket. I couldn't see very well, but his shirt was torn open and it looked like he'd pulled out Dr. Treadwell's stitches and crudely sewn the wound back up himself.

"You're going to get an infection," I said. "You shouldn't be walking around like that."

"It's nothin'," he said. His hand emerged gripping a small rectangular shape.

"You said you wanted this," he said, holding up the object. It was my crypted phone.

"What!" I had to fight to keep my voice down.

He held the phone under the brightest part of the light beam. "It still works," he whispered. "I tried it."

"How the hell did you get it back?" I said.

"You'll tell them?" he said. "How I got it for you?"

He held it out. I stepped around the corner to take it. There were blotches of what looked like blood on it.

"That's great, Benny," I said. "But you shouldn't have done that. It's too dangerous." I gestured with my head back the way I'd come.

"Come on, let's go in. I'll smooth things over with Travis and we'll get the doctor to look at you."

He drew back. "Don't like those guys."

"What's wrong with them?" I wasn't sure what they'd done that put him off. "They're trying to get rid of the government - that's good, isn't it?"

He hesitated.

"What's going on there?" the voice of the guard called out behind me. "Get back here. Are you talking to somebody? Who's there?"

I stuffed the phone under my shirt and stepped back around the corner where the guard could see me. He was walking in my direction.

"It's nothing," I called back, and tried to wave him off. He kept coming.

I turned my back on him again to talk to Benny. "Come back with me and I'll get Dr. Treadwell to sew you up again properly," I whispered. I glanced over, but he was gone.

TWENTY ONE

....

A DILEMMA

It was tough finding a hiding place for the phone. There was no 'private' space for anybody at the hideout. Travis might be okay, but I didn't trust some of the guys around him. I didn't want to tell them about the phone, and if I kept it on me someone would notice it sooner or later. I hid it behind a broken electrical panel in one of the storerooms. It wasn't that secure, but it was the only place I could think of.

The next day there was another big meeting. I wasn't a full-fledged Rebel member, so I wasn't invited. The hideout was almost empty. I rescued the phone from its hiding place, found a deserted room, and checked it out. The battery was three-quarters drained. The phone had a solar panel. It could be charged in sunlight, but I'd have to leave it out somewhere for at least a couple of hours.

I was about check for messages when the phone vibrated in my hand. The ringer was muted but it was clear what was happening - I was getting a new message.

A jolt went up my spine as I checked the display. Was it one of Fatso's cronies? Or even Fatso himself? That would make sense. A disturbing thought surfaced in my head. The phone wasn't supposed to be traceable by SecureCorp, but what if Fatso had his own special way of tracing it? He was a crook, after all. Worse still, what if he'd contacted SecureCorp and was working with them to recapture me?

The screen showed a new entry. My hand shook as I pressed the button to display it.

I talked to Richie, it said.

I tensed up. Did another person get killed trying to help me?

Who are you? I typed.

A friend, the display returned.

What did you do to him? I typed.

First, I need to know who you are, the text returned. *Tell me - what's AMP mean to the Lost Souls?*

Everybody in the Lost Souls knew the place the message was referring to. AMP stood for 'Alternate Meeting Place' - an old furniture factory not far from the Center in Tintown. I wasn't sure whether to answer him. In the end, I couldn't see what harm it would do. If he knew about the AMP I wasn't giving anything away.

Richie's fine, came the reply after I'd answered. *Don't worry. We're going to help you.*

I considered turning the phone off. Maybe SecureCorp had caught Richie and extracted the stuff about the AMP from him. Maybe they were trying to trace the call.

More text came up. *I'll be at the AMP every day at four PM, for the next week - I'll wait for one hour. Come alone.*

The message was scary enough, but what really freaked me was when I looked in the bottom corner at the sign off.

It said: *Uncle Zack.*

I dropped the phone like it was red hot and stood there staring at it. It couldn't be Fatso. There was no way he would know about Uncle Zack. The phone couldn't be traceable; if they could find me they would have taken me already. I tried to check the calling number but it was obfuscated.

But how could it be Uncle Zack? In spite of what my dad said, Zack was supposed to be dead.

Then I remembered - I was dead. At least in the eyes of the world.

Whoever it was must really have talked to Richie, or one of the others. We were the only ones that knew about it. I swallowed hard. Was Richie okay?

Uncle Zack.

Was *he* really still alive? Or was it just somebody who knew about him?

☼

The next day Travis said if I was going to stay (I still wasn't sure if I was even allowed to leave) I should be assigned a regular set of duties. I was placed on kitchen detail. I wasn't really clear on what kitchen detail was. Other than zapping hot drinks and reheating packets from FoodCorp, I'd never actually prepared a meal.

To my surprise, and mixed feelings of joy, guilt, confusion, and sadness, Laura was there too. I was assigned to help her. When I showed up, she was washing these rough, brown, oblong objects in the kitchen sink. She handed one to me, gave me this gizmo with a blade, and told me to peel it.

I stared at it in my hand. "People actually eat these things?"

"It's a potato," she laughed. "It comes from the root of a plant. You've never seen one before? You've probably eaten them yourself thousands of times, you just didn't recognize what it was."

She demonstrated how to peel it, and gave it back to me. I turned the half-peeled potato over in my hands. "I always wondered what went into the slop FoodCorp makes."

"We don't get fresh food here very often either," she said. "Usually they just hijack a delivery truck and take the food packets. This time they just happened to get one that had fresh vegetables. I think it was headed for the First Circle."

I finished peeling the potato and dropped it in a bucket. Several others who'd also been assigned to the kitchen were chopping up vegetables Laura called carrots and beets across the room.

"You don't remember me, do you?" Laura said, smiling.

"Sure I remember," I said defensively. "But...well, you looked a lot different back then."

She laughed, and again I felt a twinge of guilt, as I felt myself drawn to her. She handed me another potato and I started peeling.

She blushed as she smiled and said: "You didn't notice me following you around at co-op school like a little puppy dog?"

It was my turn to blush. "I guess I wasn't too observant—"

"You've changed too," she said. "Older, more mature. It's so courageous of you to risk everything to come and fight for our cause."

147

I cringed. She had no idea why I was here. It occurred to me that that was probably a good thing.

"It's important," I went along, though at this point I still wasn't really sure what their cause was.

"Did your dad really work for InfoCorp?" I asked, changing the subject.

She nodded, sadly. "My mom, too. She was a reporter. Dad said most people in the Corps are in denial about the political situation. Mom wanted to change that. She wrote a piece about some stuff she'd uncovered, but InfoCorp refused to run it. Dad warned her to leave it alone, but she kept pushing and digging. She was supposed to meet with an informant one night alone. Dad forbade her to go. He said it was too dangerous. She left a note and snuck off anyway. We never heard from her again."

She was choking back tears.

"I'm sorry," I said. I thought about taking her hand, but I wasn't sure how she'd react.

She continued. "Dad spent months trying to find out what happened to her, but he kept hitting a brick wall. He would have kept going, but he was worried about my safety, so we gave up and moved to the Quarters. A friend of ours managed to sneak me into a school in the Corp Ring. Once in a while a bigwig would tour the place, so I'd have to make myself scarce."

"That's when you showed up at the co-op school," I guessed.

"And that's when I first saw you," she smiled. "When the Rebel leader was killed, it left kind of a vacuum. Dad had no choice. We came out here. He was originally planning to wait until I turned sixteen - after I got my Appraisal."

"When does that happen?" I asked.

"Next month," she said cheerfully.

After all that had happened it seemed crazy that somebody could be so casual about it, but I didn't say anything. I dropped my peeled potato in the bucket with the others.

I thought about my own Appraisal. I still didn't know what it was, but from what Walter had told me...

"You can still get one - even out here?" I said.

She shrugged. "It's not that hard to do. It's just an injection. Dr. Treadwell's going to do it."

"You're not worried?"

"About what?" she said.

I stiffened. I should never have gotten into this conversation.

"Nothing," I said, smiling. "I'm sure it'll be fine."

TWENTY TWO

....

REVELATIONS

I had a problem. I was almost certain that the Rebels wouldn't let me leave. Even if they didn't care about losing me (and I'm pretty sure they *did* care), they wouldn't want me out there like Benny giving away their location. At the moment, there always seemed to be somebody paying attention to where I was, but I was free to go where I wanted. If I made it obvious I was trying to escape, that might change, and I'd never get away.

I thought about the night I'd met up with Benny. The guard had let me walk all the way to the end of the building before he tried to come after me. I came back willingly, so he'd probably let me do it again. I could walk to the spot where I'd met Benny, then just take off into the night. He wouldn't be able to stop me.

Then again, he might have talked to somebody about how far I should be allowed to go. I might not get away with that again. Anyway, did I really want to get away? Was it worth cutting my ties with Travis (and Laura) and the Rebels just to contact some guy I'd never met, who might be setting a trap for me?

I had a week to think about it. For now, I'd leave things the way they were. Maybe Travis would come through with more on Uncle Zack…

✧

I had trouble sleeping that night, my mind ticking over about Travis, his lieutenants, and the Rebels in general. When he was my teacher Travis had some outlandish views, but I felt like he'd always been straight with me.

Now it seemed like he was hiding something, but before I even considered going to see Uncle Zack, I wanted to give him the chance to explain. I found him outside on the front steps of the building, talking to a couple of his lieutenants. As I approached, they nodded to him and took off somewhere.

"Have you heard anything?" I asked. I was ready for a fight if I got the runaround again. To my surprise, he gestured toward the entrance and started walking. I followed him inside to a room they'd set up for meetings. There was a large table with chairs around it. We sat down on a couple of them.

"Okay…" he said. He sat facing me, one arm resting on the table. "Yeah, we know about the Dead Shift. And their leader is a guy named Zack. How old was your uncle?"

I shrugged. "He was my dad's older brother. He'd be in his fifties, I guess."

"Zack seems pretty young to be your uncle, but you never know with those guys."

He hesitated, like he was trying to decide how to tell me something.

"We see them once in a while," he finally said. "They're really secretive. It's different for them. SecureCorp don't really consider us a threat. They'll attack if we happen to cross paths - otherwise they leave us alone. But they're actively hunting the Dead Shift. Our groups have the same agenda, but for the Rebels it's political, for the Dead Shift, it's a matter of life and death."

Nothing was making sense. "You've got the same agenda?" I asked. "What agenda is that?"

"There's stuff you don't know."

I laughed. "Well, duh… yeah I don't know, because you and the others won't tell me."

His expression darkened as he leaned toward me. "You joked before about us trying to overthrow the government. You're actually close to being right. We *are* out to change the status quo."

"You're crazy man," I said. "We're about to have an election to get rid of them. Haven't you heard? The Enterprise party are going to eliminate more red tape and streamline the economy. They're even planning to give the CCE more say in government decisions–"

He smiled. "You haven't figured it out yet?"

"Figured what out?"

His smile disappeared. "There *is* no government."

"What are you talking about? What about President Foster?"

He snorted. "Foster's an actor."

"What about the cabinet - the parties - the opposition?"

"Actors, actors, actors." He shook his head sadly.

"Come on - so if there's no government, who's running things?"

"What's there to run?" he laughed. "Think about it. The two biggest functions of government are to enact and enforce laws, and to deliver services to the people being governed. Except for the one forcing everybody to vote, there's only one law - survival of the wealthiest.

"As for the services, the government used to provide roads, sewers, electricity, garbage collection, education, and health care for the people they governed. All that stuff is now done by the Corps. What's left for the government to do?"

I swallowed hard. I'd never thought of it before. What exactly *did* the government do? I just sat there with my mouth open. My mind had gone blank.

"A better question to ask," he continued, "is - who's in control? And that's an easy one to answer. Our true masters are on half the posters you see on the street, every other HoloTV show, and especially here—" he pointed to the HUD contact on his temple.

I was confused. I scrunched up my nose. "The CCE?"

He raised an eyebrow in confirmation.

"Bullshit," I said.

"They've been in control for decades," he said, "since long before you were born."

I laughed, shaking my head. "And how's that supposed to have happened?"

Travis shrugged and leaned back. "It was easy. From the beginning, Elite business interests had a massive influence on government.

Originally, they preferred to lurk behind the scenes, using their wealth and connections to get what they wanted, and letting the government take the blame if the result was unpopular.

"But eventually that wasn't enough. They got tired of just influencing, they wanted to be in charge. By pouring bucket loads of money into successive elections, they were able to place a core of their own people in key positions. Once they'd reached a critical mass, they just picked off the stragglers and eliminated the government altogether.

"Of course, they didn't tell the public any of this. As far as the average person knew, nothing had changed. The result is what you see." He gestured with his hand around us.

I felt like I'd entered some backwards world where the rules I knew about didn't apply anymore. "So what happens when there's an election?"

"You ever played the slots at the big casino in the Corp Ring?"

I nodded. "Cindy took me once, and gave me some money to play."

"It's kind of addicting isn't it? That's because it's designed to take advantage of human psychology. You keep playing, looking for the high when you win. If you lost every time, eventually you'd get fed up and quit playing, right?"

"Is there some point to this?"

He smiled. "The slot designers know exactly how long you're willing to lose before you give up. Just at the point where you're about to walk away, guess what?"

"They set you up to win," I said.

He nodded. "You win a little, and that gives you hope - you think your luck has changed and you keep playing. But your luck hasn't changed. You're being played for a sucker just like before."

"Yeah, so?"

"That's exactly how the government scam works - the changes in government give the public just enough hope to keep them from getting fed up and revolting."

I still thought he was full of it, but somewhere in the back of my mind his words had a ring of truth.

"But everybody's always going on about how much better things would be if the CCE ran the world," I argued. "You're telling me that they actually *do* run the world? What would be the point? Why set up this big elaborate scheme and make people hate the government and pretend you're trying to fix things? Why not just tell everybody the truth?"

"People need something to fixate on," Travis answered. "To hate. It distracts them from all their other problems, like not having enough to eat or not having proper medical care. It works especially well if an identifiable group can be blamed for everything that's wrong with people's lives, then punished, replaced, and forgotten about - until next time."

His hand on the table clenched into a fist. "Through their HUDs and HoloTV, the public are manipulated into believing that all their problems are the fault of the current government. Sophisticated software and armies of computer analysts track the public mood. When their analysis indicates that the level of dissatisfaction has reached a critical point, guess what? It's time for a new party to 'govern'." He held up two fingers of each hand like quotation marks.

His mouth twisted into a bitter smile. "It's just like with the slot machines - everybody thinks their luck has changed, that they're due for a win, but they're being played for suckers like always."

"But what about the vote?"

"The vote?" he smirked. "The ballot is tossed in the garbage as soon as you cast it. It's just for show. When people think they have a choice, they feel empowered, like they're doing something to improve their lives. Fact is, nothing at all changes. Exactly the same masters are in charge."

I was still trying to wrap my head around it all. "Anyway," I said, "if the CCE are this all-powerful force behind everything, what can you guys do?"

"There's no way we can hope to get rid of the CCE," he answered, "at least at the moment. There's too much power behind them, and the public aren't on our side - yet. But there is a flaw in their setup. Two flaws, actually."

"They better be big ones," I joked. I still wasn't sure I bought what he was saying, but it was clear there were things going on I didn't understand.

"Weaknesses as old as humanity itself," he said. "Arrogance and greed. You've got to understand about these people. They already have *almost* all the riches it's possible to possess. They could be satisfied doing without the minuscule amount that's left, continue to live better than the wealthiest sovereigns in history, and never be in danger of a revolt. But giving up something - even the tiniest scrap - isn't in their DNA."

He stared down at me. "They want everything. That's the way they're put together. They've got egos the size of these skyscrapers." He gestured out the window at the buildings around us. "The joke is, they don't even need what they already have, but that doesn't matter. They can only be satisfied by taking it all.

"That could be their downfall. If conditions get bad enough, the public will have no choice but to fight back. The Elite are incredibly wealthy, but they're a tiny minority. Their biggest fear is that the masses in the Quarters will get pissed off and revolt. That *should* limit how far they're willing to go, but their greed is tempting them to push the envelope."

"You haven't changed from school," I laughed, though I felt like I was just trying to convince myself.

He shrugged. "You can believe it or not. One way or another you're going to find out for yourself. Our hope is that we can get truth out, or at least raise some doubt. Then maybe the public will wake up and support us. What we need is some kind of catalyst. Some event or revelation that will trigger the people to act."

"Where do I fit into all this?" I asked, by now dreading the answer.

"I think you're right that it's got something to do with your Appraisal," he said. "But exactly what, I don't know."

I closed my eyes. I'd been so happy when I met up with Travis again. I thought I'd finally find out what was going on. Now I had the feeling he wasn't telling me everything he knew.

I opened them again and looked up at him. "So - what about my uncle?"

His brows came together. "Look - there's something strange going on with those Dead Shift guys - especially Zack. I didn't want to tell you about them because I don't completely trust them."

"What do you mean?"

"We have contact with the Dead Shift every once in a while. About a year ago Peter Barnes, the former leader of this group, arranged a meeting. He said it was stupid that both our groups were after more or less the same thing, but weren't working together.

"The meeting went well, and we agreed to meet again to map out a combined strategy. But a couple of days later, out of the blue, SecureCorp attacked our compound." Travis looked away. His hands clenched into fists, and his voice shook as he continued.

"Of the one hundred-twenty Rebels that were there, only seventy got out alive. That's when Peter Barnes himself was killed."

He hung his head and shook it slowly.

"We couldn't figure out how SecureCorp knew we were there," he said, looking up. "Nobody but us knew about the place. Later, one of our people admitted that he'd said something to Zack that hinted at our location. He'd been afraid to mention it, and figured it wasn't a problem, since the Dead Shift were supposed to be on our side.

"We met up with Zack later. It took everything I had not to kill him on the spot. I was sure he'd given us up. I don't know why. He claimed that he had nothing to do with it - that SecureCorp must have found us some other way. I didn't believe him."

"Maybe he was telling the truth," I said.

Travis shook his head. "I can't prove anything, but I'll give you some advice - even if we find him, don't trust that guy - there's something fishy about him."

"But he's my uncle."

"You don't know that. And, from what I've seen of him, I doubt it."

TWENTY THREE

....

A RUN

After the story he'd told me about the Dead Shift, I wasn't sure I believed Travis' claim that he was doing his best to locate Uncle Zack. I had nobody else to turn to, and I figured I was safer with the Rebels than being alone, so I stuck around. But once or twice I caught a couple of the other leaders eyeing me, especially Rolf, Travis' second in command. I still had a few days to decide whether to meet with Zack, but the deadline was coming up fast.

One day, Travis announced that we were going to conduct a raid the next morning on a SecureCorp outpost on the very edge of the Quarters, one of the closest to the Dregs. He'd gotten reports that a lot of the soldiers had been called away on a prolonged mission to deal with riots nearby (a Rebel diversion?), and that the place was only thinly defended. The Rebels were looking for weapons. I was bored, so I said I wanted to go. Travis said it was too dangerous, and insisted that I stay behind.

160

That night I heard him arguing with some of the other leaders in one of the offices. I tried to sneak closer to hear what they were saying, but there was a guard posted outside the door. The argument was pretty intense. There were lots of shouts and what sounded like fists pounding on tables. I managed to get close enough to see who came out when the meeting was over. There was Travis, Rolf, and a couple of the other guys who'd been glaring at me. None of them looked very happy.

Early the next morning Travis changed his mind and said I could come with them. I snuck away, grabbed the crypted phone, and stuffed it in my pocket, just in case something happened and I couldn't make it back. I was waiting in one of the empty rooms for the group to get organized, when Laura came to see me.

Every nerve in my body lit up as she took my hand. Again I was swamped with a confusing mix of guilt and excitement.

"Don't go," she said.

"It's just a raid," I answered, smiling, trying to sound braver than I felt. "It's no big deal. I'll be back this afternoon."

She looked up at me. "I've got a bad feeling about it. Something's going to happen–"

"I gotta pull my weight around here," I said. "I already said I'd go. I'm not going to back out now. Don't worry. Everything will be fine."

She removed a small brass medallion hanging on a string around her neck.

"At least take this," she said. "It'll bring you luck."

She reached up and hung the charm around my own neck. Then she grabbed it, pulled me close, and kissed me, full on the lips. I thought I was going to explode.

We heard footsteps approaching, and she broke away.

"Be careful," she said.

One of the fighters came through the door. He nodded at me. "Time to go."

I was gawking back at Laura, still stunned by her kiss, as the guy led me away. There was a thin, sad smile on her face as she stood and watched me go.

We gathered on the front terrace. I scanned around, and was relieved when I couldn't see Rolf anywhere. We were about to start walking when he suddenly showed up.

Travis was pissed. "I thought you weren't coming," he said to Rolf.

"Changed my mind," Rolf shrugged. "Jimbo said he'd look after things."

Travis stood and glared at Rolf for a few seconds. Finally he turned and we headed out. I'd been scared shitless during my 'rescue' from SecureCorp, so I was stressed out about the prospect of another battle as we slunk through the darkened alleyways toward the outpost.

Half an hour later we reached an area I recognized, where I'd been captured by Cash and his gang. As we entered an open square, Travis held up a hand for us to stop. I followed his line of sight and saw the reason. A half-dozen crows were feeding on something in the center of the square. The crows exploded into the sky as we approached, and a dozen or so rats scurried away.

As we got closer, I could see what was left of several bodies scattered on the ground. We approached cautiously. I guess you never know when it might be some kind of trap. At close range there was no doubt. All of them had been dead for a while.

My gut tightened when I recognized who they were. There were three of them - the guys that had captured me before. The women weren't there - they must have taken off once the party was over. We walked around the corpses, looking for anything worth taking. One thing I knew for sure they *didn't* have: the crypted phone. I fought the urge to be sick as I stood over the body of Tory, his head twisted into an impossible position, his eyes and entrails picked apart by the animals.

Travis stood scratching his head, wondering who'd killed them.

"Can't be SecureCorp," he said. "They would've just shot them." He pointed at the body closest to him. "This guy was beaten to death with something…" He wandered over to the next closest one. "Looks like this one had his neck broken."

The hair on the back of my own neck stood up. I thought about the snapping sound I'd heard outside the room where I was being held just before Benny rescued me. The bodies had nothing that interested us, so we left them alone and continued on.

A couple of hours later Travis motioned again for us to stop. This time it looked like we'd reached our destination, an open space in front of a collapsing low-rise building. He ordered Rolf, and a couple of other guys who'd been at the meeting, to scout the target outpost. Rolf didn't look too happy. He glanced at me, then back at Travis, like he was trying to decide something. Finally, he turned and went off, following orders.

When they were gone, Travis brought a guy over, one of the ones who'd originally rescued me and Benny from SecureCorp.

"I don't think you've been formally introduced," Travis smiled. For a split second he was the friendly, easy-going schoolteacher I remembered. "This is Bailey," he said.

Bailey smiled and stuck out his hand. He looked in his thirties, stocky with curly brown hair. He had a nasty scar on the right side of his face. I didn't ask how it got there. I shook his hand and said hi.

"Bailey's going to look out for you during the run," Travis said. His smile disappeared and he glared at me. "Do whatever he says."

Bailey and Travis seemed pretty tight - on better terms than the others, anyway. Fifteen minutes later Rolf and the other scouts came back. They stared again at me, then Bailey, as they went off somewhere with Travis. Bailey and I were standing beside a low cement wall. He motioned for me to sit down on it, then sat himself.

"You're just here as an observer," he said. He pulled a small gun out of his belt. "Ever use one of these?"

I shook my head.

He smiled. "There's a first time for everything."

He gave me a short lesson on holding and firing it, then handed it to me. "Don't use it unless you have to."

I took the gun and stuffed it in my own belt.

"When the fighting starts," he said, "stay right behind me. Don't ever let us get separated by more than an arm's length. Don't listen to anybody else - nobody - just me. Got it?"

164

I nodded.

He leaned in and lowered his voice. "Travis didn't want me to tell you this, but I think you need to understand. There's sort of a price on your head."

After all that had happened, I shouldn't have been surprised. He looked up and scanned the group around us. I realized what he was saying. I'd been right - it wasn't just SecureCorp I had to worry about - anybody here might decide to make their fortune by giving me up.

Travis, Rolf, and the others returned from their meeting.

"It's a go," Travis said. I swallowed hard.

There were fifteen of us, including me. We were still in the Dregs, so cameras shouldn't be a problem, though we all monitored our HUDs just in case. After about ten minutes we reached the end of an alley that fed into a wide square.

Travis pointed to the right. "The outpost is just on the other side. The cameras start here, and they get pretty thick as we get closer, so be careful."

Bailey leaned down to me and whispered, "Stay exactly behind me."

I was annoyed. I was probably better at Cam-surfing than him, or any of them, but I kept my mouth shut.

Rolf took the lead, navigating slowly along one of the inside walls. I noticed that he not only avoided the cameras, but kept out of sight of any of the viewpoints around the square as well. I had to admit, he was good - but still not as good as me.

Rolf and another guy snuck away, while the bulk of us hid in a nearby alley. A few minutes later Travis got some kind of signal on his

HUD. He motioned for us to move forward. As Bailey had ordered, I hung right behind him. A few minutes later our objective was in sight, the side door of a solid-looking concrete building. It was open, and the bodies of two guards in SecureCorp uniforms lay just inside. We had to step over them to get past.

We crept through a network of hallways, looking for the armoury. There were doors at regular intervals along them. Bailey and I were at the rear. So far we hadn't seen another soul.

We entered a hallway that formed a 'T' intersection with another running at ninety degrees. The front of the group turned left down the new one, momentarily leaving Bailey and me alone. A guard emerged from a door right beside Bailey. He jumped at the sight of us, and went for his gun. Bailey was faster. He took out the guard, but the guy managed to get off a shot. Bailey collapsed to the floor, blood gushing from his left side.

The others rushed back to the junction, but a group of guards appeared, coming the opposite way. There was a firefight. That left me and Bailey stranded in the first hallway.

I knelt down to where he was crouched on the floor. "Can you walk?"

He managed to haul himself upright, but he could barely stand. I put an arm around his shoulder and helped him stagger back the way we'd come. We emerged from the building, and had just reached some cover when he finally collapsed, unconscious. I tried to drag him to a better spot, but he was too heavy.

I stood up, trying to decide whether to go back inside. The firefight was still going on. I could still go help the others. I was turning to leave when someone grabbed my shoulder from behind.

I jumped and turned. It was Rolf. His gun was drawn.

"He'll be okay," he said, nodding at Bailey. He eyed the gun in my belt. "You won't need the gun. Just come with me."

He had the same look I'd seen at the hideout.

"What about the others?" I asked him.

"They'll catch up in a few minutes."

I didn't move. There was still gunfire in the background. "It sounds like they're still fighting," I gestured with my head. "Shouldn't we help them? How did you get out here?"

"Travis said if Bailey got taken out, I should look after you," he said. He motioned with the gun down a nearby alley. "Follow me."

I stepped back. "You're full of it."

Rolf moved toward me, his gun pointing at my head. "There's no time to argue."

I turned to run. Rolf grabbed me by the arm.

"Let me go!" I yelled.

"You got any idea what your ransom would do for the revolution?" he said, finally showing his hand.

"Screw you!" I yelled, trying to pull away.

There was a blast from behind me, and a patch of red expanded on Rolf's chest. He let go of my arm and collapsed to the ground. I whipped around. Bailey was lying there with a smoking gun in his hand.

"Get away from here," he whispered.

167

"What about you?" I said. "I can't just leave you."

"I'm in no shape to go anywhere," he answered. "If the others get out they'll help me. Go - now!"

I wasn't going to leave him lying there. I got him to his feet and managed to walk him back to our original gathering point. I hoped the others would come back there.

I laid him down by the wall we'd sat on, and opened his shirt. There was a big gash in his side that was still oozing blood. I tore off part of my own shirt and wrapped it around him, hoping to stop the bleeding.

Then I ran back to the outpost to find the others. I peeked around the corner where we'd hidden before. Two SecureCorp guys were standing at the side entrance. One of them spotted me and pointed.

The closest one raised his weapon and fired at me. I took off.

TWENTY FOUR

....

AT THE AMP

It was too dangerous to go back to the Rebels. Rolf was dead, but there were others like him. Bailey was either dead or seriously injured, and I wasn't sure whether Travis would still be there to protect me.

The way I saw it, I had no choice but to meet with whoever had called me. It might be a trap, but I'd just have to take my chances. It took three hours, crossing into the Quarters, sneaking through back alleys and skulking along walls to avoid the cameras. I finally made it to the furniture factory - the place we in the Lost Souls called the AMP.

By now it was three in the afternoon; I had an hour to kill. I spent half of that time casing the place, suspecting some kind of trap, but there was nobody there. Like a lot of the buildings, the factory was basically gutted; it was nothing but a big open space, the floor a carpet of dust, glass, and wood chips. I climbed what was left of a broken staircase and found a hiding place with a view of the entire floor below.

I sat down and waited. I thought about Travis' story. He obviously believed Uncle Zack had betrayed him, but I didn't see why it couldn't have gone down the way Zack had said. Zack was my blood relative - or at least, he might be. I had to believe he was a good guy.

Just before four PM there was a scraping sound on the north side of the building. I had to shift to see what it was. Five men were sneaking along a clear space by the north-east wall, too far away to make out who they were. They were searching for something.

I leaned out from the corner I'd been hiding behind to get a better look. I finally saw them clearly and my heart almost stopped. SecureCorp. They were following a swarm of fucking drones.

Shit! I thought. *Travis was right!*

I scoured the building for a way out. I was so preoccupied that I didn't hear the footsteps behind me until it was too late. An arm wrapped around my chest with an iron grip, and a hand clamped over my mouth. I tried to scream but nothing came out.

"Shhh," a voice above me whispered.

I tried to turn to turn my head but I was held too tight.

"Shut up and hold still," the voice said.

My captor slowly shifted backwards, dragging me with him, so that we were deeper in the shadows. I could still just barely make out the line of soldiers, their guns drawn now, scanning around them. They passed by our position and continued to the south.

As soon as they were out of sight, the voice whispered again: "I'm here to help you. I'm going to take my hand off your mouth. Scream and I'll be gone and SecureCorp will get you."

I nodded.

The hand was removed, and the arm loosened. I turned. A man stood facing me, his features blotted in the shadow.

He leaned over and whispered in my ear: "Stay exactly behind me and don't make a sound."

We picked our way, crawling carefully along a solid section of the floor. Far in the distance now I could hear the voices of the searchers. I froze when a faint hum approached us from the north. My companion heard it too. We turned and looked. A dark cloud of drones was moving toward us, their edge-detected outlines crowding together like stitches in the shadows.

My companion pulled some kind of device out of his pocket and pressed a button. The cloud stopped instantly and dropped from the air, producing a barely audible rain of clicks on the floor below. The SecureCorp guys started shouting and running back and forth looking for us. They knew we were around, but without drones they had no idea where.

My companion motioned to me and we kept crawling. After a few minutes I saw an opening in the wall ahead. We made for it and the footsteps of our pursuers faded as we passed through and outside.

We climbed down a ladder-like tangle of broken framework outside the building. I thought I was the master at getting around SecureCorp's surveillance cameras and drones, but these guys were at a whole other level. A stealth-equipped car was waiting beside the building, and a cloaking device hid us while we rushed for it. Whoever they were, they must be loaded to be able to afford gear like this.

The rear door of the vehicle slid open. My companion pushed me inside and slid in after me. The door closed with a thunk. Inside it was black as a tomb.

"We're going to cover your eyes," my companion said. "It's just a precaution."

A black bag was pulled over my head. I struggled.

"Settle down," my companion said. "It's only until we get where we're going."

We were both hunkered down in the back seat. We drove, crawling forward, for almost an hour. Nobody said a word. The only sounds were my own laboured breath, the faint hum of the vehicle engine, and the crunch of the tires on road below.

From the twists and turns and the rough ride, I figured we ended up somewhere deep in the Dregs. We finally stopped. I heard a deep rumble ahead of us, and the vehicle drove ahead a few meters. The driver knocked twice on the dashboard.

My companion put his hand under my elbow, motioning for me to get up. I sat up, and the bag was removed from my head. I was finally able to get a good look at him. The light filtering back from the vehicle's dash was dim, but I'd seen his picture enough to know.

It was my Uncle Zack.

TWENTY FIVE

....

THE DEAD SHIFT

"This is it," Uncle Zack said.

I could see his face in the dim light. From pictures I would have sworn he was my uncle, but he didn't look over twenty-five. Was it possible that this was my dad's *older* brother?

"Pretty fancy tech," I said to him, nodding at the vehicle.

"Some of us have been around a long time," he answered. "We've been able to accumulate some resources."

The lights of the vehicle switched off and we were in total blackness. It wasn't natural. It should be twilight, not night. I could barely make out the shadowy shape of the driver up in the front. We must be somewhere indoors.

The driver opened his door, got out, and opened mine.

"You can come out," he said.

I climbed out, holding onto the door frame like a blind man, and stood by the car. Uncle Zack climbed out the other side, walked around the vehicle, and joined us. We felt our way to the right, using a wall to guide us. I was still almost blind. A door opened ahead and a dim light spilled out. I followed Uncle Zack and the driver inside.

There wasn't much more light in the space we were in now, but as soon as the door closed somebody switched one on. It was so bright I had to cover my eyes until they'd adjusted. When I opened them, we were standing in some kind of storage room, with boxes and miscellaneous junk piled around the walls. But the place was clean; it looked like they'd been set up here for a while. A table, surrounded by four folding chairs, stood in the middle.

There were three of us: me, Uncle Zack (I guess - it was still hard to believe), and the driver, a guy who looked a little older than me, with blond hair and a thin mustache.

Uncle Zack turned to me.

"Welcome," he smiled.

There he was: the curly dark hair, the penetrating black eyes under expressive brows. Somewhere in his expression I could see my dad - as he must have been… It was like traveling back in time, coming face-to-face with the grainy images from the family info card. Uncle Zack seemed to be enjoying my confusion.

"Have a seat," he said. He motioned toward one of the chairs.

I put my hand on the chair back. Maybe this was just part of some kind of twisted SecureCorp scheme to recapture me. I kept my eyes on both of them as I sat down. The driver took a seat to my left, Uncle Zack sat across from me.

"Well, Alex," Uncle Zack said. "It's great to finally meet you. You're the spitting image of your father. Do you recognize me?"

"I know who you look like," I said, "but it's impossible."

"You of all people should know it's not," he said, with a patronizing smile.

"Me - of all people?" I said. So far Uncle Zack was a bit too cute for my taste.

"Well," he said, leaning back, "if you're referring to me being dead, you've probably heard that in the eyes of the world you're dead too. If you're referring to the fact that I don't look much older than you... We'll get to that."

Uncle Zack nodded at the driver. "This is Connor," he said. Connor smiled and held out his hand, which I reached over and shook, still suspicious.

"What were those SecureCorp guys doing in the warehouse," I said. "It scared the shit out of me. I figured you'd screwed me over."

"Just bad luck," Uncle Zack said. "They periodically send teams through the old buildings, hunting for 'enemies of the state'. They've stepped up the searches big time in the past few weeks."

"How come?" I asked.

"Looking for you," he smiled again.

He asked me about my father. I told him about my mother, what my father's life had been like, and how he'd finally given it up for me.

Uncle Zack looked at the floor and shook his head. "We both got screwed, in our own way."

Only he's dead and you're still a twenty-year old, I thought.

"How much do you know about what's happening?" he asked.

I shrugged. "After my Appraisal they kidnapped me, kept me prisoner in some hospital, and did a bunch of tests. A guy died helping me escape. Now everybody in the world's after me. My dad just said I

175

should find you. He said something about some outfit called 'Vita Aeterna'."

Uncle Zack raised an eyebrow. He glanced over at Connor, like he was asking what he should do. Connor just shrugged. Uncle Zack described how he'd been held prisoner after his Appraisal and experimented on, like I was, for three months. When they drugged him for transport me to a different facility, he'd woken up prematurely, in the back of a moving ambulance.

"I just opened the doors, jumped out, and took off," he said. "I went on the run. I dropped by home first, just to say goodbye." He smiled. "Your dad wanted to come with me, but of course I refused. He was just a little kid, anyway.

"But why?" I asked. "What are they after?"

"There's a lot you don't know," Uncle Zack said, "but we've got time." He stood up and paced back and forth. "You gotta understand about these guys - the Elite. They're used to getting everything they want. They want your house? They've got it. They want your wife, your girlfriend, your dog? Presto. They want you dead, you're dead. They want your life ruined, it happens."

He turned, and stared down at me. "There's only one thing they can't control: Appraisal. Nobody, not even them, can change how it alters someone's lifespan. That drives them batty. They can't stand the arbitrariness, the democracy, of it. It flies in the face of their belief in their own superiority - their divine right to lay ownership to anything they want by virtue of their power and wealth.

"They're enraged that the treatment can double the lifespan of some pathetic street bum while shortening that of one of their number." He started pacing again. "Over the years, armies of scientists, with a massive war-chest of funding, have toiled away in pursuit of one goal: controlling life extension.

"Their masters wanted Appraisal to be governed in the same way as everything else in the world: the more money you have, the longer you get to live. They wanted to be able to buy immortality the same way they buy everything else.

"But even with the trillions of dollars and tens of thousands of man-hours poured into the project, the scientists weren't able to change the treatment one iota.

"The guys paying for it all started to think the scientists were deliberately stalling - that they wanted the process to fail because of some twisted resentment of their masters' wealth, or some socialist vision of a world that didn't play favourites.

"One of the problems was that a lot of the scientists, Corp workers, and even some of the Elite themselves, were burdened by the remnants of morality."

I thought about Travis - and what Dr. Treadwell has said about him.

"They refused to perform certain types of experiments," Zack continued, "experiments that inflicted what amounted to torture on human test subjects to get the answers they wanted."

Uncle Zack stopped again and turned to face me. "So a group of the richest and most powerful of the Elite took matters into their own hands." He stuck out his chin and raised his fist. "This was the giving of life itself. Cheating death, or at least delaying it for a while, was the dream of the ages. If a few insignificant lives needed to be ruined, or even snuffed out, in pursuit of that goal, then so be it."

He turned back to me. "The group formed a secret society called Vita Aeterna - Eternal Life. Its goal was to carry the research work a step further, unbridled by the sentimental morality of the 'public' work.

"Vita Aeterna aren't constrained by any ethical considerations. Their only interest is to control the Appraisal process - at any cost. They recruited a cadre of scientists willing to do their bidding without question. Their work focuses on subjects with exceptionally high Appraisals. Such people don't show up very often. When they do, the organization is informed. They kidnap the high scorers and conduct experiments on them. They believe they can discover the secret of long life by studying people who have it.

"Over the years, some of those test subjects managed to escape, like we all did." He gestured with his head around the table. "We found each other and formed an underground resistance movement. We're all supposed to be dead, so we call ourselves the Dead Shift."

"So how do I fit in?" I asked, a feeling of dread creeping over me.

Uncle Zack sat back down and leaned toward me. "Do you know what *your* Appraisal is?"

I shook my head. "That's how this all started. Nobody would tell me, and then they're all after me."

"*I* know what it is," he said.

I tensed. The way everybody seemed to be acting about it, I wasn't sure I wanted to know. He sat staring at me. His expression reminded me of the one I saw on Chuck and the first doctor.

"Well?" I said.

He snapped up his right hand, with all the fingers spread apart. Again I was confused.

"What?" I said. I stared at his hand. Finally it hit me. "Five?"

He nodded.

"Five?" I said. "Bullshit."

He shook his head. "What it is, is the highest Appraisal anybody's ever scored. And it's yours."

It hit me like a sledgehammer. I was too stunned to say anything.

"Do the math," Uncle Zack said. "With an Appraisal of five, every fifty years you'll have aged ten. Fifty years from now your effective age will be twenty-six. In a hundred, it'll be thirty-six."

I was in shock. I was hardly conscious of what he was saying.

"In fact," he continued, "you put us all to shame. Connor, here," he nodded at the driver, "has an Appraisal of two point three. Mine's two point five. Still, if we ever have children, and those children have Appraisals as high as ours, they'll grow up, live their lives, and die of old age, and you'll still be going."

A jolt went up my spine. Everybody - everybody I ever knew, everybody I met for the next hundred years, would be dead long before I'd even reached middle age...

"You're messing with me," I said. "It's not funny."

He shook his head. I looked over at Connor. He wasn't laughing.

I felt like I was going to be sick. My eyes were wet with tears. Suddenly I was sobbing. What was I going to do? I put my hands in front of my face.

Uncle Zack put a hand on my shoulder.

"What kind of fucked-up lonely-ass existence am I in for?" I said through my tears.

For the first time since it all started I truly wished I'd never heard of Appraisal, and that had nothing to do with being imprisoned or experimented on, or having those bastards chasing me all over the city.

"Don't worry, Alex," he said. "We'll look after you. We'll make it right."

"Nobody can make it right," I sobbed. "I'm screwed, and there's nothing you or anybody else can do about it."

Uncle Zack patted my shoulder.

"We'll leave you alone for a while to think about it," he said. He and Connor left the room, left me sitting there, staring into an empty future with nobody beside me. Appraisal had reprogrammed me to live for four hundred years, but right now all I wanted was to die.

TWENTY SIX

....

UNCLE ZACK

I lost track of the time, so I'm not sure how long they were gone. Finally, Uncle Zack came through the door alone and sat down again across from me. I didn't really feel any better, but I'd come to a conclusion: this was the hand I'd been dealt. All I could do was accept it and go on. Anyway, I still had the immediate problem of a crack army of highly-trained soldiers trying to hunt me down. I'd have to think about the rest of my life later.

"By the way," he said, smiling, "under the circumstances you can dispense with the 'Uncle' bit. Just call me Zack." He leaned forward. "Now, let's get down to business. Statistically speaking, you're the holy grail. You could outlive everyone on the planet, even babies that won't be born for generations. They want you bad."

"So I'm screwed?" I asked. "I just keep on running until they catch up with me and rip me apart like a lab animal?"

"No," Zack said. "We fight back. That's the purpose of our little group here. The only chance we have of surviving and returning to

181

society is to get rid of Vita Aeterna. As long as they're around we'll be living in fear and on the run. We want to destroy them, and make sure that they never come back."

"But what hope have we got of doing that?" I asked. The whole thing sounded pretty hopeless.

"It's a long shot," Zack said. "Our best chance is to eliminate the guy who's the big mover behind all this.

"And who's that?"

He turned and stared at a poster on the wall, the same one Benny had stuck up as a shrine in his office, the one he'd kept so pristine and new.

It was like Zack had shot me with a poison dart. "Charles Wickham?" I said. "The head of the CCE?"

Zack nodded.

I swallowed, thinking back on what Travis had said about them. "Then we *are* screwed. Us against him, the CCE, and all of SecureCorp?"

Zack shook his head. "We know we can't hope to win against SecureCorp. That's the difference between us and that ridiculous Rebel group you were hanging out with."

I looked up at him, shocked.

"Why so surprised?" he said. "We know all about what goes on around here. How do you think we knew about the phone?" He nodded at the bulge in my shirt.

"How *did* you know?"

"We ran into your friend Fatso." He smiled.

My spine stiffened. "He's no friend of mine."

182

"Then you'll be pleased to know that you won't have to worry about him anymore," Zack said without emotion. "We know where you've been. We don't know exactly where the Rebels are at any given moment, but we've got a good idea what they're doing. They've got this fantasy that they can wake the general public and engineer some kind of popular uprising. We know that's not going to happen."

"Why not?"

Zack sneered and shot me a look. He was my uncle, but I wasn't so sure I really liked him.

"The public are sheep," he said. "The thought has never even crossed their minds that anything can be changed, or even *should* be changed. They've bought into the idea that if they work like dogs and are willing to screw their neighbour, someday they'll be up there with the Elite."

He shook his head contemptuously.

I felt my cheeks flush. Up until a few days ago I'd been one of those people. I still wasn't sure I believed him.

"But if they knew the truth..." I said.

Zack scowled at me. "And how's that going to happen, nephew? Are *you* going to tell them?"

I glanced at my hands, then looked back up at him. "Well, if you can't change the public's mind, what *do* you plan to do?"

He shrugged. "There's only one option. It might not change anything, but at least it's got some slim chance of succeeding."

"What's that?"

His eyes locked on mine, and a thin smile curled up on his lip. "We're going to kill Charles Wickham."

☼

We sat there staring at each other for almost a minute. I swallowed. If that was our best chance...

Zack finally spoke. "If we can get to Wickham, the organization will be crippled, maybe beyond repair. If we can couple that with getting out the word about them, in a way that they can't discredit, we might have a chance. InfoCorp controls the media, so if they say we're dead, there's not much we can do about it. We have to find a way to change that."

I still didn't say anything. I felt like I was already dead - I just hadn't fallen down yet.

"You could be a real asset," Zack continued.

"Me?" I said, snapping out of it. "What have I got to do with it?"

"Vita Aeterna wouldn't have a problem killing most of us - there's more where we came from. We're already on record as being dead, so if we make too much trouble for them, all they've got to do is get rid of us for real.

"You, on the other hand, are an anomaly - one of a kind. They'll want you kept alive so they can study you. We might be able to use that to our advantage. While they're tripping over themselves trying to get you, maybe they'll make a mistake."

I still wasn't convinced. And something about my uncle didn't seem right.

"You can bet your buddy Travis knows all about your Appraisal," Zack said out of the blue.

"No way," I said. "If he knew, why wouldn't he tell me?"

184

"He's afraid of us," Zack answered. "He told you some bullshit story about me, didn't he. About how I betrayed them - about how you shouldn't trust me?"

I stared at my hands on the table.

"He's not your friend," Zack continued, "no matter what you think. He's out to get us - all of us."

"But you and them have almost the same agenda," I said, looking up.

He laughed. "Only *our* plan actually has a chance of succeeding." He stared at the wall behind me, like he was mulling something over.

The door opened. I turned to see Connor poke his head in. He nodded at Zack, who pushed himself up and headed toward him.

"I've got some business to take care of," Zack said, reaching the door, opening it and stepping out. "Connor will look after you, and set you up with a place to sleep."

Connor came over and sat across from me. So far the only people I'd seen were him and Zack. The thought occurred to me that maybe there was actually only the two of them.

"How many people are there in the Dead Shift?" I asked.

"Right now?" he answered. He looked a little embarrassed. "Only twelve. Remember, it's made up of people who've escaped from SecureCorp. You know from experience how hard that is."

"I'm surprised there's that many," I said.

"Escapes only happen every few years," he said, "but we've been around for decades."

"So where are the others?"

He smiled. "You'll meet them soon enough. We have to be pretty careful about these things."

Connor talked for a while about how he got to be part of the Dead Shift. His story sounded a lot like mine. I guess all of them probably went through something similar. I got a positive vibe from him - a better one than I got from my own uncle. He helped me program a contact for the Dead Shift into the crypted phone, in case I was ever in trouble or got lost.

Finally, he rose from his chair. "You must be tired."

I followed him out of room, into the area we'd felt our way through when I first arrived. Now, the lights were on. I'd been right earlier; we'd actually driven inside a building. I was facing a wide-open space that looked like it was probably once a warehouse. Unlike most of the places I'd been lately, there was no garbage or debris lying around. The floor was spotless and all the lights worked - they must have been here for a while.

The stealth vehicle I'd ridden in was parked in one corner, just inside a sliding steel garage door. There was also a couple of motorcycles, and a large cabinet with shelves full of equipment. These guys were way more organized than the Rebels.

"Not all our setups are this sophisticated," Connor smiled, noticing me staring. "This is a special one. That's why you were kept in the dark on the way here. No one can know about this place."

There were doors around the perimeter. Connor led me to one of them in a distant corner. Behind it was a small room with a bed, a chair, and even a tiny desk, a step up from sleeping in the dorm-like arrangement at the Rebel hideout.

"Get some rest," Connor said, standing by the open door. "You're safe here. Somebody will contact you in a few hours."

Connor took off and I lay down on the bed. At first I couldn't sleep. So much had happened so fast. It was like some kind of accelerated nightmare. I thought back on my Appraisal. I'd been looking forward to it since I was old enough to know what it was. Everybody did. You basically put your life on hold until you got it, because everything you did after that would depend on how long you were going to live. I had all these dreams of somehow snagging a Corp job, having a career, getting past Cindy's dad and marrying her, having a family. If I had a good Appraisal I'd have lots of time to make enough money to enjoy my life...

I had to laugh. Now, in some twisted, cruel version of my dreams, I had the ultimate Appraisal. And here I was, running for my life. Cindy was dead, I might have killed her father, I'd broken out of a SecureCorp prison, and the whole world was after me. Two people, one of them my own father, had died trying to help me. I was destined to spend my life alone, outliving everybody on the planet. And I didn't know what to do. I couldn't dodge the cameras forever. Eventually I'd make a mistake and they'd catch up with me.

Finally, exhausted, I fell asleep. I woke to a knock at the door. I got up and opened it.

It was Zack.

He walked in and sat on the end of the bed.

"I've been thinking about what you said earlier," he said. "You know, about us and the Rebels being after the same thing. You might have a point there." He smiled. "What if I was to set up a meeting with

Travis? Maybe if the Rebels and the Dead Shift were to join forces we could actually accomplish something."

I was confused. Zack would reconsider working with the Rebels just because I suggested it? It didn't make sense.

"Travis would never go for that," I said. "Anyway, why now? You've had years to get together with them."

He put a hand on my shoulder. "You've added a whole new dimension to the equation. You've got a relationship with Travis *and* me. You can act as sort a liaison, the 'glue' that holds us together."

His eyes went wide, as if he'd had an idea. "You came here from the Rebel stronghold, right? You could take me to see them."

The hair rose at the back of my neck. I didn't like where the conversation was headed. Travis wouldn't want me leading anybody, even an ally, to their location. As far as that went, they'd probably moved by now. And Travis had made it clear how he felt about Zack.

"No way," I said.

"I don't suppose I blame you for not trusting me," Zack said. "It'll take longer, but we have ways of contacting them. If I set up a meeting with Travis, will you come?"

I studied him. He was my flesh and blood - my father's brother. I hadn't heard much about him growing up, but what I had heard had always been positive. His request made sense.

"I guess," I said.

The barest hint of a smile formed on Zack's lips. He got up and stood with his back to me for a few seconds.

Finally he turned again to face me. "We'll talk about it again soon. Meanwhile, let's keep this between us. Don't tell Connor or any of the others about it."

"Why not?"

"Some of them don't trust the Rebels. They don't want to have anything to do with them. If they found out we were trying to contact them, it might be a problem."

It sounded logical, especially after the way Travis had talked about Zack and the Dead Shift.

So why did my gut seem to have a problem with it?

TWENTY SEVEN

....

BETRAYAL

After a couple of days, Connor took me in the stealth vehicle to another hideout. He never said why. Like the Rebels, the Dead Shift seemed to have an endless supply of them. Once again, I had to wear the bag over my head. His claim that the first one was special appeared to be true. This new one looked more like the Rebel hideouts I was used to.

It took a few days for Zack to make contact with the Rebels. I think he was pissed with me, knowing that I could tell him where they were, but wouldn't. I didn't care. If he wanted to contact them he'd have to find them himself.

In the meantime, I was relieved when I finally met a couple of other Dead Shift people. A guy named Rick, and a woman named Monica. I talked to them both and they seemed great - we had a lot in common. I felt a little better about being there. I followed Zack's instructions and didn't tell any of them about the planned meeting with Travis, even though I wasn't sure I bought Zack's explanation of why that was necessary.

One morning Zack came and told me he'd contacted the Rebels, and set up a meeting for the afternoon of the next day.

I slept badly that night. I had doubts about Travis and the other Rebels, especially after what Rolf had done, and what Zack had said about them. But at least I knew Travis. I'd spent enough time with him to be convinced he was a good guy. But I believed what Zack said - that Travis knew my Appraisal. If he could lie about that, he could be lying about other things as well.

Zack *was* my uncle, I had no doubt. But I'd just met him. Our family had never been that close, but I'd always been raised to believe that family ties were important.

A gut instinct told me something was wrong. I was surprised that Travis had agreed to the meeting. He'd seemed pretty down on Zack when I talked to him. One thing was crystal clear: either Zack or Travis was lying to me. The question was - which one? Or was it both? And if they were lying, what did it mean?

The next day, early in the afternoon, Zack came and told me it was time. We snuck out of the Dead Shift hideout, and walked for an hour to what I assumed was the meeting place, a small square in the middle of nowhere. We waited about twenty minutes, hiding in an alcove of an abandoned building.

Finally, we heard movement. Zack gestured for me to be quiet, and peeked around the corner. A few seconds later, he turned back to me, smiling.

"It's Travis," he whispered. "Stay where you are."

I didn't understand what he was up to, but I went along.

He stepped out from the corner with his hands up. But when his jacket shifted I saw that he had a gun stuffed in the back of his pants.

"You were supposed to be alone," I heard Zack's voice say.

"You can understand why I still don't completely trust you," Travis' voice answered. "Bailey's only here for insurance. If you're being straight with me, you've got nothing to worry about."

I felt relieved at hearing Travis' voice, and I was surprised and pleased to hear that Bailey had made it back and was okay. Maybe this get together could actually come off.

"Where's Alex?" Travis asked.

"He's right here," Zack answered.

He turned his head and motioned to me, and I came out to join him. Travis was standing about ten meters away. Bailey was standing to his left. He had a bandage around his stomach, but otherwise he looked okay.

I thought they'd be glad to see me, but as soon as I showed myself they tensed up and raised their rifles.

"I thought you said he was injured," Travis said.

Before I knew what was happening, Zack had wrapped an arm around my neck and held me like a shield in front of him. He pulled out the gun and held it against my head. I couldn't believe what was happening.

"A little white lie," Zack said. "Otherwise you wouldn't have come."

I struggled against Zack, but he was a lot bigger and stronger. I couldn't breathe.

"If you want the kid to live," Zack said, pressing the barrel of his gun against my temple, "You better come with me. I have some friends who want to talk to you."

"Friends in SecureCorp?" Travis said. "You know I can't do that."

Zack working with SecureCorp? I thought. *How was that possible?*

"You think I'm bluffing?" Zack yelled, and cocked the trigger, ready to fire.

Travis shook his head. "The movement is more important than any one person's life - even his. I'm sorry, Alex." He stood with his rifle trained on us, his expression a blend of horror and determination.

"That's what I thought you'd say," Zack said.

I felt the gun barrel move away from my head. Before the others could react, Zack turned the gun and shot Travis in the chest.

"No!" I screamed.

Bailey hesitated. I guess he was worried about hitting me. Zack fired another shot and Bailey went down. Zack grabbed me by the arm and started dragging me off.

I glanced back. Travis and Bailey were lying on the pavement. Two other Rebels came running from the shadows. One knelt over their bodies. The other ran after us, firing now, not even caring whether he hit me. Zack dragged me behind the corner of a building. He locked my head in the crook of his left arm while he fired at our pursuer with his right. After a few minutes I heard a grunt and the Rebel's firing stopped.

Zack let go of my neck and jammed his gun between my shoulder blades.

"Move it!" he said.

193

Vita Aeterna

We ran through a network of alleyways. There was no sign of the Rebels. Zack didn't say a word. Tears welled in my eyes. What the hell was going on? Was Travis dead? What had I done? Twenty minutes later we stopped at a door in one of the buildings. Something smashed against my skull and everything went black.

TWENTY EIGHT

....

THE HAND OFF

When I woke up, I was in a room I'd never seen before, sitting in a chair with my hands tied behind me and my feet bound. It felt like a pile driver was slamming against the inside of my skull. It took a few seconds for my eyes to focus. When they finally did, Zack was standing in front of me.

"You fucking bastard!" I screamed. The sound and exertion made my head explode. I closed my eyes and clenched my fists against the pain. I thought again of Travis and what I'd done, and felt tears running down my cheeks. "Do you know what you've done?"

"Sorry, nephew," he grinned, in a way that made me want to smash his face in.

"Why?" I said, still choked with tears.

"The deal was you and Travis," he said. "They would have preferred him alive, but they'd accept him dead, and that was easier anyway. I don't think they really care that much about the Rebels. You're my ace in the hole. I want to keep *you* to myself until I'm sure they're going to fulfill their end of the bargain."

"Who's they?"

"Guess."

"So Travis was right about you," I said. "You led SecureCorp to the Rebel hideout."

"That was a dry run," he said. "To convince them I was serious. Turned out the Rebels weren't important enough for them to give me what I wanted. Then you came along, like a gift from heaven. I decided a long time ago that I was going to get out of this. I'm going to need a lot of money to live on once that happens. After all," he smiled, "I'm planning to live another hundred and fifty years."

"You've made some kind of deal with the Vita Aeterna?"

"I'd been thinking about it since we first hooked up," Zack said, "but couldn't decide whether to go through with it."

He paced along the wall beside me.

"But now you've accepted that you're a complete asshole," I said, "so you're okay with it."

He stopped and sneered down at me. "You're still a stupid kid. You haven't got a clue." He smashed his fist against the wall. "Don't you get it? We're going to lose. Look what we're up against."

"So you're just going to give me up? Your own flesh and blood?"

"You know how old I am?" he asked.

I twisted at the ropes binding my hands. "My only interest in your age is that you don't get the chance to get any older."

"I'm fifty-six," he said. "You hate what you've been going through for the past couple of months? Well I've been dealing with it since I was your age, forty years ago."

I shuddered, considering what might be in store for me. It was hard to imagine. I'd barely been able to cope for the few weeks I'd been on the run. Forty years? Fifty? One Hundred? But nothing excused what Zack was doing.

I struggled, trying to free my hands. "I'm your brother's only son," I said, my voice breaking. "I'm the only family you've got in the world."

He shrugged. "I'll get over it. You'll be better off anyway. You said so yourself. What kind of life would you have - outliving everybody you ever knew or loved."

"I won't miss *you*."

He snorted and turned away. He started pacing again.

"Years ago," he said, "many years ago now, there was enough of everything to go around. Even back then the majority of the population were poor. The wealth wasn't distributed equally, but in theory it could have been.

"That option ended forty years ago, about the time I went on the run. Now, there's resources for about one percent of Humanity to live in luxury. The rest are screwed. In order for somebody to join that one percent, somebody already in it has to leave voluntarily."

Zack stopped pacing and stared down at me. "What do you think the chances are of that happening?"

Again I thought of Travis, whose death I probably caused. Again tears welled in my eyes.

Zack continued. "Since then, the Elite and the Corps have taken every opportunity to eliminate people they don't think are of any use to society - which basically means the rest of us."

I stared up at him.

"Why do you think there's so many abandoned buildings?" he sneered. "Didn't you wonder where everybody went?" He shook his head. "Natural death from squalid living conditions and lack of heath care, elimination of anyone they've determined won't be missed, and regular sweeps of death-squads through the Dregs have helped. But the process has been too slow for their taste. I have it on good authority that there's an 'ultimate solution' in the works - a plan to 'cull' huge numbers of the population."

I swallowed hard.

"Robots do almost all the factory work," he continued. "The ruling class need a certain number of human drones around to do what's left - and a minimum gene pool as test subjects until they learn to control the Appraisal. The rest are a liability. Every body removed means one less HUD to be installed, and one less potential threat to deal with. The only question is how? How to do it without causing a revolution. Maybe a plague - but then there's a chance everybody, even the Elite, could get it."

"They're monsters," I said.

Zack shrugged. "They'll come up with something, don't worry. Probably some kind of poison. It'll look natural. They'll spin something out on people's HUDs - nobody will question it."

He moved in front of me and stopped. "They said if I got rid of Travis and delivered you, they'd move me out of the danger zone and leave me in peace. I've got a chance to finally have a life. I'm gonna take it. Can you blame me?"

I glared up at him. "And what kind of life is that gonna be - Uncle?"

"Shut the fuck up!" he screamed. He backhanded my face.

"We're not gonna lose," I said, breathing hard, my right cheek burning with pain.

"What makes you so sure?" he laughed.

"'Cause if we lost I wouldn't want to live anymore, and I'm planning to be around for another three hundred and eighty-four years."

Zack grabbed a roll of tape from the bench and tore off a piece. I moved my head back and forth trying to stop him, but he finally managed to stretch it across my mouth. I closed my eyes. It was over.

The worst part was what Laura would think of me after what happened. It was like I'd been standing on a platform and the pillars supporting it were kicked out from under me. Maybe the Dead Shift were some kind of bullshit con set up by SecureCorp to reel me in. And I'd walked right into it. It was like a black well opening up beneath my feet.

Zack left the room and I passed out. When I woke I couldn't check with my hands tied, but I figured I'd been out for half an hour. Zack was talking to someone over my crypted phone in the other corner of the room. I couldn't hear what they were saying. I tugged again at the ropes, but they weren't going anywhere.

Zack stopped talking and headed for the door. He didn't look at me. For that much I couldn't blame him.

✿

A half hour later Zack came back. He avoided making eye contact. Big surprise. He untied my feet, hauled me up and dragged me out the door and down an alley. I had trouble breathing with the exertion and the tape across my mouth. He finally removed it.

"Are the rest of the Dead Shift in on this?" I asked him as we moved.

"Shut up," he said.

We stopped in an open space at the convergence of several alleys. He shoved me through the open door of an abandoned building and prodded me up a narrow flight of stairs. We entered what looked like it was once a hotel room, with a commanding view of the space below.

He pointed to a single chair in the middle of the room. "Sit," he said. "And don't try anything." He patted the gun in his belt.

"What, you're gonna shoot your precious bargaining chip?" I said.

"Shut up, or I'll tape your mouth again."

Ten minutes later Zack talked again to somebody on the crypted phone. He crouched down and peered over the window sill, waiting. In a few minutes I heard movement in the street below. A voice called something. I couldn't make out what it was. Zack spent a few minutes scanning the area, checking for a trap, I guess.

Finally satisfied, he grabbed me by the collar and dragged me back down the stairs to the door.

He let go and leaned in toward me, whispering, "If you know what's good for you you'll keep your mouth shut until I come and get you."

As bad as things were, I figured I was still better off with Zack than whoever he was trying to sell me to. I stayed where I was.

I guess Zack still wasn't convinced we were safe; he peeked around the corner of the wall for another few minutes before he finally stepped out.

"You said you'd come alone," he said to somebody.

"We call the shots here," a voice said. It sounded familiar.

"Let's see the money," Zack said, "and the letter."

"First, the boy," the other voice answered.

There was a pause. Zack came back, grabbed me, and hauled me out from behind the corner. A few meters away stood Weber, the SecureCorp guy who'd wasted the gangster leader, Cash. Beside him were a couple of his goons.

Zack held a gun to my head. "You better not be trying to screw me," he said to Weber.

Weber's mouth turned up in sort a sneering smile. "We'll take care of you, don't worry."

Weber reached into his jacket. The hand holding the gun against my head was shaking.

Weber pulled out a paper folder. "Come and get it," he said to Zack.

"Show me," Zack said.

Weber held the folder open to display a fist-thick bundle of bills, a fancy-looking MoneyAll card, an ID card, and some papers with an official-looking seal at the top.

"Throw it down here," Zack nodded at the pavement in front of us.

Weber shrugged. He raised his hand to toss the package, but instead of throwing it at the ground, he threw it at Zack's head. Zack flinched for a second, lifted the gun from my head, and stepped back.

A rifle cracked. He grunted and staggered sideways. He was hit. A second shot missed its mark. Zack dragged me back behind the corner as another shot blasted a chip out of the wall beside us.

"Get them," shouted Weber.

We ran back the way we'd first come. There was the sound of pounding feet behind us. We headed down an alley, seconds ahead of the pursuers. Zack pushed on what looked like a solid section of wall and it swung open. A hidden door. Now I saw why he'd picked this building. He shoved me through, stumbled in after me and closed it behind him. Seconds later the footsteps ran by without stopping.

He turned to me. There was a patch of red spreading across his gut. He put one hand over it and shoved me forward with the other. The pounding feet and shouting voices faded into the distance. We traveled down a long hallway, made a few turns, and finally reached a door. Zack held a finger to his lips, and pushed it open a crack. It led to the outside.

"The bastards!" he said half under his breath. "It was all a setup."

"Big surprise," I laughed. He delivered a weak punch to my gut and grimaced. I think it hurt him more than me.

He pushed me out the door and we stumbled down yet another alley. "I know a place," he said. "It's not far."

TWENTY NINE

....

A MISSION

We walked for another five or six blocks. Minute by minute Zack was getting weaker. He was losing a lot of blood.

"You better do something about that," I said.

"Shut up," he said, and drove me forward.

I guessed that he was headed for another Dead Shift hideout. He probably would have arranged to make the hand-off somewhere close to one. But if it was more than a few blocks away, he wasn't going to make it.

We emerged from an alley into a huge wide-open space with a gigantic warehouse-looking building in the middle of it. He hesitated for a few seconds. I think he wanted to run straight across. It would be safer, but slower, to stay close to the edges.

Finally he rushed into the open, dragging me toward the warehouse. We were about ten meters away when there was a gunshot behind us. On the far side of the square, a half dozen SecureCorp soldiers were charging across the broken pavement toward us. The guys we'd escaped from had found us again.

"Shit," Zack said, under his breath.

There was no time to run anywhere. He shoved me toward the front door. It was intact but the lock was broken.

We rushed inside and Zack slammed the door shut.

"Get over there," he said, motioning toward a broken pile of crates. The place must once have been a storehouse for toys. Arms, legs, and torsos of broken dolls, along with toy cars and trucks, and gaming pieces, littered the floor.

Zack staggered toward a couple of intact crates and pushed, trying to slide them against the outside doors. He was weak, he was still bleeding, and he still had the gun in one hand. It was pathetic.

"Untie my hands," I called to him, "and I'll help you."

He stopped and stared at me for a second.

"I don't want them to get to us any more than you do," I said.

The shouts from our pursuers were getting closer. He came over and untied me. Together we slid the crates forward to barricade the entrance.

We stumbled across a debris-strewn floor to an inner section with another door, which we quickly barricaded as well. Zack scanned around, hunting for another exit. The entire southeast corner of the building, where there might have been another door, was piled several meters high with garbage and debris. There was no way we'd dig through it all before our pursuers caught up.

We made our way to a storeroom at the back of the building. I'm not sure why. It was only a matter of time until they broke in and got to us. We had nowhere to go.

We sat barricaded in the storeroom. The explosive thuds of the soldiers hammering on the outside doors echoed through the building. There was an even louder crash as they must have broken through.

Zack's wound was bothering him. Blood was still seeping into his shirt and dripping onto the floor. He nodded off for a second, then jerked himself awake. He noticed me glancing at the gun in his belt and smiled as he rested his hand on it.

"What did you think was gonna happen?" I asked him. "You say you're so old and experienced. Didn't you figure they'd double-cross you?"

He stared at me. "Yeah, sure. Sure I figured that. What you don't get is that I had no choice. There's nothing left for me."

He grimaced, closed his eyes and grabbed his side. The SecureCorp guys were battering on the second door. I had to do something. I jumped up and rushed at him, to grab his gun. He heard me, opened his eyes, and jumped to his feet. He was a foot taller than me. He caught me with a kick in the stomach that knocked the breath out of me. I fell to the floor, gasping.

"You poor little shit," he said. He pulled the gun from his belt and pointed it at my head. "You've been nothing but a pain in the ass. And now you're worth nothing to me."

He cocked the mechanism. I lay there helpless, frozen in terror.

He hesitated, his face contorted in pain. He closed his eyes. He opened them again and smiled. "But then, after all, you *are* my nephew." He turned the gun, drew his arm back, and pressed the barrel against his own temple.

"No!" I screamed.

"Bye now," he said, as he pulled the trigger.

I sat for a few seconds, stunned. Finally I snapped out of it and twisted the gun from his dead hand. His body was blocking the door. I dragged it away, and rushed out to check on the inner door. A crack in it was expanding as the SecureCorp guys pounded on it. They'd be through it in minutes. I thought about the crypted phone. I rushed back and grabbed it out of Zack's pocket. Zack had accepted that the situation was hopeless, but I wasn't going to give up without a fight. I had another quick look around. There was only one door, and the goons were about to bash their way through it.

Right beside it was a large crate, about a meter square and about two meters high. I rushed back to the storeroom and wedged Zack's body into a sitting position in the doorway, with his shoulder and left arm visible, and his head wound turned away. Returning to the door they were pounding on, I slid a smaller crate up beside the large one, climbed up, and lay in the shadows with my gun drawn.

A few seconds later the door burst open and the SecureCorp goons crowded in. They scanned around quickly but didn't notice me. One of them pointed to Zack's torso. The main body of the group edged toward it, while a few others fanned out to check the rest of the warehouse. My plan was desperate, but it was all I had. I crept out to the edge of the crate and looked down. I could just make out the toes of a pair of boots outside the door. They'd posted at least one guard.

The main group all had their backs to me and by now were at least twenty meters away. I climbed back down to the floor, hid behind the smaller crate, and peeked around. They were occupied with Zack's body and the debris at the back, and still hadn't noticed me. They were about to reach the storeroom door.

It was time to go. I formed a mental image of where the outside guard was standing, then tore around the crate and through the open door, gun firing. I hit the surprised guard and he collapsed.

I took off across the warehouse floor, heading for the main doors. Shouts and pounding feet echoed from inside and the soldiers soon emerged. I reached the outer door and ran for my life across the square. In seconds the others were outside and running after me. At the edge of the square, I tore down the nearest alley, and flew around a corner into a cross alley.

The SecureCorp guys were right behind me, but right now they weren't in sight. I hunted desperately for some kind of opening to crawl into, but there was nothing. I glanced back. A couple of soldiers rounded the corner. They were gaining on me. I hit another cross alley and raced down it. I wasn't going to last long like this. I needed a hiding place, or a way to open some distance between me and them.

I scanned the surrounding walls as I ran, crazy with fear. Down another alley I saw a patch of blood - this was the way we'd come. I retraced our route back, and breathed a huge sigh when I finally saw it - the wall with the secret door Zack had used to escape from the others.

I wished I'd paid more attention to how he'd actually opened it - my heart thumped in my ears as I groped frantically for the release mechanism. Nothing. Frustrated, I punched a spot near my head, and the door popped open. I rushed inside, jammed it shut, and lay against it shaking as my pursuers pounded by seconds later, yelling at each other.

I waited for a long time after their shouts and footsteps had faded away. Finally, stressed out and exhausted, I fell asleep. When I woke up, my HUD said I'd been out for about an hour. I listened at the door for ten minutes, but couldn't hear a sound. I opened it a crack. Nothing.

I took off and ran deeper into the Dregs. The level of decay and destruction, which had been bad enough before, got even worse. The ground was littered with debris and garbage. Some of the buildings had even collapsed, and were now giant piles of rubble that completely blocked the street. I just ran - away from the death, the terror, the betrayal, away from everything life had dealt me since I was born. I ran until I couldn't run anymore. I found an alcove hidden in the shadows, and sat gasping with my head in my hands.

Everybody I really cared about was dead. Two of them died trying to save me. Lifelong attachments were over for me - for the rest of my incredibly long existence, stretching into the hundreds of years, I'd be alone. SecureCorp, and a remorseless secret society with bank loads of money, led by the most powerful man in the world, were turning the city upside down to find me.

The Rebels, the one group that could have provided me some kind of safety, now probably hated me and thought I was a traitor. The

Dead Shift, or at least my Uncle Zack, my only remaining relative, had betrayed me, and now Zack was dead.

Zack's gun was still stuffed in my belt. I hauled it out and I stared at it. It was still slimy with Zack's blood. For a moment I considered following his example. At that moment, the phone in my pocket vibrated. I dreaded looking at it, but finally broke down and took it out. I had a message.

It was Connor. *Where are you guys?* it said. *We haven't been able to contact Zack for four hours.*

I sat for a few seconds staring at the phone. I didn't believe him. As far as I was concerned, the Dead Shift had screwed me once already - why not again?

I texted Connor: *Zack's dead, and good riddance. He murdered Travis. Fuck you guys.*

After a few seconds of hesitation, Connor texted back: *We knew nothing about it. Come and meet us.*

He described how to get to a meeting place in an area I was familiar with. I ignored it, turned the phone off, stuffed it in my pocket, and leaned back against the wall with my eyes closed. Now that everything was quiet I realized that the cards, which I had in my other pocket, seemed to be getting warm.

I pulled out the bag holding them. The two morphing ones had completed the process. The result was a single card, deep violet in colour, and still with the stylized letters VA in one corner. It now had a single red flashing number - thirty thousand - near the top, and a map, with some kind of route overlaid in green. Beside it were the words: 'Aug. 3rd, 1900 hrs'.

I'd seen that kind of thing before. It was a beacon. It indicated a location, probably for some kind of meeting. A glow that intensified as it approached the outer edge of the card indicated the direction. The number was the approximate number of meters to the target destination: thirty thousand - thirty kilometers. As you got closer, the number would decrease, sort of like the card saying: 'you're getting warmer' as you moved around.

When it hit zero, you'd arrived. But where was it directing me to? Wherever it was, I didn't see how it could be good. The beacon wouldn't work inside the bag, because it couldn't communicate through the conductive mesh. The number and direction must be measured from where I first got the cards, before I put them in the bag.

Again I studied Zack's gun. Before the raid with the Rebels, I'd never even held one in my hands let alone fired it at anybody. I fought to keep from puking as I wiped the worst of the blood off, held the gun up, sighted down the barrel, and shuddered. I shoved it in my belt.

The card was still warm. It was still working on something. Part of me wanted to toss it in the gutter and run as far away as possible. But based on the logo and where I'd gotten the original ones, the meeting was probably linked to Vita Aeterna. If that was true, I'd be needing the card.

Especially now.

I'd come to a decision. Zack had turned out to be a traitor, but he was right about the Rebels. They didn't stand a chance against the CCE. Vita Aeterna would never give up - they'd chase me to the ends of the earth. As long as they were around, I'd be running like a hunted animal for the rest of my long life, or until I got fed up like Zack and took the final way out.

There was only one solution. It crystallized in my mind as I turned the glowing violet card over in my hands. I was going to carry out the mission Zack had talked about.

I was going to kill Charles Wickham.

Even if all of this went away, even if SecureCorp left me alone and Vita Aeterna disappeared, I'd still be a freak, outliving everybody on the planet. At least Wickham's death might give my life some purpose.

If Wickham was taken out, Vita Aeterna would be crippled, and the CCE would be thrown into confusion - at least temporarily. Maybe that would give what was left of the Rebels, and the Dead Shift, if they were for real, a chance to make an impact.

I guessed that the beacon would take me somewhere close to Wickham, maybe even directly to him. If the meeting concerned Vita Aeterna, the secret society's leader would probably be there. But I couldn't use the map at this distance. It didn't show any detail, and there was no way to enlarge it. I could bring up maps on the HUD, but they only covered the Corp Ring - the Quarters and the Dregs didn't count, I guess.

Wherever I was going was in the Corp Ring. To start with I could make my way there. Once I got close enough I'd take the card out of the bag periodically, long enough for it to update, and check the direction indicator. That would probably allow SecureCorp to figure out where I was, so as soon as the beacon was updated, I'd have to cover it up again and run to a new hiding place. And I'd have to keep that process up until I got to the meeting location.

To accomplish my mission, I'd need to be mobile. I set off for the spot we'd seen Tory and the other dead gangsters. It wouldn't be much use in the Dregs, but back in Tintown I could cover a lot more ground if I had my board. I fought to keep my stomach contents down as I gave the bodies a wide berth and searched the area. There was no sign of my pack, but I found the board lying in a pile of other booty they'd locked in a nearby room.

Before I started, there was one connection I had to make. I'd had it with the Dead Shift, and I still wasn't sure about the Rebels, but somehow I had to contact Laura and explain what happened. I had to make sure she knew I wasn't a traitor.

I made my way back to the last place the Rebels had been. Of course, they'd moved. Alone, I'd probably never be able to find them. I was still new to the Dregs; I wouldn't even know where to start. But it occurred to me that I knew somebody who was an expert.

THIRTY

....

LAURA

It took a whole day to find my way back to the building where I'd first met Benny - his 'headquarters'. My plan was just to hang around and hope I'd run into him, assuming he was still alive. The last time I saw him his wound looked pretty gruesome.

When I reached his 'office', there was no sign of him, but judging from the patches of blood on the chair he usually sat in, he must have been there recently. It didn't look like his wound had gotten any better. I realized that I was exhausted. I lay down on the floor and went to sleep.

A noise startled me awake. I looked up. Benny was standing in the doorway. I wasn't sure how he'd react when he saw me. I was relieved when he smiled.

"You came back," he said.

I checked out the wound in his side. His crude stitches had partially pulled loose and it was festering yellow and purple, oozing a mixture of blood and pus.

"You need to get that looked at," I said, cringing at the sight of the wound.

He got anxious and stepped back. "No way."

"You're going to die if you don't—"

"They're not gonna touch me," he said, his voice shaking. "I'm getting better."

"Okay, okay," I said. "Settle down."

I got up and stood in front of him.

"I need your help," I said.

"For the CCE?" he whispered.

I hesitated. "Yeah, that's right."

I gestured for him to come closer. He came and leaned down toward me. I lowered my voice. "I'm going to meet Mr. Wickham."

He stood up straight and stared at me in awe. Technically it was true, but I didn't tell him why. I felt like a shit lying to him, but I needed his help and it was the only way.

"First I need to connect with the Rebels," I said. "But I've got no idea how to find them. Will you help me?"

His face fell.

"It's important," I said. "Everything depends on it."

He stood motionless, staring at the floor for almost a minute, wrestling some inner demon.

Finally he looked up. "Wait here," he said. "I'll be back."

He took off without another word.

☼

Benny was gone for two days. Luckily, the expired food packets were still lying around, along with the stale crackers and biscuits. I stuck to the most recent date-stamps, and they didn't make me sick, so I kept eating them. I found a secluded spot outside where there was enough sunlight to charge the crypted phone. Then I just hung around and waited.

Finally, early on the morning of the third day, he returned.

He led me through a maze of garbage and rubble strewn back alleys for five hours. We stopped in a part of the Dregs I'd never seen before, climbed to the fourth floor of an abandoned building, and peered through a window opening.

"There," Benny whispered, pointing down at what might have once been some kind of bus station.

"You've seen them?" I whispered back.

He nodded.

We hung around for a couple more hours, watching. He was right. I saw a few guys I recognized. I didn't see Laura. I was hoping against hope I'd see Bailey, or even Travis, but neither of them showed. The next problem was going to be how to contact Laura without alerting the others. I wasn't sure how they'd react to me after what happened.

I waited until the guard was at the farthest extent of his patrol, then snuck up to opposite end of the building. I removed Laura's medallion from around my neck, threw it on the pavement in plain sight, and took off. Back at the hiding place I watched the guard return to the corner where I'd been. He picked up the medallion and looked at it, then looked up. I ducked away from the window as he scanned the surrounding buildings. Eventually he wandered to the door, and called to somebody inside.

A couple of guys came out and searched the immediate area. We were ready to run if they expanded their search, but I don't think they had the manpower. They gave up and went back in. My only hope was that Laura would hear about the medallion and get the message.

☼

Later in the afternoon, my heart jumped as she appeared at the entrance and stood talking with the guard. They argued for a few minutes, probably about how unsafe it was for her to be walking around alone. Finally, the guard waved his arm around, indicating something like: 'stick around this area'.

She wandered straight ahead for a few minutes. I got ready to move. When she'd gotten about fifty meters away, she ducked behind a corner and took off. The guard reacted, and started to chase after her, then realized he didn't dare leave his post, and came back.

I rushed downstairs and outside to intercept her. After a few minutes I heard her whispering for me. I headed toward her voice and found her standing in a cramped square, in the shadows. When she saw me, her face took on this look of something like loathing. I felt sick to my stomach.

"How can you show your face around here after what you did," she said. She nodded her head toward the hideout. "If they catch you they'll probably kill you - and you'd deserve it. I won't give you away, because part of me still cares for you, but you'd better leave."

She explained what she'd heard from Hank, the Rebel fighter I'd seen bending over Travis and Bailey before Zack dragged me away. He'd reported that Zack and I were working together. His partner had died in the firefight with Zack. Both had been waiting as 'insurance' some distance away, in case things went off the rails.

"My father's dead," Laura said, her eyes welling up and her lower lip quivering.

I felt sick, my worst fears confirmed. "I'm sorry," I said. I stepped forward to comfort her.

She jumped back and pushed out her hands. "Don't come near me. This is all because of you. You and Zack."

"Zack's dead."

Her eyes went wide for a second. "I don't believe you." She shook her head slowly. "After all my father did for you..."

She said Bailey was alive, but moving in and out of consciousness. Hank had contacted the Rebels, who'd brought Travis, Bailey, and the dead fighter back to the hideout. Of course, they'd all had to move again.

"It's not like you think," I pleaded. "I didn't—"

"I don't want to hear any more from you," she said.

She was shaking, and the tears started to come. Instinctively I reached out to her. She backed away.

"Please leave," she sobbed. "And don't come back."

She turned to walk away.

"Wait," I called after her.

She stopped without turning.

"Benny's up there waiting for me," I said. "His wound is really bad. He needs a doctor."

She turned and stared at me for a second, like she thought maybe I was lying.

"He had nothing to do with any of this," I said.

"I'll keep an eye out for him," she finally said. "If he shows up, I'll make sure they don't hurt him, and maybe Dr. Treadwell can look at him. That's all I can do."

"Thanks," I said. "Laura—"

She shot me one last contemptuous look. "Come back here again and I'll give you up - or kill you myself."

She turned and walked away.

☼

I felt like part of me had died as I watched her disappear into the shadows. I couldn't leave things like this - but I had to. Maybe someday she'd understand. For now, there was nothing I could do.

It seemed like I didn't have a chance in this world. It made me even more determined to complete my mission. Back at our hiding place, I tried to convince Benny to see Dr. Treadwell, but he didn't want to go anywhere near the Rebel hideout.

I appreciated him helping me find Laura, but I couldn't take him where I was going. I'd have to have to ditch him at some point, but I wasn't sure how to do it. I wished I hadn't told him about Wickham - now he was all hot to go with me, for the chance of meeting his hero. He wouldn't be so happy with me if he knew what I was planning.

For now, it was good to have him around. He knew how to navigate the Dregs to avoid the thieves and gangs, and if we did get into trouble, he was there to help me. I didn't want to think about what would happen when he figured out what my mission was. For now, his excitement at the prospect of meeting Wickham was overriding his fear of leaving the Dregs. I hoped that once we got close to the borderline, his fear would win out and he'd give up on following me.

I left him for a few minutes and slipped the card out of its protective bag. The beacon light started flashing green. I mapped out what direction I should go, and checked the distance - thirty-two kilometers. I'd actually been closer the last time the card was updated, when I'd first entered the Dregs.

The meeting would probably be packed with assholes like Chuck - all the people that were after me. It would be like stepping into a swarm of killer drones. Zack had said that the main goal should be to kill Wickham. Zack wasn't around anymore to accomplish that task, if he ever intended to do it in the first place.

But I might be holding a free pass for a ringside seat to Zack's target.

THIRTY ONE

....

A VISITOR

Benny lightened up when I said we were finished with the Rebels. It was late in the afternoon, and we didn't want to travel at night, so we found a hiding place in an abandoned building not far from the Rebel hideout, and spent the night.

The next morning we took off, headed in the direction I'd figured out from the card. The first day went without a hitch. We reached the edge of the Quarters. As I'd expected, Benny started getting jumpy and anxious, torn between his fear of leaving the Dregs and his desire to meet Wickham. His fear seemed to be winning, which was fine with me. Tomorrow we'd be in my territory. I knew well enough how to get around there. We stopped just outside the border and found a hiding place for the night.

I couldn't sleep. Benny was snoring beside me as we lay on an upper floor of yet another abandoned building. I kept thinking about Laura. The look of disgust she'd given me at the hideout was etched into my brain. I knew she was wrong, but that didn't matter. A new

220

goal was taking shape in my psyche like a gathering storm cloud. If I caught up with Wickham, not only could I take out my rage on somebody, I could end this nightmare once and for all, with Zack's ultimate escape.

I heard voices in the alley below, two male, one female. Then I heard a woman scream. I sat up, stuck my head out the window, and peered down. Lit by a pale patch of moonlight, two guys were dragging a girl toward the building across the street. It was obvious what they had in mind. The girl was screaming and fighting them. They moved closer to the light and I jumped up - it was Laura.

I leaned down and shook Benny's shoulder. "Benny, wake up!"

He sat bolt upright and grabbed me by the throat. "It's me," I barely managed to croak. He loosened his grip.

"It's Laura," I whispered, nodding toward the window. "She's down there. A couple of creeps have got her. We've got to help her."

He got up and leaned out the window. Laura was still screaming. We raced down the stairs, and got outside just in time to see the guys drag Laura into the building's smashed front door. We crossed the street and ducked behind the open doorway.

There was almost no light inside, but I could hear scuffling, and the sound of tearing clothing. Laura was screaming and her attackers were laughing. I had the gun, but didn't want to risk hitting Laura. As my eyes adjusted to the dim light, I scanned the floor for some kind of weapon. I spotted a length of two-by-four, but it was out in the center of the floor. I'd be in plain sight of the rapists if I went for it.

I was trying to decide what to do when Benny made my decision for me, running full-speed at the guys. I ran after him, picking up the two-by-four on the way.

Benny grabbed the closest one by the shoulder and tore him away from Laura. Before the guy even had a chance to scream Benny had snapped his neck. The other one turned to see what was going on. I could just make out a gun in his belt. He pulled it out and aimed it at Benny. I took a flying leap and brought the two-by-four down on his skull. The gun went off, but the bullet ricocheted off the floor. The guy went down, blood spewing from his head.

I grabbed his gun and held it on him, still breathing hard. He didn't move. Laura was on the ground. She staggered to her feet and swayed, like she was going to fall. I rushed over to hold her up.

"Can you walk?" I asked her.

She nodded. I took her hand as the three of us rushed out of the building. Outside, in the moonlight, we stopped and I checked her out. She was still shaking. Her shirt was ripped open, and her right eye would be black tomorrow, but otherwise she looked okay.

"We better get out of here," I said to Benny, stuffing the gun in my belt. "The gunshot will attract people."

We took off, putting as much distance as possible between us and the rapists. Benny found us another good hiding place and we hunkered down for the night.

"What the hell are you doing out here by yourself?" I asked Laura once we were settled. Moonlight streaming through the numerous window openings bathed her features in an eerie pale blue. Benny lay in a corner, snoring again like nothing happened. Laura and I sat on the floor, with the wall as a backrest.

Tears welled in her eyes. "Bailey finally regained consciousness and I talked to him," she said. "He told us Zack had a gun to your head. And our sources confirmed what you said about Zack being dead. I couldn't live with myself, the way I treated you. I had to find you and apologize."

I felt like a ten-tonne weight had been lifted from my shoulders. I turned and took her in my arms. Suddenly she kissed me, full on the lips. Again, I felt a stab of guilt about Cindy. But part of me thought back on what I was doing here and how my quest was likely to end. Would Cindy blame me for finding a tiny interval of love within the horror my life had become?

Then I was lost in Laura's kiss - lost in the warmth of her, in her innocence, her love. For a few seconds there was nothing else.

I leaned back, still holding her. "Thank God we were there to help you," I said, sobbing myself now.

I told her how her father had died, how I was kidnapped by Zack, and all that had happened after that. I didn't mention anything about my 'mission', or even where I was going. I knew she'd try to stop me. Anyway, there was no way I was going to say anything while Benny was around.

I closed my eyes and pulled her close. For a brief moment I felt safe and at peace. I could forget about the nightmare unfolding around me and lose myself in her warmth and love. For the first time since all this started, I was happy.

She finally broke away. We sat back in each other's arms.

"Who's in charge now?" I asked. "Now that..."

Her eyes went moist, but she got control of herself. "Bailey's taken over," she said. "He'd lost a lot of blood, but his wound wasn't that bad. He's been taking it easy - he's healing incredibly fast. It's tough for everybody, but we've been through it before. We all knew what life was going to be like when we got involved in the movement."

She wiped away a tear, and smiled. "I've got some good news..."

Her smile was infectious. I put my hands around her waist and smiled back. "I could use some of that."

"I got my Appraisal," she said

My throat tightened. "What was it?"

"Guess," she said.

"How should I know?" I blurted out. I cringed when I realized there was anger in my voice. She didn't seem to notice.

"One point four," she said, beaming.

She still didn't know. For a second I closed my eyes.

"What's wrong?" she said.

I opened them again, and forced a smile. "Nothing," I said. "That's great news."

"You've never told me what yours is," she said, teasing.

My gut clenched. I hesitated.

Her smile disappeared. "Oh God, is it bad?"

I smiled. "I guess great minds think alike - it's the same as yours."

She leaned forward and hugged me. "That's so wonderful. See, we're compatible in so many ways."

Benny was still snoring in the corner. I hated to spoil Laura's moment of happiness, but we had to talk. I held my finger to my lips and led her into another room.

"You can't come with me," I whispered when we were out of Benny's hearing.

The expression of joy still lighting her face collapsed. "Why not?"

I looked at the floor.

"What are you going to do?" she said.

I looked up. She was trembling.

"I can't tell you," I said. "But it's going to be dangerous."

"I don't care."

"Don't argue," I raised my voice. "You have to go back."

I heard Benny move in the other room. I snuck back to check on him. He'd just rolled over.

"Benny can take you," I whispered, nodding in his direction. "Neither of you can be where I'm going. Maybe you can convince him to get Dr. Treadwell to look at his wound..."

She started to cry. I took her in my arms. "Look, if what I'm planning works out, I'll come back, I promise."

"And if it doesn't?" she said, her voice choked with tears.

I looked away.

"I don't want to talk about it anymore," she said. "If you don't want me around, say so. Otherwise, wherever it is you're going, I'm coming with you."

THIRTY TWO

....

CUTTING THE CORD

The next day the three of us continued toward the border of the Dregs and Tintown. I gave the gun I'd taken from the rapist to Laura, for protection. Benny let it slip that we were going to meet Wickham. When Laura heard, she gave me this suspicious look, but she didn't say anything.

Laura and I talked as we walked. As always, I was torn between Cindy's memory and the feelings that were building inside me. I kept reminding myself about Laura's Appraisal, that we could never have a life together, but part of me refused to believe it. Maybe the doctors had been mistaken - maybe there was some way to fix it after all. They kept saying there was no way to lengthen your Appraisal, but had anybody tried to shorten it...?

Benny got more and more jumpy as we approached the border of the Dregs. I prayed that his fear would win out. There was no way I could take either him or Laura where I was going.

226

I started seeing stuff that was familiar. Late in the afternoon we crossed the fuzzy transition between the Dregs and Tintown. There were more people, who looked at us suspiciously. Once or twice a passerby gawked at the scar on Benny's right temple, where his HUD should be, at the absence of a controller on his wrist, and at the oozing wound in his side.

Every time we passed someone Benny would get more anxious and slow down, like he was being held back by some invisible force. I had to Cam-surf all the time now. Benny's eyes would go wide as he stared up at the cameras we were passing.

Late in the afternoon he started hanging back. He'd stand talking to himself, like he was trying to convince himself to keep going. I was stressing out too, as we got close to my old apartment. The image of my dad's face when I told him about my Appraisal, the sound of the SecureCorp guys interrogating him, and his body smashing to the pavement, rushed through my brain.

Benny started lagging farther and farther behind. Finally, he disappeared altogether. I probably could have gone back and tracked him down, but he couldn't be part of what I was planning, so I let him go. Anyway, I had a feeling he'd show up again before this was all over.

Now I had the problem of getting away from Laura. I'd been hoping that Benny could take her back to the Rebel hideout, but that option was gone now. As we got further into Tintown I felt more at home. Finally we were only a few blocks from where I was headed - the Center, our old meeting place. There was a danger that SecureCorp might know about it, but for what I wanted to do, it was necessary.

227

When we got there, I left Laura in one of our hiding spots nearby and staked the place out. It looked the same as always. I went back and got her. We pushed through the secret entrance, and settled in for the night. Again I told her to wait, and took off for a while. I had to make a phone call.

Sorry about your uncle, Richie texted over the crypted phone when I got through. I'd told him about Zack's betrayal, and how he finally died.

You said you were looking for him, Richie continued. *He had proof who he was...*

It's not your fault, I texted back. *Neither of us knew how things would turn out.*

He told me about the other guys in the Lost Souls. Jake had an Appraisal of 1.1. Not great, but acceptable. I envied him. Richie hadn't heard from Spiro since my 'death'. That couldn't be good...

I worried that SecureCorp could somehow trace me through the crypted phone. Richie and some of his buddies are a lot more tech-savvy than I am. He convinced me that the phone really was safe - that even SecureCorp couldn't hack into the signal.

I need a favour, I texted. *It's totally fine if you don't want to get involved.*

You're dead, remember? he texted back. *You need all the help you can get.*

I described my plan to him, and he agreed.

Back at the Center, I talked to Laura. "A friend of mine's coming to meet us tomorrow morning."

"Why?" she said.

"He's going to help us get to the Corp Ring without getting caught," I lied. The lie didn't really make that much sense, and anyway I hadn't told her why I wanted to go to the Corp Ring, or what I wanted with Wickham, but she seemed to buy it.

I smiled. "So, if you see a big lug with curly blond hair coming at you in the dark, don't freak out and shoot him - it's just Richie."

Her eyebrows came together. "What do you mean? You'll be there too, won't you?"

"Yeah, sure," I said. "I was just joking."

She looked at me funny. We were both exhausted. I brushed the dust off the old mattress we used to sit on when we hung out here, and we both lay down on it. I put my arms around her. She didn't resist.

"You know how I felt about my girlfriend, Cindy," I whispered to her. She nodded. "I really like you," I said, "but I'm still trying to work all that stuff out."

"Sure, I understand," she said.

I held her more tightly. "No matter what happens, know that I'll always care for you."

Her body stiffened, but she didn't say anything. A few minutes later we were both asleep.

☼

I woke up, the HUD alarm beacon I'd set earlier flashing. I was still wrapped around Laura. She was asleep, breathing heavily. I carefully worked my arm out from under her and moved away. She twitched a couple of times, but didn't wake up. I took one last look at the dark wavy hair flowing over her shoulder. She was so beautiful I had the urge to bend down and kiss her, but I didn't dare.

I couldn't just run off and leave her. I'd contacted Bailey and arranged for somebody from the Rebels to come and get her, and Richie had promised me that he'd look after her until they showed up. I knew I could trust him, but I had to be sure he'd even make it here. SecureCorp knew he was my best friend - they'd be watching him.

I climbed up high into the rafters of the building, where I'd be out of sight. I could still see Laura lying there, her knees drawn up and her hands together like she was praying, a childlike form on a torn-up mattress in a crumbling building in a dying city.

I must have nodded off for a while, because I was jerked awake by voices below. In the shadows, Richie was moving toward Laura with his hands raised. She was cringing behind a pillar with her gun drawn, and glancing desperately around, looking for something - someone - me.

I wished I'd found a spot that was closer. I couldn't hear what they were saying. Richie got within an arm's-length. He said something to her. She lowered the gun, but started yelling at him. I still couldn't hear what she was saying. Richie was shrugging and trying to calm her down. She glanced around one last time. Finally she just seemed to collapse inside. She hung her head and started to cry. Richie put a hand on her shoulder and she batted it away.

I felt tears running down my own cheeks. I wanted to go down there - to jump up from where I was crouching in the dark like a coward and tell her I was sorry - to make it all go away. But I stayed where I was.

Richie gestured for Laura to follow him. She resisted at first, and yelled something else at him. In the end, she stuffed the gun in her belt and followed. She didn't have any choice. As soon as they were out of sight I made my way down.

I checked my pockets: the crypted phone in one, the bag of cards in the other. Once I was far enough away I'd check the melded card again to see what direction I should go.

I told myself I'd done Laura a favour, and I knew it was true. I couldn't form any attachments; not ever, but especially now. Nothing could stand in the way of my completing my mission.

THIRTY THREE

....

TRAIN HOPPING

Now that I was back in the Quarters it was slow going. If I used the beacon too often I was bound to get caught. I only felt safe checking it a couple of times a day. Each time, I'd have to make a note of the number indicator to make sure I was actually getting closer. Once or twice I drifted in the wrong direction and the next time I looked I was actually farther away. The location the card was guiding me to was far to the west. I traveled west in the Quarters for as long as possible before turning south and crossing into the Corp Ring.

Something else had been scratching at the back of my brain since the beacon appeared. Apps like this always came with some kind of security. You didn't want some creep who stole your card to end up at one of your private meetings. But there was no hint of that with this one. Was the card leading me into some kind of trap? After all, it was the melding of cards for Vita Aeterna and SecureCorp. For now, I shoved the idea into the background. Chances were that I wouldn't live long enough to get that far. If I did, I'd deal with the consequences when I got where it was taking me.

In the afternoon, two days after I'd snuck away from Laura, I contacted Richie and he confirmed that somebody from the Rebels had shown up and taken her back home. He said she'd been upset, but in the end, had accepted it. She should be back at the Rebel hideout by now. I hadn't seen any sign of Benny. Had he gone back to the Dregs and forgotten about me, or would he overcome his fear and try to follow me to Wickham?

☼

On the third day I finally made it to the edge of the Corp Ring. Now I had another problem. The distances I'd been traveling up to now had been small enough that I could make good time on my board. But according to the card display, there was another twenty kilometers to go inside the Corp Ring. Not only was that a long way to board, but there were far more cameras here. For every one of those kilometers I'd be under tight surveillance.

I decided to try a trick the kids used sometimes in the Corp Ring - train-hopping. It was a good way to travel long distances without being seen (or paying anything), but it was also incredibly dangerous. Hardly anybody I knew was wacko enough to do it on a regular basis, and a lot of kids had died trying.

The idea was to find a hidden spot, usually some kind of overpass, that spanned a transit line. First, you climbed up underneath the structure to a position directly over the line (which was dangerous enough

- I knew kids that had died just doing that). The spot you chose had to be on a hill or a curve, someplace that the train would slow down (to at least give you a fighting chance of surviving what followed).

Then, when the train passed under you, you fought to keep from shitting yourself and jumped, and hung onto the roof by your fingernails until either you got bounced off and died, or got where you were going. The train made regular stops, so you could get off pretty easily (though doing it without getting caught was another issue).

I'd only ever done it once, and I had no desire to ever do it again. I like danger, and I like taking risks, but there's a difference between taking risks and committing suicide. The line between the two was really thin for train-hopping.

The joke was, I still had the four hundred dollars in my shoe. For the first time in my life I could actually afford to pay for a ticket, but I couldn't take the chance that I'd be recognized.

The spot I'd jumped from that one time wasn't far from my current position, just inside the Corp Ring. I swallowed hard as I approached it - a truck overpass with a latticework of supports that spanned a line running in the right direction. Images flew through my head of the time I'd nearly died doing it before.

There were cameras on all the access points, but the crazies who were into train-hopping usually broke them as soon as they were installed. I gaped up at the angular web of steel above my head, and was grateful to see they'd kept up that tradition. I was lucky; right now there was nobody else around. With my board slung over my back, I climbed up the supports and made my way to a location directly above the tracks.

When I got to the jumping point, I was ten meters in the air. I held on tight. There were trains every few minutes. Whenever one passed below, my perch vibrated like an earthquake hit it. If I was to fall, and if by some miracle the fall didn't kill me, I'd probably get run over by the train.

I let a couple of trains go by, mentally rehearsing what I would do when the time came, and working up the nerve. Finally, I couldn't stall any longer. I was facing away from the oncoming train, but I could hear it rumbling behind me. In seconds, it was directly under my position. The vibration almost knocked me off as I straightened up, getting ready to leap to my doom.

I waited for the lead car to pass, then leaned out and tensed my legs. I could see my distorted reflection in the stainless-steel roof of the car flying below me: squat and ugly, like the toad I was about to imitate. I said a prayer, and jumped. I landed okay, but the shaking bounced me toward the edge of the slippery-smooth roof. There was nothing to hang onto. I was an arm's length from being tossed over the side and cut to pieces by the wheels. I scanned the roof in a panic. A finger-sized knob, an antenna or something, stuck out a couple of meters away. I kicked at the slick metal and got enough traction to propel myself at it. If I missed, I was dead.

As I jumped, the car jerked sideways and knocked me on my back. I saw the knob go by, but I was bouncing sideways. It was all over. I rolled off the rounded edge.

I was waiting for the end, but stopped with a jerk in mid-air. I twisted my head around and looked up. The strap of my board had caught on the knob. I was hanging from it, with buildings and streets flying by at eighty kilometers an hour, the steel wheels grating on the rails below. I turned my head and looked in the window. Inside the car, a middle-aged woman stared at me in horror.

The strap was old and frayed. It wasn't going to hold for long. I twisted my body enough to grab it, and hooked my right toe onto the gutter of the window beside me. My muscles screamed with pain as I hauled myself back up. After what seemed like an eternity, I worked my way onto the roof and held on.

So far we hadn't made a stop, and I knew we still had a long way to go. I wondered whether the woman who'd seen me would say anything, but when we made the first stop, nothing happened. If you were pressed flat on the roof, you weren't visible from the platform, so if she kept her mouth shut, I'd be safe - until I tried to get off.

I hung on, vibrating and bouncing around like a marble in a slot machine, for five more stops. The blur of buildings flying by gradually grew in size and got fancier, as we approached one of the wealthiest sections of the Corp Ring. I'd managed to sneak a look at the card at one of the stops, so I knew the almost empty station we were approaching was close to where I wanted to go. Now it was time to get off.

Somehow I had to do that without running into SecureCorp.

☼

The train slowed as it approached the platform, with me still lying in plain sight on the roof. There were hardly any SecureCorp people watching. That was unusual. It occurred to me that a lot of them might have been siphoned off to look for me in the Quarters.

I heard the stations had algorithms that analyzed the camera scans of the train and picked out anybody riding on top. It was dangerous, but I decided to get into position while the train was still moving. There was a spot at the very front of the car I was on, near the exit doors but away from any windows. My plan was to slide down onto the platform at the exact moment the train stopped. Then I could merge with the crowd pouring out of the exit.

It was easier than I was expecting. Once the train slowed, there was almost no vibration. The few guards I could see were looking the other way. I crawled along the roof and got into position. A female voice echoed through the sound system announcing our arrival. The train finally shuddered to a stop, and the bell dinged to say the doors were opening. I slid down and jumped to the platform just as a mass of humanity started pouring out. An alarm went off - the cameras had seen me. A couple of SecureCorp guys rushed over, but I was lost in the crowd.

I smiled. Something had finally gone right. I was alive *and* free. We were almost at the main exit.

That's when I heard it - a woman's voice shouting: 'that's him there'. I glanced around. The woman who'd seen me hanging outside her window had ratted me out after all. She was standing with two SecureCorp soldiers and pointing at me.

"Shit," I said, and took off.

"Stop!" yelled a voice behind me.

The exit turnstiles were straight ahead. There was a soldier to one side. I flew toward the opposite side and took a flying leap over them.

"It's him!" I heard a voice yell.

I had a big head start, but I had no idea where I was going, and I was in too much of a panic to Cam-surf. I turned down the nearest corner, then down another one. The excited voices behind me faded, but I heard cars starting, sirens wailing, and a chopper approaching in the distance. This wasn't like the Quarters - there were almost no abandoned buildings to sneak into.

They'd be monitoring the camera feeds and rushing to this spot. I willed myself to relax, Cam-surfed down the alley to a larger street, and spotted something that could be my salvation. A RoboTaxi, coming right toward me, and slow enough to hitch a ride.

I'd have to wait until the front fender passed. I ducked behind the corner of the alley and unslung my board. There was a humming noise behind me. My spine stiffened as I recognized it. I turned to look. A swarm of twenty or thirty drones was hurtling my way from the other end of the alley. It was too early to jump. The swarm was half way along now, their high-pitched whine growing constantly louder. They'd be on me in seconds. Finally the taxi's fender appeared. As it passed I ran, jumped on my board, grabbed ahold of the back bumper, crouched down to avoid the cameras, and hitched a ride.

The swarm was right behind me. They couldn't keep up to a vehicle going full speed, but we were still on a side-street, where the taxis were programmed to go slower. The drones were catching up. One fired a tranquilizing dart that clanked off the metal trunk I was holding on to. I was about to let go and run for it, when the taxi turned right onto a main street and sped up.

We pulled away from the drones. But now I had a new problem. Normally I would have let go by now - it was almost impossible to board behind a vehicle going at full speed. But this time I had no choice. I just hung on for dear life. The wheels of my board were rattling on the pavement. If we kept this up, they'd soon start breaking off.

We rounded a curve and the drones were out of sight. But I still couldn't let go - we were going too fast. After ten minutes of expecting to die, we finally turned onto a side street, and slowed down. I let go, coasted to a stop, and stood there for a couple of seconds, hunched over, hyperventilating.

I could still hear the choppers and sirens in the distance, but they were now far away. I relaxed a bit. I got control of myself and started Cam-surfing. The blood pounded in my ears as I tried to put as much distance as possible between me and the last spot where I'd been visible.

THIRTY FOUR

....

STAKEOUT

For some reason, I'd pictured the meeting place as some big, flashy celebrity hangout, like the ones they used in their stupid Safety Award shows, but it was wasn't like that at all.

In fact, staring down at the beaten-up brick building that must have been built a hundred years ago, at first I thought I'd gotten the location wrong. But that couldn't be. It was the right address, and the number on the melded card read less than fifty.

I was hiding out on the roof of a building across the street, deep in the Corp Ring. When I'd finally been able to stop long enough to catch my breath after train-hopping, I checked the card, and found that I was only a kilometer or so from my destination. I Cam-surfed the rest of the way without any problems.

My hideout was some low-level BuildCorp warehouse, so security was pretty slack. There were no guards at the doors, even the main ones, and all the cameras were visible. I just waited until somebody went in the side door, snuck in behind them before it closed, and found my way to the roof.

It was night now, the night before the date now flashing green on the melded card - the date of the meeting. It was a crazy scheme, but I was desperate; I'd never get another chance at Wickham. The truth was I hadn't really thought any of it through. Right now, my only idea was to keep watch on the building and hope the right opportunity came along for me to sneak in. What was the right opportunity? I guessed I'd know it if I saw it.

Now that I'd made it here, and had some time to think about it, it hit home that after all the effort I'd put into getting this far, I had no idea what the meeting was about (or even that there *was* a meeting - maybe it was all a trap), and whether Wickham would actually be there. Anyway, I couldn't get to Wickham if I couldn't make it inside, and I'd never do that alone. If I was to have any hope of accomplishing my mission, I'd need some kind of help.

☼

I need another favour, I texted Richie over the crypted phone. It's going to be tough, and probably really dangerous.

Hey, I'm getting used to all that by now, he texted back.

He didn't respond for a few seconds after I described what I needed from him and his hacker friends. At first he thought I was kidding - hacking a high-level Corp meeting?

241

Once he'd gotten over the shock he told me he needed half an hour to contact his friends and talk over whether it was remotely possible.

Now that I knew where the meeting was I didn't need to unblock the melded card again, which meant SecureCorp could no longer track me. Of course, they'd probably been monitoring the beacon all along, which meant they didn't need to track me, since they knew where I was headed. They'd be waiting. Thus the need for the mother of all hacks I was asking for. The only way I had any chance of a shot at Wickham was to fool their system somehow.

It was more than an hour before Richie finally got back to me. *No way we can hack the doors open,* he texted. *Whatever's happening at this place, it must be big. It's got security up the ying-yang.*

So I'm screwed, I texted back.

Not necessarily, he answered. *We can't hack the doors open. But maybe we can do something else. Security for the entrances and exits are tight, but there's other systems they haven't paid much attention to - like the lighting, heat, sound.*

How does that help? I texted.

He texted back. *We can create a diversion.*

☼

By the next night I was as ready as I was ever going to be. It was too dangerous to move around. I slept at my rooftop hiding place, and spent the day lying low and keeping my head down.

Now I was relieved to have the comfort of darkness again to hide in. The card was ticking down, now reading less than two hours before the meeting time. I peeked over the edge of the roof. The main entrance of the target building was still as dark as a tomb. It didn't look like there was anything going on. But then, Vita Aeterna was a secret society - it wasn't going to broadcast its meetings to the public.

The plan was that if conditions were right, I'd text Richie from the crypted phone, and he and his hacker friends would stomp on all the building's systems they could access. If there was enough confusion, maybe a door would be left open when nobody was watching.

I headed down, snuck around the place, and found a tiny entrance at the back, with a single dim light above it. I expected that it would be less heavily guarded, but even that one had a guard. That was a good indicator that I had the right place - something big was going on.

I hid in a camera-less shadow behind a corner of a building across the street, where I still had a partial view of the main entrance. I waited, and twenty minutes later a big black limo slid up to the curb at the entrance, and a light at the front blinked on. A guy got out. It was too dark to make out who it was. He stopped in front for a few seconds, I guess to pass through security or something, then went in.

Over the next half-hour about twenty vehicles pulled up. Their owners all went through the same routine as the first guy. So far I hadn't seen any way inside. The guard on the side door didn't look like he was going anywhere, and even if he left, the door he was guarding would be locked and alarmed.

Ten minutes later, a TechCorp van pulled up by the little door I was nearest to. A workman got out and strolled over to talk to the guard. The guard contacted somebody over his HUD, then nodded at the workman. The workman went back to the van, opened the hatch, and unloaded a trolley with what looked like media equipment: speakers, floodlights, video projectors.

Finally it looked like I might have caught a break. I got ready with the phone. The media guy locked up again and wheeled the trolley to the side door. The guard frisked him, then sifted through the stuff on his cart. They talked again for a few seconds, and bingo! The guard reached over and opened the door.

I typed 'Go' and held my finger poised above the phone. The guard stood aside and held the door open, and the media guy wheeled the trolley towards it. As soon as the trolley was blocking the door, I hit the 'send' button.

All hell broke loose. Alarms sounded, lights flashed, and I could hear shouting inside the building. The guard talked to somebody on his HUD, then rushed toward the main entrance. The trolley and the media guy were left still blocking the door.

I jumped up with the gun in my hand and ran toward him, taking a route I'd already picked out to avoid the cameras. The media guy was standing there, stunned. I pointed the gun at him and shouted, "Get lost!"

He put a hand on the trolley.

"Leave it!" I yelled.

He put his hands up and ran towards his van.

I shoved the gun in my belt, pushed the trolley out of the way, and rushed through the door.

✿

I tore down the hallway, avoiding the cameras. Alarms blared from several locations in the building, and both the emergency and the regular building lights were flashing.

"Good job, Richie," I said under my breath.

I wondered what the media guy would do. I hoped he was scared enough to take off and not say anything, but I had to assume that the security people knew about me. At least I was inside.

There was nobody around. I guess they were all dealing with what they assumed was some kind of emergency. A sign ahead said 'Conference Room One'. I found the door. Big surprise - it was locked. It had a small window in it. I stood on tip-toes and peered inside. It was a small theater. There were rows of chairs and a stage at the front with a lectern. I guessed that the meeting they were planning would probably happen here.

I looked up. A balcony wrapped around the room at the next level. There were stairs leading up to it. It might make a good hiding place. I was debating whether to sneak up there when the alarm suddenly stopped, and the lights quit flashing.

I panicked. I felt like the whole of SecureCorp were going to descend on me at any second. Without the alarms it was eerily quiet. I was too exposed down here. I took the stairs to the next floor. A hallway running parallel with the back of the meeting room had two doors spaced evenly along it. I rushed to the first one and tried the handle. It was locked, but it had a window like the other one. I looked inside. It was an entrance to the balcony.

So far nobody else had showed up. I gave up on the balcony and ran down the hall looking for another place to hide. I turned corner into another corridor. On the left wall was a door marked 'Maintenance'. No window in this one, but light was pulsing off and on through the crack underneath it.

A card scanner with a red light was mounted beside the locking mechanism. I put my hand on the cards in my pocket. They were warm. I thought about the melded card. If it was partly a Vita Aeterna card... But the beacon would tell them where I was. I took out the protective bag still holding the cards, held the open end around the detector, and passed the melded card over the surface.

The card was changing - the surface swimming in colours that seemed to be coalescing into some kind of image. I didn't have time to worry about what was happening. I looked over at the detector. Its light turned green and there was a click inside the lock.

I tried the handle. It turned. I opened the door.

There were footsteps and shouts heading toward me. I stepped inside and shut the door. The room was jammed with electrical panels, communications boards, and heating equipment - a maintenance room. Two or three large ducts ran up to the ceiling. Suddenly the lights quit blinking. I heard the click of the auto-lock on the door and stared down at the open bag still in my hand. A few seconds later footsteps of several people ran past. Someone tried the door handle. I held my breath. It was now locked. More footsteps rushed away and I exhaled deeply.

But why had it unlocked it for me - and who locked it again behind me?

There was a grate in the ceiling for the ventilation system. I stacked a couple of boxes on top of each other, climbed up, and pushed on it.

It lifted easily. I wasn't high enough to see inside. I stacked another box and poked my head up through the hole. Air ducts, big enough for me to squeeze into, branched off in several directions.

There was still shouting and the pounding of feet in the distance. I figured I was dead if I stepped outside the door. There was nothing else here, so the ducts looked like my only choice. All my life I hated being such a little runt. For once I was glad. I hoisted myself into the duct opening and pulled the grate back into place. After taking a few seconds to visualize the position of the theater I'd passed earlier, I moved in that direction. Occasionally I'd pass other grates in the ceilings of different rooms.

The running and shouting had died away now. All was silent. I peered down through a ceiling grate above the balcony I'd passed earlier. There was another one just ahead - one that I guessed would give me a clear shot at the stage.

THIRTY FIVE

....

THE MEETING

A door opened somewhere below, in the direction of the outside hallway. I pressed my back against the duct. People started shuffling into the theater, and mumbling voices filled the space below. For ten minutes I lay there, frozen. Soon they'd all be seated and the room would be quiet.

Shit! I thought, as it occurred to me that I should have been heading for the closer grate while there was still noise to cover the sound. I started moving now. I'd hardly gone anywhere when the shuffling and talking died down and the room went silent. Now I was stuck about a quarter of the way from the balcony grate and the one nearer the stage. The light pouring up through the theater grating dimmed, and there was polite applause.

A male voice started speaking. I couldn't hear what he was saying, but it sounded like some kind of introduction. In a few minutes whoever it was finished talking, and there was a thundering applause. I took advantage of the noise and slid closer to the grate near the stage.

248

By the time the applause died down I was about two-thirds of the way there. The new arrival at the podium started speaking. I could catch snippets of what he was saying.

I heard. "...slip through our fingers."

I took a chance and edged slowly toward the grate. In a few minutes, I was close enough to see the stage and the speaker at the lectern. The hair at the back of my neck rose, as I recognized him from countless appearances on HoloTV, and on posters everywhere I went.

It was Charles Wickham - the CEO of SecureCorp, the head of the CCE, and the force behind Vita Aeterna - the man I was here to kill.

Several other men and women were lined up on the stage behind him. I recognized the uniforms some of them were wearing: SecureCorp, TechCorp, MediCorp.

Where Chuck's face was smarmy and devious, Wickham looked downright evil. His eyes were like bullet holes, black and empty. At one point, he stopped talking and lifted his head. He seemed to be staring right at me. I froze. I was sure nobody could see me from down there, but...

He lowered his head again. I relaxed a little.

"This is an unprecedented opportunity," he continued. "Never before has such a multiple been available for our study."

I shivered. I had a bad feeling I knew what he was talking about.

Wickham finally shut up and went to sit in an empty chair, as one by one the others on stage got up and talked. They sounded like scientists or doctors or something. They went on for about an hour. I couldn't catch all they were saying, but the overall gist seemed to be that whatever they were trying to do wasn't going very well. With each speaker Wickham's expression got angrier.

I heard the final guy say: "It's as if an insurmountable barrier has been placed in our way, a barrier that we cannot cross - as if God has drawn a line in the sand and said 'this far and no further'."

This really seemed to piss Wickham off. His face turned red. He stood up and grabbed the back of the chair beside him, and for a minute I thought he was going to lift it up and throw it at the guy.

Wickham finally got ahold of himself, and said: "That is completely unacceptable. *We* control our fate. *Nothing* is insurmountable. That's just a pathetic excuse for failure."

The scientist looked scared. "We've been working like slaves—"

"Well work harder!" Wickham shouted him down. He pounded his fist on the back of the chair. "And find the boy! He's the key! Our sources tell us he's headed this way. How can one pissy little low-life shit evade the whole of SecureCorp?"

A couple of the people on stage bowed their heads. The SecureCorp guys tried to avoid his gaze.

Wickham strode up to the lectern, pushed the scientist guy away, and spoke again. "Some of you are lucky enough to have Appraisals that could allow you to live productive lives for well over one hundred years..." He scanned around the room. "Don't jeopardize that gift by continuing to fail me!"

As Wickham was shouting I edged my way the final distance to the grate. I was now looking straight down onto the stage. He was no more than ten meters away. He paused, and there was silence around the room. Somebody at one of the tables cleared their throat. It looked like Wickham was wrapping up. He'd be leaving the stage within a few minutes.

I worked the gun out of my belt, released the safety, and gripped it in my hand. He was right in front of me, but I figured the mesh of the grate would deflect, maybe even stop, a bullet. From the one I'd climbed through at first, I knew the grates were held in place by a set of clips. If I pushed hard enough on the one below me it would fall out and I'd have a perfect line of sight. But as soon as the grate fell everybody would know I was there.

I realized that I'd been naive about this mission. In the back of my mind, I'd been telling myself I could take out Wickham and somehow still escape. Now it was obvious that there was no way I'd get out of here if I took the shot. I had to choose, and I didn't have much time. Tears welled in my eyes. For a second I considered going down there and giving myself up. How long could I keep on running?

Then I remembered why I was here. This was bigger than just me. I stared at the gun, shaking in my hand. What kind of life was I going to have anyway, even if I managed to get out of here. Running for years like Zack, getting more and more desperate, watching everybody I knew die before I did. If I could get rid of Wickham, at least I'd give future generations a chance at a life.

I looked up. Wickham had finished talking, and was turning to leave the stage.

I slammed my fist down on the grate. It bent open but didn't fall. There wasn't enough room in the cramped duct to get a good punch at it. Shouts went up from below. I hit it again and it finally dropped to the floor. Wickham was startled and rushed from the stage, surrounded by bodyguards. I held up the gun and fired. One of the guards went down. Wickham was running now. I fired again, but didn't hit anything.

One of the guards turned to shoot me, but Wickham's voice yelled, "No, it's him! I want him alive!" It was over. I'd failed. I couldn't turn around in the duct so I crawled forward. My only hope was to find a grate in another room, climb down, and run for it.

The duct I was in ran straight ahead for about twenty meters. That's the direction they'd expect me to go. But a couple of meters ahead was another duct angling off to the right. I took it instead, and followed it into another duct running at ninety degrees. There was another grate about five meters ahead. I crawled to it and looked down. Below was an empty room.

I stuffed the gun in my belt, punched out the grate, and dove through it to a desk underneath. I landed unhurt, but realized that the gun had fallen and was still up in the duct. There was no time to go back for it. I jumped from the desk, rushed to the door, and opened it a crack. An army of feet were pounding down the hallway, headed in my direction. They sounded like they were about to turn the corner to my left. I took off in the other direction and flew around a corner myself, buying a little time.

The alarms started sounding again. I had no idea whether it was Richie and his hackers or the Security guys controlling them. I spotted a door to the outside. Was it possible I could get away after all? I crashed into it and to my surprise it opened. I took the steps to the street two at a time, reached the ground, and tore up an alleyway. I ran until I thought my lungs would burst.

I had to stop and get my breath. I spotted a dumpster and squeezed in behind it, gasping for air.

Shouts, car engines, and running feet echoed in the distance. As soon as I had the strength I raised myself up and got ready to take off again.

I froze when I heard a muffled voice coming from the pocket of my pants. I reached in, like I was expecting a trap to snap shut on my fingers, and pulled out the packet of cards.

The MoneyAll was missing. I fished around in the pocket and found it. The elastic holding the bag had fallen off. The bag had opened, and the MoneyAll had fallen out. I turned it over. Its surface was filled with the video of a face - the face of Charles Wickham.

"You can't run, boy," Wickham said, a sneer curling up on his lips. "We've had you all along."

I felt sick. "You're lying," I yelled at his picture.

I tossed the MoneyAll in the dumpster, with Wickham's face still frozen on it. I looked at the bag. The melded card was now glowing. I considered tossing it too, but it had helped me find Wickham and get access to the maintenance room; it might still be good for something else. I wrapped the elastic securely around it, took off my shoe, shoved the bag and card into it along with the money, and put it back on.

I took one last deep breath and stepped out from behind the dumpster. A line of SecureCorp soldiers stood facing me, their guns drawn. I turned to run. I heard a sound behind me. Before I could turn around, a muscular arm wrapped around my neck and squeezed. After a few seconds I blacked out.

☼

A few seconds later, when I regained consciousness, there was a face hovering a few inches above mine. My eyes weren't focusing properly yet, but I didn't need them to recognize who it was. I'd know the stench of his breath anywhere.

Brickhead.

He reached down and clamped a hand around my throat.

"Lucky for you Wickham wants you alive," he snarled.

He pushed down, compressing my windpipe until I almost passed out again. He finally let go, probably worried that he'd kill me. I gasped for breath. He dragged me to my feet.

The line of soldiers had moved closer.

Brickhead shoved me toward the leader. "Take him to headquarters," he said.

Two of the soldiers dragged me toward a SecureCorp vehicle parked nearby. One of them frisked me. He dumped the crypted phone, the money, and the card, which was now pulsing on and off, into a big envelope, and tossed the envelope onto the seat of the driver's compartment. His partner slid open the side door. They handcuffed me and dragged me inside. The back was empty, except for a bench on each side. They sat me down on the far one, strapped me in, and slid the door shut. A few minutes later we started moving.

It took a few minutes of twisting and stretching, but I managed to unbuckle the strap holding me in. I thought back on Zack's story about his escape. Crouching to stay below the window of the cab, I made my way to the side and rear doors of the vehicle. Both were locked; I wasn't getting out that way.

I returned to the bench and peered through the side windows at the buildings flying by. They got bigger and fancier with every block - mirrored glass, concrete polished as white as a cloud. And we kept going, deeper into the Corp Ring than I'd ever gone before.

Finally I sat back on the bench and closed my eyes, exhausted, powerless, and defeated.

That's when it happened. A deep blue glow appeared on my HUD, and a shape coalesced in front of it - the head and shoulders of a human being.

But it wasn't human. It was like a 3D representation, an avatar. Eyes, a nose, and finally a mouth, gradually formed. When the mouth was finished forming it started to speak.

"Hello, Alex," it said.

THIRTY SIX

....

A FRIEND

I sat up straight. The glow had faded but now it was pulsing on and off. For a second I thought I was hallucinating. I shook my head and blinked my eyes. The image was still there.

"W...Who are you?" I asked the cartoon guy.

"A friend," the voice answered. It sounded male, but with a weird overtone, like the computer-generated voices on the vending machines, only way more natural.

"Do not be alarmed," it said. "I have been attempting to help you for some time, but until my complete integration I was unable to communicate with you directly."

Integration? I thought. *What was this thing?*

Finally it dawned on me. "You're the card," I said.

I thought about where the melded card had come from, how the meeting location and date had appeared with no security, and the way it had opened and locked the doors at the building where I tried to assassinate Wickham. Now it had spawned some kind of bizarre

256

mutant being that could communicate with my HUD. Why had I kept the stupid thing in the first place?

The card spoke again. "I represent the fusion of the artificial intelligence components of the two cards from which I was formed. I'm happy to report that I have successfully cross-referenced the mission statements of both SecureCorp and Vita Aeterna, and resolved all resulting semantic conflicts."

"What the hell is that supposed to mean?" I said. A square, black region formed beneath the speaking image in my HUD. The title *SecureCorp* appeared, and bulleted lines of text scrolled down below it. It was too fast for me to catch them all, but I saw:

- *Maintain the Peace*
- *Protect Property*
- *Prevent Crime*

The title *Vita Aeterna* followed. Again, I only caught a few of the entries:

- *Study the effects of the Appraisal process*
- *Locate and protect subjects with extraordinary Appraisals*
- *Identify means to control life extension*

"So what's all that got to do with me?" I asked, still not convinced it was all real. I had no idea what this card creature, or whatever I should call it, was, but if it came from the melding of a SecureCorp card and a Vita Aeterna one, I didn't see how it could be good.

"Since I became aware, a few weeks ago," it answered, "I've been attempting to divine the purpose of my existence. My analysis of the above mission statements has led to the conclusion that my most important function is to maximize your well-being."

"Maximize *my* well-being?"

"In other words, to help you."

"What?" I said, staring at the avatar. "Not that I'm not complaining, but are you sure you read those mission statements correctly?"

"There is no doubt," the voice answered. "You are an anomaly - an outlier of the highest order. The continuation of your life and health is my most vital concern. In addition, I have identified your greatest threat."

I laughed. "I already know my greatest threat."

"As you have demonstrated," the voice said. "On that point, we are in partial agreement. Clearly, for you to survive and thrive, Charles Wickham must be eliminated."

I actually pinched myself - I thought maybe I was dreaming, but after the pinch it was all still happening. I wasn't sure how it was coming up with its world-view, but I was pretty sure that it didn't have a handle on the real purpose of SecureCorp, and I was positive it didn't have one on the real purpose of Vita Aeterna.

But at this stage, I wasn't going to argue.

"Wickham is a threat," the voice continued, "but there is a greater, more immediate one."

"Y...Yeah?" I stuttered. I was still stunned by the conversation I was having.

The figure spoke again. "Mr. Wickham, and the other Elite, have a plan to eliminate those members of society they consider superfluous."

"Superfluous?" I'd never heard that word before.

"Unnecessary," the voice said.

My spine stiffened. Zack had claimed they had this 'Ultimate Solution' in mind, but I hadn't believed him.

"They have constructed a factory deep in the Corp Ring," it continued, "to produce a toxin that they plan to unleash on the Dregs and the Quarters, resulting in the deaths of millions.

"If they succeed, your life can only be preserved if you become their prisoner and test subject. Their experiments will almost certainly cause you serious harm - possibly even result in your death."

"And..." I started off, worried now that I might say something that would make it change its mind, "you know a way to stop them?"

"The factory must be destroyed," the voice said.

"I'm supposed to destroy a factory?"

"You will require help." The image had a creepy way of moving its lips as it spoke. It continued. "My analysis of net traffic indicates serious errors in the Elite's assessment of the public mood. A number of riots have broken out already, and my evaluation predicts major events in the near future.

"The coming chaos will siphon off much of the security surrounding SecureCorp installations. The Rebels, and others with an interest in destroying the factory, can take advantage of the resulting vulnerability."

I was confused. This 'card being', or whatever it was, could be lying (really?), but I didn't have a lot of friends right now.

I turned to face the driver's compartment, where the card lay in its envelope. "How the hell are you doing all this, anyway?"

259

The creepy lips moved again. "I can hear you by monitoring the audio input on your HUD controller. I can also monitor the feeds of any nearby cameras to see your image. I will do my best to help you, but my abilities are limited. I can hack into buildings, unlock and lock doors, and control functions such as lighting and heat."

"Can you unlock my handcuffs and open the doors of this van?" I asked.

"The van is an older model I cannot control," the card answered.

"No offense," I said, "but in that case your skills aren't all that useful right now."

The image spoke again. "Through your crypted phone I can connect to the network, and devices attached to it, and make certain changes."

"Like what?" I asked.

"Sorry to interrupt," the image said, "but your phone has just received a text message from a 'Connor McLean'. I will forward it to you."

I'd already told Connor where to shove it once - I wondered why he'd be contacting me again.

We knew nothing about what Zack was planning, Connor texted. *We were as surprised as you were.*

I didn't believe him, but I thought about how Zack had insisted that I not tell the others what we were doing. I decided to at least hear him out.

Connor continued. *I've contacted the Rebels. Bailey and I have gotten together and worked out our differences. The deaths of Travis and Zack affected both of us. We're after the same thing, and there's no way we're going to get it unless we join forces. We're here to support you if you need us.*

"Can I reply to him?" I asked the avatar.

"I can re-route your reply to the crypted phone," it answered.

Okay, I texted from my controller, too stunned to know what else to say.

Are you with us? Connor texted.

I sat there, confused.

I'll let you know, I finally texted, still in shock.

I told the card being to end the call. Its image was still floating in my HUD.

"What if I want to 'summon' you or something?" I said to the avatar. "What am I supposed to call you?"

"Call me whatever you choose," it said.

I heard a story once, from long ago, about this guy who had something called a Genie in a bottle that would grant him wishes. I felt like that guy, with this force that was supposed to be working for me.

"I'll call you Gene," I said.

"Very well," Gene answered.

I thought about what Connor had said. I'd always gotten a more positive vibe from him than from my uncle, but after all that had happened...

About five minutes later, I got a text from Bailey. He backed up Connor's claim that they were working together. He also confirmed what Laura had said about Zack's betrayal and Travis' death, and that no one blamed me. In the end, the run we were on when Rolf attacked me had been successful. The Rebels had come away with a valuable cache of weapons. Bailey was healing quickly, and was now able to actively lead.

Connor asked before if I was with you, I texted him. *I am in spirit, but I'm sort of unavailable right now.*

I explained where I was, about Gene, and about what was happening. I filled him in on the 'Ultimate Solution' Gene had talked about. There was a long pause. He was probably having a hard time believing me.

We'll look into the factory thing, he finally responded. *There's not much we can do to help you at the moment but I'll talk to the others about it.*

A few minutes later, the van stopped. The door in front of me slid open, and my captors motioned for me to jump down. I stood for a second with my eyes bugging out. Fifty meters ahead of us stood a massive, pure white wall at least ten meters high.

The First Circle - the forbidden zone.

I didn't know anyone who'd been inside - not even Cindy. An equally huge and equally white gate was set into the wall. I was half expecting to get machine-gunned or something - there actually were parapets mounted up high on each side, and I could see the tops of what looked like machine guns sticking up over the openings.

My captors dragged me toward a small door to the left of the main gate, and contacted somebody on their HUDs. Seconds later there was a click. The guards opened the door, and shoved me through.

I gawked around me. It was night, but the whole place was lit up like a fireworks display. It was like passing through the gates of paradise: gleaming silver and glass skyscrapers, spotless streets, not a broken window or streetlamp in sight. I stopped short as something else occurred to me - according to my HUD there were no cameras - anywhere! I guess that's how confident they were that nobody could get in. It was a joke that the two places I'd been that didn't have cameras were the Dregs and the First Circle.

My captors chained me to a metal post, then walked over and talked to some other SecureCorp people at an out-building nearby. I noticed that one of them was carrying the envelope with the melded card and crypted phone.

I stared back at the massive gate, and turned so that the guards couldn't see me talking.

"Gene, are you still there?" I asked, still feeling like a moron talking to a cartoon.

The image, which had faded, reappeared in my HUD. It was a bit less distinct, I guess because the crypted phone was farther away.

"You say you can open doors," I said. "What about these ones?" I nodded at the gates. It was partly a joke.

He answered, "If they are opened without authorization, the authorities will immediately attempt to close them again. But I can set in motion a series of workarounds that will hold them open for approximately one hour."

I stared at the avatar, stunned. "I don't believe it," I said. "You're shitting me."

There was a deep rumbling sound, and the giant gates started to move. The doors were swinging open, all by themselves. I stood there with my mouth hanging open, staring at the empty space behind them. The guards my captors had been talking to rushed forward.

Dozens of soldiers were running around, shouting, trying to understand what was happening. Several of them jammed themselves against the massive doors, trying to push them shut.

"Okay, I believe you," I said to the avatar. Almost immediately, the gates began to close again.

Minutes later, a new SecureCorp vehicle showed up. My captors unchained me from the post and shoved me inside. The vehicle took off. I peered through the tinted window of the vehicle's cab. The envelope with the card and phone lay on the seat. The soldier sitting beside it was completely oblivious to what was going on.

About a half hour later, Gene routed through a new text from Bailey.

There's a new urgency now, he said, *with your news about the factory.*

The Rebels had confirmed Gene's claims about 'Ultimate Solution', and, with the Dead Shift's help, located the factory that was to produce the toxin. Their tech guys had managed to hack the blueprints for the building, and had come up a plan to destroy it. But the plan required high explosives, and the factory was heavily guarded. They'd need a major diversion in order to gain access.

I told him about Gene's ability to control the gate. *That would be fantastic!* he answered. *The open gate would be the ultimate diversion. Any idea when this could happen?*

I called to Gene. His image appeared, now brighter with the closer proximity of the crypted phone. "Obviously you *can* open the gate," I said, "but *will* you - if I ask?"

I explained Bailey's idea of using the open gate as a diversion to draw off soldiers from the factory.

Gene answered. "Article four of the SecureCorp mandate states: *Protect the lives and well-being of citizens.* The elimination of large segments of the population is clearly contrary to this goal. Opening the gate would facilitate the factory's destruction. However, it would have to be done in the next twenty minutes."

"Why is that?" I asked.

"Because," Gene answered, "we are about to reach our destination. Chances are that the crypted phone will be removed from my proximity."

I relayed Gene's answer to Bailey. After a long pause, he signed off, saying he wanted to discuss what had been said with the other Rebels, and with Connor.

We kept driving, past lush gardens, spraying fountains, and glittering towers of glass and steel. I hoped I'd hear from Bailey soon. I had a feeling we were almost where we were going.

Bailey finally texted back. *We're gathering all our forces as we speak. We've got our two stealth vehicles and the motorcycles, and we can steal RoboTaxis and other vehicles along the way.*

The plan is to split into two groups. One will head for the gate immediately. If it's open we'll fight our way in and mount an attack on SecureCorp headquarters. That's guaranteed to freak out the Elite and occupy a huge number of SecureCorp soldiers. The other group will break into a SecureCorp armaments warehouse not far from the factory, which we hope will be thinly guarded by then, and steal the explosives we need.

Ask your friend to wait as long as possible, then open the gate. We'll be there as soon as we can.

I closed my eyes. Would Gene really open the gate, or was it some trick by SecureCorp? Vita Aeterna already had me. If Gene was lying, they could ambush both the Dead Shift and the Rebels, and eliminate their only opposition.

But what if Gene was telling the truth? I'd already blown my one chance to kill Wickham. I'd never get another one without major help - help that even the Dead Shift and Rebels combined couldn't give me. I looked ahead at my future, either caught and experimented on until I wasted away like Walter, or running scared for the rest of my incredibly long life like Zack.

I swallowed. Gene had convinced me that he could lock and unlock doors, and even open the forbidden gate. What I couldn't be sure of was *why* was he doing it.

I might be leading the people who'd helped me and taken care of me, who trusted me, into a trap. Worse than that, if the Dead Shift and Rebels were wiped out, there'd be nobody left to change anything.

But this might be the one chance we had to make a difference.

THIRTY SEVEN

....

WICKHAM

About twenty minutes later, the vehicle rolled to a stop. My captors opened the sliding door and hauled me out. Straight ahead was a massive, open concourse with trees and spraying fountains. At its center loomed a gigantic, ultra-modern structure - a palace of mirrored glass deep inside the First Circle. I called for Gene, but there was no answer. Far in the distance, a soldier carrying the envelope headed for the building's entrance.

For a few seconds I stood frozen, gaping up at the incredible structure, like nothing I'd ever seen before. A single guard appeared at the front, then several others. They patrolled around the massive plate glass facade, beneath the giant, black 'SecureCorp' sign above the entrance - SecureCorp headquarters. My captors dragged me forward. As we approached the huge glass doors a light on a security panel flicked green, and they swung open.

The lobby must have been a hundred meters across, and the ceiling was another thirty meters above my head. The furniture and fixtures were luxurious in the extreme: plush leather couches, polished wooden tables and chairs, carpets so thick it felt like I was walking on air.

Soon we were joined by Brickhead. I noticed that he now walked with a limp. He rubbed his bad leg and sneered at me. We headed for a row of gleaming, stainless-steel elevators on the east wall. Brickhead pressed the Up button for the closest one. When it arrived, my original handlers took off, and Brickhead and I entered it alone. He pressed the button for the tenth floor, and we sped upwards.

It stopped, and we stepped out into a long hallway. There was nobody around. It was creepy. At the end, to our right, one door was open; a bent rectangle of light spilled out into the corridor. Brickhead prodded me toward it.

When we reached the open door, he gave me one last kick and I stumbled inside. There, sitting in a high-backed leather chair by a massive plate-glass window, framed by a stunning view of the glittering lights of the First Circle, was the man I'd sworn to kill - Charles Wickham.

He swiveled to face me and smiled. "Hello, Alex. We finally meet."

He nodded at my handcuffed wrists, and Brickhead reluctantly bent down and removed them.

Wickham ignored me for a few seconds, while he talked to somebody on his HUD. I wondered whether the feed for his HUD was the same as mine. No way. His body twitched. I smiled. There was stuff going on he didn't understand any more than I did.

I just stood staring at him. The call might have been about the open gate. I wondered if he knew about the gathering Rebel force, or the melded card, or that it had said it wanted him dead. I wasn't sure if I believed that myself.

Wickham composed himself and smile broadened. "Our tracking of your movements implies that you've been looking for me. Now that you've found me, what are you planning to do?"

"Give me a gun and find out."

He laughed. "You have a lot of rage inside you for one so young."

"Maybe that has something to do with you ruining my life and killing everybody I ever cared about."

He shrugged. "That's the way of the world - nothing personal. A week from now, most of the people you 'cared about', as you say, would have been gone in any case. By that time there will only be three Corps," he continued, a smug expression on his face. He rose from his chair and strolled across the room, absently glancing out the floor to ceiling windows.

I had to laugh. "Three Corps? I thought you guys were supposed to be big on competition."

He stopped and turned to face me. "Well, you know how it is with competition. Somebody loses and somebody wins." He smiled. "When I've finally won against all my competitors - and I *will* win - there will only be *one* Corp, and I will be at its head. After all, that's the ultimate intent of all competition, isn't it - to produce a single winner? In order for that to happen, all the other competitors have to be eliminated."

I scanned around the room for some kind of weapon. Brickhead seemed to have disappeared. As far as I could tell Wickham and I were alone. It was my one chance. He was old, but he was still a lot bigger than me, and he looked in good shape. There was no way I could over-power him by myself.

He paused, getting some communication on his HUD.

"What!" he yelled. "Still! Well close them for God's sake!"

He looked really rattled. I liked that look on him.

He turned away and contacted somebody else. Minutes later, Brickhead and another goon appeared behind me. Each of them grabbed one of my arms, and they dragged me toward the elevators.

☼

A half hour later I lay on a bed in a room one floor down, my heart sinking into my gut. It was like déjà vu, like I'd never escaped the first time. The room was just like the one Chuck had kept me in before. I was back in a hospital gown, and my feet were bare. I had no idea what had happened to the crypted phone, the money, the melded card - and Gene. And again my HUD was no longer working.

A few minutes later, the door opened, and Wickham appeared again, flanked by Brickhead and the other thug. The two grabbed my arms.

Wickham was smiling, but he still had that look like somebody had punched him in the gut. Something was screwing with his world. Tough break for him.

"You know," he said, glancing around the room, "it's ironic. You have the potential to live for another four hundred years." His fists clenched as he said it.

He turned his head and glared at me. "But you can die as quickly as anybody else."

I struggled, but I couldn't break free. I had nowhere to go anyway.

"You know what I can't stand?" Wickham said.

I just sneered at him.

He took a step toward me. "That worthless little shits like you and your miserable uncle, who have never accomplished anything, never dedicated their lives to anything, never pursued anything, and above all else," he turned again and stared out the window, "never sacrificed anything…" he turned back and brought his face up so close I could smell his breath, "have been blessed with this miraculous gift, while fine, ambitious, visionary people are cursed with early death."

"Life's a bitch," I said. "Get over it."

He drew back his arm and back-handed me across the face. "I never asked for your opinion."

He turned and strolled toward a tiny window in the west wall. "You should be grateful. Thanks to me, you may actually contribute something to society. Who knows, the tests we perform on you may lead to the breakthrough that allows the Appraisal to be controlled, to be enhanced for those who truly deserve it. Of course, it's possible, even likely, that you will suffer, and possibly die, in the process, but you will be able to rest easy knowing how you have helped the cause."

"Yeah, that gives me a warm feeling inside," I said.

The light above struck his face at a weird angle. The wrinkles on his skin stood out like river valleys on some ancient map.

"By the way," I asked, "what was *your* Appraisal?"

He stiffened and started shaking, like there was some kind of storm whipping up inside him. He strode over to me and punched me in the gut - so hard that it took my breath away. I collapsed. The two thugs had to hold me up.

"Proceed with the tests," he said, and marched out of the room.

THIRTY EIGHT

....

THE FINAL SOLUTION

Brickhead called somebody on his HUD, and a few minutes later a guy in a white lab coat showed up and took my blood pressure and checked my heart rate right there in the room. As he left I overheard him say that the tests were scheduled for tomorrow morning.

Eventually they all took off and I was left alone. I collapsed on the bed and clamped my eyes shut. I no longer had contact with Gene, but from the way Wickham was acting, I guessed that the gate was still open.

I passed out. I must have been exhausted, because when I woke up and checked my HUD, several hours had passed. Something had woken me - a sound. I listened and heard it again. A garbled, digitized voice that was barely audible.

A faded, grainy image of Gene's avatar appeared and spoke, a little more clearly this time. "Are you receiving my transmission?"

"Gene," I said.

"I've tapped into the building's communication system," the avatar said. "That has allowed me to amplify my signal, but I don't know where I am. You must locate me so that I can help you."

I laughed. "Hey, no problem. Just get me out of here and I'll get right on that."

I heard a click. I jumped off the bed and went to the door. It was open.

"What the hell are you?" I whispered.

"I can detect your proximity through the building's security system," Gene answered. "Just start walking and I'll direct you to me. I believe I'm on the same floor as you."

I wasn't sure how far I was going to get skulking around the hallways with my bare ass hanging out, but I didn't have too many other options. I opened the door a crack and checked the hallway. There was nobody around.

I left the room and started walking.

"Wrong direction," Gene said. "Go the other way."

I could see this was going to be a lot of fun. I turned back, keeping an eye out for Brickhead or the other thug. I got to the intersection of two corridors.

"Now what?" I said.

"It doesn't matter," Gene said. "Start moving, and I'll let you know."

I continued like that for almost an hour, weaving back and forth through hallways, with Gene telling me if I was getting 'warmer' or 'colder'. His image on my HUD gradually intensified and came into focus. I turned down a hallway and Gene said I was very close. There were doors all along it. About halfway down, one of them was open, and the lights were on.

"You've arrived," Gene said in my HUD.

I jumped when I saw a shadow move inside. I snuck in closer and tiptoed into the center of the hall for a better look. Finally I saw the full silhouette on the wall, the squarish head, the pumped-up arms and torso, and I knew whose office this was.

Of course, I thought, clenching my fists. *That's just great.*

☼

I was about to back away when a familiar voice echoed from inside the room. It was Wickham. I moved back against the closest wall. I could only catch snippets of what he was saying.

"... never seen it before," Wickham said. "...it's like a Vita Aeterna card, but..."

"...they should never have messed around with that nanotechnology shit," Brickhead's voice answered.

"...still open...," Wickham said. "...Rebel mobs marching...First Circle. SecureCorp...conflicting information."

I'd been edging closer and closer to the door, trying to hear what they were saying.

"I'll get rid of the damned thing," Brickhead said. I heard the click of his gun being primed.

"Not that way," Wickham said. "And not yet. Before we restart testing, we need to find out from the kid what the hell else this thing's been doing. I've got a card shredder in my office. In fact, I don't know if that would be enough. We might have to incinerate."

I was almost at the door opening. Suddenly an arm reached out and grabbed my wrist, dragging me inside. Brickhead was squeezing so hard I thought my wrist would break, and his gun was pressed against my forehead. Wickham stood beside a desk. The melded card lay on it in front of him. Gene - it was close enough for me to reach out and touch it.

"Don't kill him," Wickham said.

"This won't kill him," Brickhead snarled, hauling back to club me with the butt of his gun.

"Gene - do something!" I yelled.

The room lights went out and I ducked. I heard the whoosh of air from Brickhead's blow pass over my head. It was pitch black. Gene must have done all the lights in the building. I pictured where Brickhead had been standing, and kicked as hard as I could at a point I figured would be between his legs. He screamed and let go of my arm. His gun went off, but it missed me.

I jumped toward the desk and groped desperately for the card lying there. My fingers finally touched it, but other fingers grabbed my wrist. I closed my hand on the card, twisted my arm away and started running. It was still totally black. I bashed sideways into the right-hand wall and veered away. I had no idea where I was going. I glanced back and saw Brickhead's image lit up as he fired his gun into the darkness.

"Don't shoot!" Wickham yelled.

"Fuck you!" Brickhead yelled back.

I tried to do a serpentine thing as I ran. Brickhead kept firing, but none of the shots hit me. I used the light from the gunfire to follow the wall to an intersection with another hallway. As soon as I turned the corner, the card started to glow, enough for me to see where I was going. I held it up in front of me like a beacon as I ran. I turned another corner.

Gene's avatar appeared in my HUD. "Next left," he said.

We snaked through a maze of hallways, Gene directing me. The lights started flicking on in each hallway when I entered, and off again as soon as I left. We finally reached one that looked familiar. I realized it was where I'd escaped from earlier. As I ran by, the locks on every door I passed clicked open. From one or two of them people emerged, stunned, dressed in gowns like me. Most looked young, a couple were ancient and withered like Walter.

I heard a shot and a bullet whizzed by my head. I looked back and froze. Brickhead was standing at the far end of the hall behind me with a flashlight in one hand and a gun in the other. He raised his arm to fire.

A gowned woman from a doorway nearby pointed at him and screamed: "It's him!"

She dove at him. He turned and shot her, but she kept coming, grabbing his gun hand. Several of the other gowned people joined in. He managed to shoot one or two of them but by now there were a least a dozen. They pulled him down and his screams echoed through the hallway as they tore him apart.

"We must go," Gene said, shocking me back to the present.

☼

He directed me to a storeroom, where I found my clothes and put them on. On a shelf above them sat the crypted phone. I grabbed it, and Gene led me through another series of hallways.

As I moved, Gene talked to me. "SecureCorp have access to a 'presence' beacon in your HUD, which indicates whether your bodily functions are currently active. I am attempting to install a hack that will allow you to disable that beacon. Activating the hack will make it appear that you've ceased to exist."

"They'll think I'm dead," I said, too busy running for my life to pay much attention.

"The hack should be operational shortly," Gene said. "A skull-shaped icon will appear with all the others when the process is complete."

We finally reached an open concourse. Directly ahead was a row of elevators.

I can finally get out of this place, I thought.

I flew to them and hammered on the Down button a couple of dozen times. Sirens, explosions, and gunfire echoed from outside. I took a step toward the window next to me and looked down. Far below, a massive crowd were descending on the building. A line of muzzle flashes from defenders ran the length of the entrance.

Gene spoke. "The crypted phone has once again enabled me to connect to the network. According to the chatter, the Rebels have fought their way into the First Circle through the open gates, and wedged them open with vehicles. On the way they've gathered thousands to their cause. They're headed for this building."

I wondered if Connor and Bailey were down there fighting. And Laura...

One of the elevators finally thudded to a stop, and the Down arrow flashed on. My first impulse was to jump in, head down and join in the fight. Then I realized that in all the confusion I'd forgotten my original mission.

"I've got to find Wickham," I said to Gene.

"Eliminating Mr. Wickham should not be your primary objective," Gene said.

I ignored him and instead, pressed Up, and took the elevator back to the tenth floor. Thank God - my HUD started working. Most of the building was still dark, but Gene continued lighting hallways and rooms as I entered and darkening them behind me. I made my way to Wickham's office. Gene lit it for me, and I stuck my head around the open door. The office was empty. I rushed over to Wickham's gigantic metal desk, hunting for a weapon.

There was a paper memo on the desktop. I bent down to read it. The title read: 'Test Results for Psychotropic Nerve Agent XC-5.' Below was a table full of numbers and a graph. The Y axis of the graph was labeled 'Death Rate'. The line beside it shot almost vertical.

"Nerve agent?" I said, half to myself.

"It's extremely effective," a voice said behind me.

I looked up.

Wickham stood at the office door, holding a small flashlight. Another thug stood beside him, his gun drawn.

"So it's true - about the Final Solution," I said.

279

"Why so surprised?" Wickham said, smiling. "The only reason any citizen has ever been kept alive is to be of use to us. Be thankful you're one of the few who fall into that category."

Wickham nodded at the thug, who moved forward, grabbed both my hands in one of his own gigantic ones.

"No more tricks from your little friend," Wickham said.

The hallway lit up, and a faint glow replaced the blackness outside. The building's lights were back on.

Wickham glared at me. "Where is it?"

"Where's what?" I answered him.

The thug started going through my pockets with his free hand. He found the melded card and tossed it to Wickham.

"Where did this come from?" Wickham asked, holding up the card.

I didn't answer. The thug hauled up on my right arm. I still said nothing. He hauled back his gun to pistol-whip me.

"No," Wickham said. "I don't want him injured."

Wickham turned to me. "I don't need you to tell me. I have other ways of finding out. Anyway, as you know, we have bigger plans for you."

There was a commotion somewhere outside, on our floor, followed by shouts and gunfire. The thug accessed his HUD.

"Rebels," he said. "They're inside. Coming this way."

"How did they get past security!" Wickham shouted.

The goon shrugged.

"We've got to get him out of here," Wickham said, nodding at me. "Over there." He gestured with his head at a private elevator in a far corner of the office. Wickham and his helper dragged me toward it.

The gunfire was getting closer. Wickham pressed the Up button. The door slid open. Wickham stepped in and the thug started dragging me inside.

Pounding feet and shouts echoed through the hallway. "There they are!" a voice yelled from outside the office door. A fighter appeared and raised his weapon. The thug let go of me and pulled out his own gun. Both fired. Both were hit and went down. I froze in the confusion. Wickham grabbed me and hauled me inside. Gunfire ricocheted off the bullet-proof door as it slid shut. We traveled up to the very top - the eleventh floor. Wickham dragged me out and down the hall.

"You've had it," I yelled at him. "It's all over for you."

"Shut up," he said, jerking my arm so hard he almost yanked my shoulder out of its socket.

Gene appeared in my HUD. "I believe I have a way to distract him."

I nodded, not wanting to speak.

"Be ready," Gene said.

We reached a thick metal door - what looked like the entrance to some kind of bunker. Beside it was a retinal scanner. Wickham clamped one hand on my wrist while he leaned his face into the device to open the door. The thing beeped, but nothing happened.

"Shit," Wickham said.

He dragged me closer and tried again. Same thing. There was major gunfire happening on the floor below. He tried again several times, each time getting more and more angry.

He turned to me. "It's you, isn't it!" he yelled. He pulled the card from his pocket. "You and this abomination."

He hauled back and pounded on the retinal scanner. For a split second he loosened his grip on my wrist. I twisted away and took off down the hallway. He turned and chased after me. As I ran, I tried the handle of the doors I passed. All were locked. I finally hit one that opened and rushed through it.

Inside was a set of stairs going up. I glanced at the door behind me for some way to jam it shut, but there was nothing. I flew up the stairs. After a couple of flights I reached another door. I pushed through it and cringed at the rush of cooler air. I was on the roof. There was nowhere else to go. Sirens, gunfire and circling choppers echoed in the darkness below as I rushed to the edge and stared down at the panorama of the glittering city.

The melded card was still in Wickham's pocket. Gene's image was already fading, but still visible.

"Any ideas?" I asked him.

THIRTY NINE

....

TWO BATTLES

Seconds later, Wickham burst through the door and onto the roof. He was talking on his HUD. He didn't approach me, he just stood there smiling. I soon realized why, when the whirring drone of a chopper approached in the distance. A few seconds later, the machine appeared, hovering over us, its blinding searchlight scanning the rooftop, a machine gun mounted on its undercarriage.

The searchlight found Wickham and he waved and pointed in my direction. There was a helipad in the northwest corner. In seconds the chopper would land and a new set of goons would climb out of it and grab me. Once that happened, I was screwed.

My only avenue of escape was the door back down, and Wickham was blocking that. Somehow I had to get him away from it. I had an idea. I stepped up to the very edge of the roof, and stood there, like I was getting ready to jump.

"No!" Wickham screamed.

"Why not?" I yelled back. "So I can spend the next three hundred and eighty years being hacked apart by Vita Aeterna?"

His face fell, as he realized I was right. I glanced down. The Rebel force had filled the square surrounding the building, and was driving toward it. Hundreds of SecureCorp defenders formed a wall protecting it, while a ring of choppers dove at the Rebels, machine-guns blazing.

As I'd hoped, Wickham rushed toward me. The chopper overhead hovered, its searchlight bathing the roof below my feet in giant pool of white light. Now that the door was clear, I could circle around Wickham and run back through it. But just as I was about to move, the searchlight caught my eyes and I was blinded. Then Wickham was beside me. He reached out and grabbed my wrist. We were both standing on the very edge.

"Make him let go," Gene's voice came through my HUD. "Step away from him."

"How am I supposed to do that?" I yelled.

I knew the melded card was still in Wickham's inside jacket pocket. When he looked away for a second, gesturing orders to the chopper, I reached in with my free hand, fished around, and brought out the card. Wickham grabbed for it with his own free hand, but I had a firm grip; there's no way he could pry it loose.

He punched me hard in the stomach. My hand opened as I doubled over in pain. The card flipped into the air. It hovered there for a fraction of a second, just beyond the edge of the roof.

Wickham let go of my other wrist and reached out to save the card. He actually managed to grab it out of the air, but he was off balance.

Following Gene's instructions, I jumped back as far as I could away from him. I took a step toward the door.

Gene's avatar appeared in my HUD. "Take the southeast elevator to the third floor. From there you can climb down the back way."

Wickham was still dancing on the roof edge, off balance. He flapped his arms at his sides. It looked like he'd finally gotten his footing, when the chopper's searchlight swung away from me and blasted directly into his eyes, cranked to maximum intensity. The chopper pilot's expression was a blend of bewilderment and panic as he frantically hauled on the unresponsive controls. The CEO of SecureCorp and head of Vita Aeterna stumbled backwards, blinded by the light.

His left foot slipped and he staggered off the edge, the melded card still in his hand. I peered down at his falling shape. His screams stopped about half way down.

My distraction was broken as the chopper's searchlight beam began swinging erratically back and forth. I looked up. The machine was pitching from side to side, its main rotor almost touching the ground.

I skirted around the careening chopper and dove for the exit door. Once inside, I stopped and peered around the jam. The machine was rocking violently, the roar of its engines interspersed with the screams of the occupants. The main rotor finally clipped the roof. The whole machine flipped over and the still-turning rotor drove it toward me. I flew down the stairs to the first landing. There was a massive explosion above, and fire licked past the open doorway. Then the only sound was the crackling of flames, and the gunfire and shouting from the square below.

It occurred to me that I still needed a gun. I snuck back up the stairs and poked my head out. The blackened hulk of the chopper lay smoking about ten meters away. The burnt, mangled bodies of a couple of the goons were lying close by. I could see the bulge of a weapon on the belt of one of them. Fighting my nausea, I crept up to the body and touched the weapon. It was still so hot it burnt my fingers.

I circled around the smouldering chopper, ventured to the edge of the roof, and stared down at the ground far below. The dark was still lit up with hundreds of flashes from gunfire. A circle had opened up around Wickham's sprawling body.

The battle slowed, then stopped altogether, as I guess both sets of fighters were trying to digest what had happened. As I watched, a huge knot of SecureCorp soldiers worked their way to that location, and the crowd around Wickham's body expanded. A searchlight from one of the choppers swung in my direction. One of the SecureCorp soldiers looked up, spotted me, and pointed. Guns started firing again, this time at me. I jumped back from the roof's edge. It was time to get out of here.

By now the weapon on the dead goon had cooled off. I grabbed it, ran for the exit door, and flew down the stairs. I located the southeast elevator, and punched the Down button. An eternity seemed to pass as I waited for the doors to open. I got to the third floor and rushed out into the open concourse, hunting for the escape route Gene had described.

I finally spotted it, through the windows on the western wall. A fire escape outside led down into a small grove of trees. There was a window with a latch on it. I pulled on the latch - it was stuck. There was a coffee table and a set of metal chairs across the room. I ran and grabbed the closest chair, turned my face away, and smashed it against the glass. The window shattered. I cleared the shards off the bottom of the frame and climbed onto the fire-escape, praying that there was nobody nearby to hear the racket I'd made. There was still lots of gunfire echoing around, but it was coming from the other side of the building.

I flew down the steps and jumped to the ground, gasping for air. The question now was: where could I go? I took a couple of deep breaths and tried to think. I was effectively behind enemy lines. The SecureCorp defenders stood between me and the Rebels. I no longer had Gene to help me, and I didn't dare try to get the melded card back, since it would now be surrounded by SecureCorp soldiers. My only option was to search for the gate, and pray that somehow I could get through.

I'd taken a single step when an arm wrapped around my chest from behind, forcing my own arms behind me.

"You thought you could fool me," a familiar voice whispered in my ear, "but I saw his body. I saw you on the roof. You lied. You don't work for the CCE. You work for the government. It was you. You killed Mr. Wickham."

I recognized the voice.

It was Benny.

I tried to reach for the gun in my belt, but a single giant hand pinned both of mine behind my back. Benny's free arm wrapped around my neck.

"What are you doing here?" I croaked, barely able to speak.

"Maybe Mr. Wickham's gone," Benny said. "but I'm gonna finish what he started. We're gonna put an end to you all."

He squeezed. I could hardly breathe.

I figured it was time for honesty. "It's true," I said, gasping. "I don't work for the CCE. But things aren't the way you think—"

"You government bastards have tried to confuse me before," he said. "Never again."

"Believe me," I said. "I don't work for the government."

"You're lying." His grip around my neck tightened.

"It was self-defense," I said. "He was trying to kill me."

"Yeah?" Benny said. "Too bad he didn't - time to finish the job."

He squeezed harder. I was about to black out. He could have killed me instantly. He was hesitating.

I made one last desperate plea. "Benny, I thought you were my friend."

For a split second his grip loosened. He made a sound like he was choking down a sob. I twisted my right hand free and grabbed my gun.

The grip of his left arm tightened again and he reached his right forward trying to grab the gun. I turned it to point behind me. I couldn't tell where I was firing - I might even hit myself, but I only had one chance. I pulled the trigger.

The blast was deafening. Benny grunted as his body jerked backwards and he let go of me. I jumped away and turned to face him, my gun still drawn. He staggered back a couple of steps, a red blotch soaking across his stomach. Benny looked down, confused. His crude stitches had completely come apart, and a festering wound covered most of his left side. He looked up again, his face twisted in rage, and rushed toward me.

"Benny, no!" I yelled. He kept coming.

I fired again. Once again he wrapped his fingers around my neck. I fired twice more, point blank. He finally collapsed, dragging me to the ground with him, and fell on top of me. Soaked with Benny's blood, I struggled out from under his motionless body.

✧

I knelt for a second beside my friend. He was still breathing.

"I'm sorry," I said, sobbing.

His eyes opened and he looked up at me. His breath was coming in gasps.

"I don't work for the government," I pleaded, tears running down my cheeks, praying he could hear me. "I'm going to change things - I promise."

He blinked, and his body shuddered as the life force left him. He lay still. The shadows and red flashes bleeding through from the battle washed over him. The guy who'd saved my life more than once - who'd protected me and been my friend. How many people had to die for my sake? The worst thing was that I'd never be able explain to him, make him understand.

I couldn't hang around. I shoved the gun in my belt and took off, trying to figure out how to get back to the gate.

I slunk from shadow to shadow among the glittering, pristine glass towers, feeling like I was floating through some dream world, past block after block of mind-bending wealth and luxury. There didn't

289

seem to be much in the way of security inside the First Circle. I guess nobody ever expected lowlifes like me to actually make it in. Or maybe they were all off fighting the Rebels.

There was hardly anybody around. Once or twice I saw a silhouette running by a few blocks ahead, or diving into a doorway. I think everybody was cowering indoors. Maybe there'd been some kind of announcement on their HUDs about the Rebels. This was probably the first time the outside world had ever invaded their little cocoon.

After countless wrong turns and backtracks, I breathed easier as the top of the wall became visible in the gaps between the palace-like structures. Minutes later I was within sight of the gate. I hid behind the corner of a nearby building. When I peeked out, my throat tightened. The gate was closed, and the guards were back in their towers, scanning the area, hands on their turreted machine guns. I wished I hadn't lost the melded card and Gene.

The gunfire in the distance got closer. It seemed to surround me. I wasn't sure where to run. Anyway, what was the point in running? As far as I knew, the gate was the only way out. I heard a gunshot very close. I took off, running in the direction away from it, glancing behind me as I ran. I was so distracted I almost ran into a group moving up the alley toward the gate.

A dozen guns were instantly trained on me. I raised my hands.

FORTY

....

ESCAPE FROM THE FIRST CIRCLE

"Lose it," one of the group yelled, nodding at the gun in my belt. "Slowly - make a sudden move and you're dead."

None of them were wearing uniforms. At least they weren't SecureCorp. But they didn't look familiar.

"I'm on your side," I said, as I slowly reached down, pulled the gun out of my belt, and dropped it on the ground. "I'm a friend of Bailey's."

"Step away from the weapon," the leader said.

I raised both hands again and stepped back slowly.

"I'm with you guys," I said. "Do I look like SecureCorp?"

"He's okay," a woman's voice came from farther back.

The front line of Rebels split apart.

My heart raced, as out walked Laura.

"Thank God," I said. It was great to see her, but I wondered how she'd react after what I'd done.

291

She walked up to me, scowling. "I should let them shoot you, for running out on me like that." Finally she broke into a smile, came forward, and hugged me.

"I had to take out Wickham," I said, my eyes welling up. "I couldn't let you be part of it."

Laura and I let go of each other, and I stood facing the others.

"Wickham's really dead?" the leader asked.

I nodded. Whispers swept through the crowd at the news. The fighters stood staring at me like I had two heads or something.

"Where's Bailey?" I asked, breaking the silence.

"He's wrapping up the Rebel attack on SecureCorp headquarters," Laura answered. "He'll be joining us soon. Connor's leading a smaller group on the other side," she nodded toward the wall. "They're fighting their way into the SecureCorp weapons storehouse. If they make it inside, we'll have lots of firepower, and even explosives."

A few minutes later we got word from Connor's group. They'd lost a few people, but had gotten what they'd come for. While we waited for Bailey, Laura and the others filled me in on what had happened while I was going after Wickham.

Just after my conversation with Bailey, a hack had mysteriously appeared on his HUD. Normally, the 'common' citizen could only reach a half-dozen people at a time. The hack removed that restriction. That meant that the Rebels could broadcast their message to everybody equipped with a HUD, which was pretty well everybody.

Gene, I thought.

The Rebels leveled their charges against Wickham and the CCE. Of course, a lot of people didn't buy into what they were saying, but there were enough who finally understood the truth, and saw that this might be their only chance to fix things.

Then the word went out that the gate to the First Circle was open. When people from the Quarters got over their initial shock, they headed there, first just to see if it was true, then to venture inside, to finally see with their own eyes a place that was so far removed from their lives that it was like sneaking into heaven itself.

Some of the ones who'd entered just ran off to experience the wonders of the place, but after seeing it, many joined the Rebels. They now had a force of thousands. Since there'd never been any large-scale resistance movement, SecureCorp wasn't set up to deal with it. They were spread so thin that the arms storehouse that Connor's people were after was left almost unguarded. As word began to circulate that Wickham was dead, things really started to unravel.

Bailey and the rest of his group soon appeared in an alley, headed towards us. Both Bailey's torso and his right leg were now wrapped with bandages. I was still worried about how he'd react when we met again - after what happened to Travis.

I was relieved when he smiled and wrapped me in a bear hug. We exchanged information about Wickham's death and the Rebel attack on SecureCorp headquarters. Bailey said the Rebels couldn't hope to hold the building. Their diversionary mission had been accomplished, so now they could concentrate on other targets.

I told him and Laura about Benny, and how he'd died. I also told him that the gate was locked and guarded again.

"Thank God for that card," he said. "I don't think all this could have happened if it hadn't opened the gate."

I looked at my feet and felt the warmth rushing to my cheeks. I hated to admit that I'd lost the card. I explained the details about what happened, and how Gene had actually killed Wickham.

Once again Bailey and the others stared at me, not quite believing what I was saying.

"We could sure use that card now," Bailey finally said. "You figure it was on Wickham's body?"

I nodded, still embarrassed.

"Well, there's no way we're going to get it back, then," he said. He put a hand on my shoulder. "Don't worry about it. You've single-handedly struck a crippling blow to the CCE and SecureCorp. Anyway, we've got alternatives - we've got the explosives."

I explained to them what Gene had told me about the 'final solution', and the memo I'd seen on Wickham's desk.

"The first thing we've got to do is get out of here," Bailey said. "Now that the gate's locked again we're trapped - us, and a lot of people who just wandered in to see what was on the other side. Once the confusion dies down, SecureCorp can sweep through sector by sector and kill anybody who doesn't belong."

We marched to the gate. On the way, we met some resistance, but most of the SecureCorp guys were preoccupied with the tens of thousands of people from the Quarters, and even the Dregs, who'd wandered in through the gate while it was open.

When we were about a block away we stopped, and some scouts Bailey sent out came back to report that, as I'd said, the gate was closed. The guards were back in place in their turrets, and a small army of SecureCorp soldiers were now posted in front of it.

Bailey got in contact with Connor on the other side. Together, they came up with a plan to blow the gate. Connor's group had plenty of explosives, enough for the gate and the factory as well. Two contingents of fighters would march to the gate - one on each side. The one on our side, led by Bailey, would keep SecureCorp occupied. A smaller one on the other side, led by Connor, would plant an explosive to blow a hole in the gate.

The groups headed out and we waited. A few minutes later, an intense firefight echoed in the distance, followed soon after by a massive explosion. As soon as we heard the blast, the rest of us rushed for the gate. When we got there the firefight was still in progress, and we joined in.

I glanced at the gate and smiled. A giant hole had been blown in the center, easily big enough for our people to get through. Once our force had eliminated the opposition, thousands of us filed through the opening and crossed back into the Corp Ring.

We stopped at the first opportunity, and Bailey, Connor, Laura, and I huddled for a meeting. We'd lost a lot of people, but we still had a substantial force, and more were finding their way to us and joining all the time.

It was decided that Connor would lead the main group to capture InfoCorp's communications center, deep in the Corp Ring. That would give them control of the 'news' coming from the CCE and its puppet government. From what little we'd had time to monitor, the official line was still that nothing was happening. If Connor and his group were successful, the news feed would change very soon.

A second force would remain at the gate, holding it open for as long as possible to help any non-Elite still inside to escape.

Laura and I both joined a third, smaller group, led by Bailey, that would head for the factory, about an hour away by foot. Directions to the factory, how to break in, a map of the inside, and instructions on where to plant the explosive, were all made available on our HUDs.

On the way we met only token SecureCorp resistance. We guessed that the bulk of their soldiers were off battling the main Rebel force, and trying to secure and reseal the gate.

About half-way there we reached an isolated square with a strategic view in every direction. Bailey posted lookouts at all the accessible alleys and called for a ten-minute rest stop. I wandered off into a distant corner with Laura.

She turned to me. "Connor told me about your Appraisal."

I froze. "I'm sorry I lied to you. You were already upset about your father, and I didn't—"

"Five?" she said. "Really?"

My eyes stung as I fought back tears. I nodded.

"But we could still make it work," she said, her voice breaking. "It's a big difference, but—"

I shook my head. I'd already done the calculations.

"Think about it," I said, looking into her eyes and watching her world collapse behind them. "After one hundred years, your effective age would be eighty-seven. Mine would be thirty-six. And by one hundred twenty—"

"But we'd still have at least fifty or sixty good years together," she said, a tear coursing down her right cheek.

"You'd end up hating me," I said. "You'd be getting older and I'd still be young—"

"Never!" she pleaded. "I could never hate you."

I smiled and took her in my arms. "Maybe you're right," I whispered, not really believing it. "We'll see when this is all over."

We started off again, meeting almost no resistance. A half-hour later we were within a block of the factory, according to the Rebel's map. We sent a couple of scouts to check the place out. The plan was to break in through a side door that led to a loading bay. The scouts said several SecureCorp soldiers were currently guarding that door. We were going to have to fight our way in.

We might not have time once we got inside, so Bailey called another meeting to plan the strategy for demolishing the factory. We stopped in a nearby alley.

There was a problem. The only way to reach the crucial point the Rebels had identified was by crawling into the building through a ventilation duct, like I'd done at the Vita Aeterna meeting. The duct could be accessed from the loading bay, but only two people in our group were small enough to get through it: Laura - and me.

"You have to let me do it," I said.

Bailey stared at me like I was nuts. "Too dangerous. We need you. You're the guy who killed Charles Wickham. You made all this possible. You're a hero to all those people out there."

"I can be a hero whether I'm alive or dead," I argued. "Better I die a hero than get captured again by SecureCorp. That would be disastrous for the movement. I want to make up for losing the card. Anyway," I smiled at them, "I'm not planning to die."

297

"That's crazy," Laura said. "Let me do it. I'm the obvious choice. And I can strike a blow for my father."

Bailey studied both of us for a few seconds.

He finally turned to her. "You sure?"

"No way!" I said. I grabbed her by the arm. "Don't!"

She nodded to Bailey.

I tried to talk them out of it but Bailey's mind was made up.

A couple of the technical guys had analyzed the building plans. I listened in while they explained to Laura how to get to the critical spot they'd identified. Bailey introduced us to their resident bomb expert, a beaten-up guy with three days growth of beard and a small pack on his back. He gingerly hauled a box about thirty centimeters square out of the pack, held it up, and explained how to set it.

There were two switches: a black safety switch on the left-hand side, and a red detonator in the center. Both were mounted in a T-shaped trough with a small button at its apex. You had to move the button out of the way, then slide the switch itself into the T-trough, to prevent you from flipping the switches accidentally.

You armed the bomb by flipping the black safety, then started the timed explosion by flipping the red detonator switch. A dial on the right-hand side allowed you to lock in a delay before the explosion, which the demolition guy said would be huge.

After triggering the detonator, Laura would crawl to an exit grate they'd identified above an isolated storeroom, drop down to the floor, and run for her life. The bomb guy preset the timer for a fifteen-minute delay, and slid the box back in the pack.

We headed for the factory. Unlike the glittering steel and glass structures around it, the building was squat and ugly, formed from rough-hewn concrete. For a few seconds I worried that the Rebels had made a mistake. When we had a good look at the maps and diagrams, it was pretty clear that this was the place.

We reached the side door, and took out the guards easily, but one had time to communicate something over his HUD.

"We've got to move fast," Bailey said. "There'll be more where these ones came from."

We used another small explosive to blow the door open, and a bunch of us crowded inside. Bailey led a group of fighters, including me and Laura, to locate the ventilation duct, while the bomb guy set the bomb on the ground, waiting for the go-ahead.

The duct was in the northeast corner, almost at ceiling height. We piled up some packing crates to reach it. Bailey climbed up, ripped off the metal grate, and stuck his head inside, then climbed down to where the rest of us were standing. He called the bomb guy over.

"It's a go," Bailey said, turning to Laura.

"Let me do it," I made one last ditch attempt. She just shook her head.

"Give it to me," she reached out her hand for the bomb pack.

The bomb guy held it out for her. Just as her fingers touched it, the place exploded with gunfire. The crowd at the doorway split apart and a group of SecureCorp soldiers burst through. A bullet caught the bomb guy in the chest and he went down.

FORTY ONE

....

ASSAULT ON THE FACTORY

Everybody dove for cover. The pack with the bomb had fallen behind a stack of packing crates. The bomb guy's body was lying beside it, blood pooling around him. Nobody was paying any attention. The Rebels were locked in a firefight with about a dozen SecureCorp soldiers. Laura was pinned down behind a small crate, with no room to move.

I slid over, grabbed the bomb pack, and crawled along the floor, with the stack as cover, headed for the duct. Bullets were still flying as I climbed the packing-case stairway. A few blasted divots out of the wall behind me, but I was partially shielded by the stack, and none of them hit me. I reached the duct and squeezed into it.

"Alex!" I heard Bailey's voice yell behind me as I crawled as fast as I could. A couple of bullets punched holes in the duct behind me. I kept going, the noise of the firefight gradually fading.

After a few minutes everything was quiet, as I guess they'd taken all the SecureCorp guys out. I started getting messages on my HUD.

"That was a stupid thing to do, Alex," Bailey said. "You've put this whole operation at risk."

"Sorry," I answered him. "Laura's got a proper life to lead. I know what has to be done."

"We've got no choice now," Bailey said, "so just keep going. Keep us informed."

I crawled along the duct, following the instructions, pushing the pack with the bomb ahead of me, as the bomb guy had suggested. The hackers had identified a central point directly above the heart of the factory floor. According their calculations, a large enough explosion at that point would demolish the entire building. As soon as it was set, I'd drop down through the closest grate and get the hell out of there.

After a few twists and turns I located the target point. The escape drop was about ten meters ahead. It took a few minutes to manipulate the pack so that it was behind me. That way I'd be able to move quickly once it was set. I opened the pack and carefully removed the bomb.

I described my location to Bailey. His voice came over my HUD. "According to our map you're in position. It's a go, whenever you're ready. We've hacked into the building's security. Once the bomb is set, we can watch you with the security cameras, and help you find the way out."

I stared down at the bomb, with its levers and lights. So much destructive power in such a little package.

"Alex?" Bailey's voice came through again.

"Yeah, I'm doing it right now," I answered.

I released the safety, and activated the trigger.

"It's set," I said.

301

"Okay," Bailey said. "You've only got fourteen minutes. Get going."

I didn't answer him. My muscles had been primed to take off as soon as the timer was set, but now it occurred to me that all I'd have to do is stay where I was, and this nightmare would finally be over for good. It would be quick; I probably wouldn't feel anything. I sat staring at the bomb for more than a minute.

Bailey came back on. "Alex, there's no sign of you on the cameras. Are you okay? You've got to hurry."

After all, I thought, no matter what happened I was screwed. The CCE and Vita Aeterna were crippled, but there was no way they were defeated. I'd be on the run for the rest of my life - and that would be many, many years. I'd be cursed to continue living long after everybody I ever cared about was dead. I'd never be able to form any long-term relationships - I'd live the rest of my incredibly long life alone.

"Alex," there was an edge of panic to Bailey's voice. "What's going on? Get out of there. The place is going to blow. We'll be out of touch for a minute or so while we get clear ourselves."

Suddenly I remembered what Gene had said about a hack to make it look like I was dead. Had he actually had time to finish it? He'd said there'd be an icon when it was ready. I checked through the hack list in my HUD. There it was - a white skull, just as he'd described.

Bailey's frantic voice returned a minute or so later. "Don't do this, Alex," he pleaded, finally guessing what was on my mind. "We'll find a way. Your life is worth living. Get out of there while you still can."

With Gene's hack, I had another alternative. In spite of all I'd be in for, I still wanted to live. But there might be a way to at least make my life bearable, to take the heat off so I wouldn't end up like Zack...

I had to get moving. I made my way along the duct to the exit point and smashed through the grating in the ceiling. I jumped down into the storeroom, made my way to the door, opened it and peeked out. The hallway was empty. I checked my HUD - there were no cameras immediately in front of me, but there were a couple near an intersection farther down. I took off. It was just like old times - I was Cam-surfing.

I followed the Rebels' map, dodging cameras as I went. I felt bad for the people I was deceiving and leaving behind - especially Laura. I stopped for a second and clamped my eyes shut as I thought about her. I'd already abandoned her once. Now I was going to do it again. For good this time. I checked the countdown - ten minutes. It was slower going, Cam-surfing - I wasn't sure if I was going to make it. And if I didn't? Maybe it would be just as well.

As bland as the building had looked from the outside, inside it was ultra-modern, jammed with labs and high-tech equipment. I spotted a couple of workers and guards as I moved, but managed to dodge behind a corner or into an alcove before they saw me. There weren't many people around. I guess everybody was off fighting the Rebels or something.

As I moved, Bailey's, and then Laura's, voices pleaded over my HUD with ever-increasing desperation.

I made it to the final hallway. I could see an exit door at the end. Two minutes. At some point I'd have to activate the 'death' hack, but I couldn't do it too early…

I rushed toward the outside door.

Vita Aeterna

Laura screamed into my HUD, "Alex! For God's sake! Get out of there!"

I was halfway there when a guard stepped out right in front of me from an office door. We both jumped. He was as surprised as I was. It took a few seconds for him to figure out that I didn't belong there. By that time I had my gun out. I glanced at my HUD display - one minute.

He jumped at me just as I raised the gun to shoot. He was a big guy; there was no way I was going to take him in a fight. I tried to fire but he grabbed my gun wrist and twisted it backwards, driving me to my knees. Thirty seconds. He fumbled for his own gun in the holster on his belt. I pulled the trigger of mine. The bullet missed him, but the blast startled him and made him hesitate. Fifteen Seconds. He grabbed again for his weapon. Ten seconds. I braced myself.

He was drawing the weapon from his holster when the whole building lit up. The shock wave knocked us both off our feet. The guard fell back and let go of my wrist. I fell on my ass. My gun went off, which reminded me that I was still holding it. I staggered to my knees and held it in both hands.

The guard was stunned, but he recovered and pushed himself up from the floor. He fumbled again for his weapon. The whole building was shaking. The walls were swaying around us. I could barely hold on to my gun as I pointed it at his chest and pulled the trigger. With the deafening bomb blast, I didn't even hear the shot. A patch of red bloomed on the guard's chest and he dropped to the ground.

The walls started to give way as I took off, racing for the door. I got there, turned the door handle and pushed. It wouldn't budge. The building's frame had buckled and jammed it in place. I took a flying leap and slammed my shoulder against it. Nothing.

The hallway itself started to collapse around me. I was screwed. For a few seconds I stood there, waiting to die. The ceiling started to cave in. The door frame twisted sideways. The door popped out from the pressure, but the gap was too small to fit through. I took another run at it with my shoulder. It scraped open just enough to squeeze through.

I was out, standing in an alley next to the building. The whole structure was swaying back and forth, and the sky was lit up with flames from the roof. The place was going to collapse. I flew across the alley and behind a nearby building.

When I was sure I was out of danger, I paused, turned off the crypted phone, and activated Gene's death hack.

"Alex!" Laura was screaming into my HUD as I took off like a bullet.

FORTY TWO

....

DEAD AGAIN

A month had passed since my 'death' at the factory. In a building so deep in the Dregs that if you climbed to the top floor, you could actually see wilderness, I'd set up what was to be my new home. The good thing about the location was that I could forage for stuff to eat in the forest (as long as I carried a gun). In my explorations of the surrounding abandoned buildings, I'd come across some tossed-out books on seeds and plants. Someday I might even be able to set up some kind of garden.

Gene's 'death' hack was still in place. I hadn't dared to contact anybody, but I could monitor what was going on. Since Wickham's death, the CCE had been crippled, and the elected government had been shown up for the fantasy it was. Most importantly, without Wickham, Vita Aeterna was crushed. The Elite were still entrenched, but the belief in them as god-like masters had been broken.

The factory had been completely destroyed, though, of course, they could always build another one. Connor's group had succeeded in capturing the InfoCorp communications center. It had taken a week for SecureCorp to take it back, and for all that time, the Rebels were able to broadcast the truth.

After the place was recaptured, the new head of the CCE fought desperately to pretend that nothing had changed, but by then the Rebel force had exploded in size. They regularly attacked SecureCorp, and were making progress every day.

And lately other pretty damaging hacks were showing up. Just knowing that stuff like that could be done gave people a feeling of power. I heard that both Richie and Jake had joined the Rebels. I never heard what happened to Spiro. Maybe someday I'd be able to thank Richie for all he'd done. Things were changing for the better, but nobody, including me, knew what the final outcome would be.

I'd spent weeks setting up the security barricades around my new home, hooking up a crude water supply, and working out various ways to get food. I cast my mind ahead, and shuddered as I imagined living in this place for the next almost four hundred years. Best not to think about that. Maybe someday, like Uncle Zack, I'd decide that my life wasn't worth living. Right now, in spite of all that had happened, and in spite of my circumstances, I wanted to be here.

My long-term hiding place was coming together, but I wasn't there right now. I was holed up in what was left of an office on the top floor of a building a few blocks from the current hideout for the newly combined Rebel/Dead Shift coalition. I was getting to know the Dregs pretty well by now, and the group were a lot easier to find, since there were now thousands of them.

I'd sent a message to Connor and Bailey over my crypted phone, and convinced them to come and meet me. I wouldn't tell them who it was they were meeting, just that I was a friend who had valuable news about the movement. I knew they'd be able to identify the phone, and wouldn't be able to resist finding out who had it. I stipulated that they had to come alone, and that I would take off if I heard they'd told anybody else, or brought anybody else with them.

My hiding place had the twin advantages of an unobstructed view of the Rebel hideout and multiple avenues of escape. The building was huge, and I'd spent a couple of days mapping out getaway routes, just in case. In rummaging through the abandoned buildings near my new home, I'd come across an ancient pair of binoculars. The left lens was smashed, but the right one worked perfectly. I peered through it now at the Rebel hideout.

Connor and Bailey exited the front door and, ten minutes later, scanned warily around them as they approached the entrance to my building - alone, as I'd stipulated. I was ready to run if I found they hadn't followed my instructions.

They had their guns drawn as they entered the building. I heard their footsteps and whispers as they stalked through the hallways of the top floor, following my instructions. They finally reached the room I was in. Connor just about fainted when he stepped through the open doorway.

"You!" he said, the words catching in his throat. I had to laugh. It reminded me so much of Richie's reaction when he first realized I was still alive after my Appraisal.

"But how?" Bailey asked. I was glad to see that he'd finally healed, and his bandages were gone.

I gestured toward two chairs I'd set up for them. They put away their guns and sat down. I explained what had happened at the factory, how I'd activated Gene's hack, made my way out of the Corp Ring, laid low, and finally set up my own hideout.

"They're never going to leave me alone as long as they know I'm alive," I said. I smiled. "So now I'm dead - for the second time."

They both stared at me like I really was dead. But their expressions told me that both knew I was right. It was the only way.

"But how are you going to live?" Bailey asked.

I shrugged. "It's probably best if I don't tell you anything about how or where I'm living. I'll contact you once in a while and let you know that I'm still alive..."

"Alive," Bailey said, "but for what purpose?"

"That's something I've got to work out for myself. Maybe there's some way I can be of help to you guys. Maybe my long life can be of some use to your cause."

"I've got a contact in FoodCorp," Connor said. "We might be able help you there - leave caches of food at designated points, or something."

Bailey smiled. "And maybe we can scrape together some money and open a bank account for you. It wouldn't have to be that much. The interest would eventually be enough to support you. It would take a long time, but..."

"Time is something I've got lots of right now," I said. "But you two are the only ones that can know. If I hear that you've told anybody else, you'll never hear from me again."

Both their faces fell, as the reality of the situation hit them.

"Wickham's dead," Connor argued. "The CCE are mortally wounded. They may not survive. The public are in a surly mood, especially the ones at the bottom, who are the vast majority. Maybe it's not forever." But the lines on his face seemed to say he knew otherwise.

"To the world - even to what's left of Vita Aeterna and the CCE, you're dead," Bailey put in. "Nobody's looking for you. You've got time on your side. The highest guy in the CCE is a one point eight but he's already ancient. He'll be dead in fifty years. By that time your effective age will be twenty-five."

I stayed in the shadows. Even sitting across from the two human beings who'd done the most to keep me alive and free, I felt the need to be hidden. The scary part was that I was getting used to hiding and being on the run. And I was going to get a lot more used to it.

"Nobody but you two," I repeated. "Nobody."

"Not even her?" Bailey asked. He gestured outside with his head. "She's right down there. I haven't told her anything."

I clenched my fists. "Especially not her."

"I'm sorry," he said, finally acknowledging what we all knew. "I'm sorry it had to be this way."

"Hey," I smiled. "Like you said, maybe it's not forever."

We talked for an hour or so about the movement, their lives, and how I would stay in touch. Then they said their goodbyes and left me alone. I snuck to the window, pulled down a slat of the hanging remnants of a Venetian blind, and peered down the block with my makeshift telescope. My chest tightened as Laura wandered out of the entrance of the Rebel building, staring ahead, as if she was searching for something.

A few minutes later Connor and Bailey appeared beside her, and the three spoke for a few seconds. Connor put a hand on her elbow. She hung her head as he led her inside.

I imagined her future. She'd hook up with some Rebel guy with about the same Appraisal. With luck, they'd both live long enough to get married and have children. Her children would grow. I dared to hope that the movement we'd started would allow them to live happy and healthy lives.

She and her compatible husband would age, slowly - for them. Their children would grow to adults, and have children of their own. In a hundred and twenty years or so, if Laura and her mate survived everything else life throws at you, they would die of old age. If her children were blessed with similar Appraisals, they'd die about forty years later.

By that time, I would be... I did the mental calculations. I closed my eyes and hung my head - I'd have an effective age of about - forty-five.

I dropped the blind slat and turned from the window. I'd seen enough.

It was time to get going. I had a life to live.

AUTHOR'S NOTE

Thank you for reading Vita Aeterna!

I know there are millions of books out there for you to choose from, and I'm honored that you chose mine. It's a challenge for relatively unknown authors like myself to reach new readers, and this is where you can help.

If you enjoyed this book and think it would be of interest to other readers, please visit and write a customer review on Amazon.com. Positive reviews are the best way to attract new readers, and I'm grateful for each and every one I receive.

JAY ALLAN STOREY

ABOUT THE AUTHOR

Jay Allan Storey has traveled the world, passing through many places in the news today, including Iraq, Iran, Afghanistan, and the Swat valley in Pakistan. He has worked at an amazing variety of jobs, from cab driver to land surveyor to accordion salesman to software developer.

Jay is the author of four novels, *THE ARX, THE BLACK HEART OF THE STATION, VITA AETERNA,* and *ELDORADO*, a novella, *CHOPPER MUSIC,* and a number of short stories. A new novel is currently in the works. His stories always skirt close to the edge of believability (but hopefully never cross over). He is attracted to characters who are able to break out of their stereotypes and transform themselves.

He loves both reading and writing, both listening to and playing music, and working with animals. He's crazy for any activity relating to the water, including swimming, surfing, wind-surfing, sailing, snorkeling, and scuba diving.

Jay is married and lives in Vancouver, BC, Canada.

Contact Jay at:
   Website: www.jayallanstorey.com
   Email: jayallanstorey@gmail.com
   Sign up for Jay Allan Storey's mailing list

JAY ALLAN STOREY

ALSO FROM JAY ALLAN STOREY

THE ARX

A year ago, after a mental breakdown, homicide detective Frank Langer was placed on medical leave from the squad he was once hand-picked to lead. Now he spends his days drinking and chain-smoking, and his nights waking up screaming from a horrific recurring nightmare.

So when he shows up one day with a wild story about a conspiracy to kidnap children, his former colleagues pat him on the back and tell him to go home. When he digs deeper into the mystery and finally connects the pieces, the answer is deadlier than he ever imagined.

But can he find someone to buy his story before it's too late?

"...One of the best books I've read this year." — Eleanor

"...makes page-turning easy, driven by suspense and carried forward by vivid imagery." — Kimberley Fehr

Vita Aeterna

"...Hitchcockian plot is part noir mystery, part sci-fi, part social commentary." — Martin Roy Hill

"...Great mix of thriller with a little sci-fi" — Ed E. Morawski

ELDORADO

In an energy-starved future, Richard Hampton's world is blown apart when his younger brother Danny disappears and the police are too busy trying to keep a lid on a hungry, overcrowded city to search for him. Richard has to make the transformation from bookish nerd to street-smart warrior to survive when he jumps the 'Food Train' for the disintegrating suburbs in a desperate search for Danny and his dog, Zonk.

"...I was hooked right from the get go, on the edge of my seat throughout the whole thing, and I couldn't put it down." — Tahnee Justus

"...the plot and the backdrop of this book are so well written that they are completely believable, which makes this a page-turner" — BigBangBookGeek

"...Amazing read of an amazing futuristic journey" — P. J. Winn

317

THE BLACK HEART OF THE STATION

How did we get here? Where are we going? Those are the questions Josh Driscoll, a teenager living in The Station, a city built one kilometer beneath the surface of a frozen, lifeless earth, is determined to answer.

Josh comes to believe that the Black Heart, a computer complex buried in a sector critically damaged in a massive asteroid strike centuries ago, holds the answers to all his questions, and is vital to their future survival.

"...It's a long time since I've stayed up until 2 o'clock in the morning to finish a book, but I honestly couldn't put it down." — Eleanor

"...The Black Heart of the Station is a riveting young man's adventure." — KimberleyFehr

"...This story is an action packed ride which evokes emotional responses and paints vivid characters." — Monica

84815663R00178

Made in the USA
Columbia, SC
23 December 2017